LIVING FOR YOU

Praise for Jenny Frame

Longing for You

"Jenny Frame knocks it out of the park once again with this fantastic sequel to *Hunger For You*. She can keep the pages turning with a delicious mix of intrigue and romance."—*Rainbow Literary Society*

Hunger for You

"[Byron and Amelia] are guaranteed to get the reader all hot and bothered. Jenny Frame writes brilliant love scenes in all of her books and makes me believe the characters crave each other."—*Kitty Kat's Book Review Blog*

"I loved this book. Paranormal stuff like vampires and werewolves are my go-to sins. This book had literally everything I needed: chemistry between the leads, hot love scenes (phcw), drama, angst, romance (oh my, the romance) and strong supporting characters."—*The Reading Doc*

The Duchess and the Dreamer

"We thoroughly enjoyed the whole romance-the-disbelieving-duchess with gallantry, unwavering care, and grand gestures. Since this is very firmly in the butch-femme zone, it appealed to that part of our traditionally-conditioned-typecasting mindset that all the wooing and work is done by Evan without throwing even a small fit at any point. We liked the fact that Clementine has layers and depth. She has her own personal and personality hurdles that make her behaviour understandable and create the right opportunities for Evan to play the romantic knight convincingly…We definitely recommend this one to anyone looking for a feel-good mushy romance."—*Best Lesfic Reviews*

"There are a whole range of things I like about Jenny Frame's aristocratic heroines: they have plausible histories to account for them holding titles in their own right; they're in touch with reality and not necessarily super-rich, certainly not through inheritance; and they find themselves paired with perfectly contrasting co-heroines…Clementine and Evan are excellently depicted, and I love the butch:femme dynamic they have going on, as well as their individual abilities to stick to their principles but also to compromise with each other when necessary."
—*The Good, The Bad and The Unread*

Still Not Over You

"*Still Not Over You* is a wonderful second-chance romance anthology that makes you believe in love again. And you would certainly be missing out if you have not read *My Forever Girl*, because it truly is everything."—*SymRoute*

Someone to Love

"One of the author's best works to date—both Trent and Wendy were so well developed they came alive. I could really picture them and they jumped off the pages. They had fantastic chemistry, and their sexual dynamic was deliciously well written. The supporting characters and the storyline about Alice's trauma was also sensitively written and well handled."—*Melina Bickard, Librarian, Waterloo Library (UK)*

Wooing the Farmer

"The chemistry between the two MCs had us hooked right away. We also absolutely loved the seemingly ditzy femme with an ambition of steel but really a vulnerable girl. The sex scenes are great. Definitely recommended."—*Reviewer@large*

"This is the book we Axedale fanatics have been waiting for…Jenny Frame writes the most amazing characters and this whole series is a masterpiece. But where she excels is in writing butch lesbians. Every time I read a Jenny Frame book I think it's the best ever, but time and again she surprises me. She has surpassed herself with *Wooing the Farmer*."—*Kitty Kat's Book Review Blog*

Royal Court

"The author creates two very relatable characters…Quincy's quietude and mental torture are offset by Holly's openness and lust for life. Holly's determination and tenacity in trying to reach Quincy are total wish-fulfilment of a person like that. The chemistry and attraction is excellently built."—*Best Lesbian Erotica*

"[A] butch/femme romance that packs a punch."—*Les Rêveur*

"There were unbelievably hot sex scenes as I have come to expect and look forward to in Jenny Frame's books. Passions slowly rise until you feel the characters may burst!…Royal Court is wonderful and I highly recommend it."—*Kitty Kat's Book Review Blog*

Royal Court "was a fun, light-hearted book with a very endearing romance."—*Leanne Chew, Librarian, Parnell Library (Auckland, NZ)*

Charming the Vicar

"Chances are, you've never read or become captivated by a romance like *Charming the Vicar*. While books featuring people of the cloth aren't unusual, Bridget is no ordinary vicar—a lesbian with a history of kink…Surrounded by mostly supportive villagers, Bridget and Finn balance love and faith in a story that affirms both can exist for anyone, regardless of sexual identity."—*RT Book Reviews*

"The sex scenes were some of the sexiest, most intimate and quite frankly, sensual I have read in a while. Jenny Frame had me hooked and I reread a few scenes because I felt like I needed to experience the intense intimacy between Finn and Bridget again. The devotion they showed to one another during these sex scenes but also in the intimate moments was gripping and for lack of a better word, carnal."—*Les Rêveur*

"The sexual chemistry between [Finn and Bridge] is unbelievably hot. It is sexy, lustful and with more than a hint of kink. The scenes between them are highly erotic—and not just the sex scenes. The tension is ramped up so well that I felt the characters would explode if they did not get relief!…An excellent book set in the most wonderful village—a place I hope to return to very soon!"—*Kitty Kat's Book Reviews*

"This is Frame's best character work to date. They are layered and flawed and yet relatable…Frame really pushed herself with *Charming the Vicar* and it totally paid off…I also appreciate that even though she regularly writes butch/femme characters, no two pairings are the same."—*The Lesbian Review*

Unexpected

"If you enjoy contemporary romances, *Unexpected* is a great choice. The character work is excellent, the plotting and pacing are well done, and it's just a sweet, warm read…Definitely pick this book up when you're looking for your next comfort read, because it's sure to put a smile on your face by the time you get to that happy ending."—*Curve*

"*Unexpected* by Jenny Frame is a charming butch/femme romance that is perfect for anyone who wants to feel the magic of overcoming adversity and finding true love. I love the way Jenny Frame writes.

I have yet to discover an author who writes like her. Her voice is strong and unique and gives a freshness to the lesbian fiction sector."
—*The Lesbian Review*

Royal Rebel

"Frame's stories are easy to follow and really engaging. She stands head and shoulders above a number of the romance authors and it's easy to see why she is quickly making a name for herself in lesfic romance."—*The Lesbian Review*

Courting the Countess

"I love Frame's romances. They are well paced, filled with beautiful character moments and a wonderful set of side characters who ultimately end up winning your heart...I love Jenny Frame's butch/femme dynamic; she gets it so right for a romance."—*The Lesbian Review*

"I loved, loved, loved this book. I didn't expect to get so involved in the story but I couldn't help but fall in love with Annie and Harry...The love scenes were beautifully written and very sexy. I found the whole book romantic and ultimately joyful and I had a lump in my throat on more than one occasion. A wonderful book that certainly stirred my emotions."—*Kitty Kat's Book Reviews*

"*Courting The Countess* has an historical feel in a present day world, a thought provoking tale filled with raw emotions throughout. [Frame] has a magical way of pulling you in, making you feel every emotion her characters experience."—*Lunar Rainbow Reviewz*

"I didn't want to put the book down and I didn't. Harry and Annie are two amazingly written characters that bring life to the pages as they find love and adventures in Harry's home. This is a great read, and you will enjoy it immensely if you give it a try!"—*Fantastic Book Reviews*

A Royal Romance

"*A Royal Romance* was a guilty pleasure read for me. It was just fun to see the relationship develop between George and Bea, to see George's life as queen and Bea's as a commoner. It was also refreshing to see that both of their families were encouraging, even when Bea doubted that things could work between them because of their class differences...*A Royal Romance* left me wanting a sequel, and romances don't usually do that to me."—*Leeanna.ME Mostly a Book Blog*

By the Author

A Royal Romance

Courting the Countess

Dapper

Royal Rebel

Unexpected

Charming the Vicar

Royal Court

Wooing the Farmer

Someone to Love

The Duchess and the Dreamer

Royal Family

Home Is Where the Heart Is

Sweet Surprise

Royal Exposé

A Haven for the Wanderer

Just One Dance

Wild for You

Hunger for You

Longing for You

Dying for You

Living for You

Wolfgang County Series

Heart of the Pack

Soul of the Pack

Blood of the Pack

Visit us at www.boldstrokesbooks.com

LIVING FOR YOU

by
Jenny Frame

2023

This Trade Paperback Original Is Published By
Bold Strokes Books, Inc.
P.O. Box 249
Valley Falls, NY 12185

First Edition: November 2023

Credits
Editor: Ruth Sternglantz
Production Design: Stacia Seaman
Cover Design by Jeanine Henning

Acknowledgments

Thanks to Rad, Sandy, and all the BSB team for all their hard work. I couldn't hope for a more supportive publishing team.

Huge thanks to Ruth, who helps and encourages me so much.

And finally, thanks to my family for being so supportive in all that I do.

For Barney and Lou—We three are family.

CHAPTER ONE

The Debrek London mansion was alive with the sounds of laughter and happy chatter. How things had changed in such a short time. It was only a few weeks since the Debrek vampire clan fought the malevolent witch Anka and her followers at Stonehenge.

Anka had disappeared into the night with her people, and the Debreks were coming to terms with what lay ahead.

Everyone knew this was the calm before the storm. War was coming in the paranormal world between those that wanted to live in harmony with humans, and those that saw humans as merely dirt beneath their boots, inferior, and only fit for serving the nefarious side of the paranormal world.

Bhal scanned the room but found her gaze settling on one woman. Being in a roomful of people and only seeing one person was a growing occurrence for Bhaltair. She was a Celtic warrior, bound by honour to protect the Debrek clan and, more specifically, its current head—Byron Debrek.

But more and more it was the other Debrek sibling that caught her attention, Byron's younger sister, Serenity. She stood at the other side of the room, standing with Alexis and her blood bond, Katie, and a couple of other friends. But although their conversation was lively, Sera was not present. She had checked out from their conversation a while ago.

Tonight, Byron was throwing a drinks party in honour of her parents' visit home, and to officially welcome her cousin Torija back into the fold. The former Dred clan leader had turned against her clan and the darkness when she and Daisy became blood bonded and fell in love.

Bhal kept her eyes on Sera as she put her half-drunk glass of champagne on the tray of a server and walked over to the drinks cabinet to pour a glass of malt whiskey.

Before Bhal could think about it, she was walking over to Sera. "Can I have a top-up?"

Sera gave her a hard stare, then filled up her glass. Sera and Bhal had a rocky relationship. It had been Bhal's duty to train Byron and Sera in combat up to the age of eighteen, when they became full-blown born vampires.

The Debreks, unlike other vampire clans, had the ability to procreate, with each generation being stronger than the last. They remained mortal but with increased strength and speed until they were eighteen years old, when they had the choice to remain human or to be reborn as a born vampire at their ascension ceremony.

Byron, firstborn and most powerful daughter of her parents, Michel and Juliana, apprenticed to her father for a long, long time before taking over as Principe and letting her parents retire.

She had been a dream to train, taking instruction and practicing religiously. Sera, on the other hand, did not take kindly to instruction. She argued, talked back, and was generally a pain in the arse.

Despite this, Bhal always tried to take care of her, but this never went down well. It frustrated her that Sera had so many gifts, was so capable in combat—although she would be better if she had taken her lessons seriously, and she was intelligent, but she chose to spend most of her immortal life partying and trying to have fun.

"Is there something you want, Bhal?" Sera said.

"No, not really. I just wanted a top-up and to see if you were all right."

"Wow. I should get kidnapped more often, then maybe you'd have cared about my feelings before now."

In an effort to show her sister that she was valuable and worthy of responsibility, Sera had gone against Byron's orders and used her initiative when pursuing their enemy Anka. It got her imprisoned and threatened the lives of the humans Anka had taken hostage.

"Of course I care…" Bhal's words trailed off as Sera just walked away from her. The night Sera was captured was the night everything changed for Bhal. The fear she felt that night broke something inside her.

Before, her concern was to protect Sera as a Debrek, but now it was all the more personal, and Bhal didn't like to think about the reasons too much. But whatever it was, Bhal worried about Sera every time she went out, which was a lot more than she used to, and found herself gazing at her, memorizing every part of her—Sera's silky blond hair, her blue eyes, and her petite nose.

But like Bhal, Sera seemed to have changed from that night. Her eyes had tired, dark shadows around them, something that shouldn't be seen in a vampire.

The normal sparky, annoying Serenity Debrek was replaced by a slumped, sad vampire, but even still, that haunted look could not disguise her beauty. Nothing ever could.

"I think I can guess what you're thinking."

It was the Grand Principe, Michel, Byron and Sera's father. Bhal almost jumped at being caught gazing at his daughter.

"Sorry, Grand Principe?"

"You've noticed something isn't quite right with my little girl."

"She does not seem her usual self, Michel."

Michel poured himself a drink. "I think Sera is a little bit lost."

"Lost?" Bhal asked.

"Look at Byron. She was born to this role." Michel pointed over to Byron who had an arm around Amelia and was laughing with Juliana, Torija, and Daisy.

"Byron's had her ups and downs, but she's always had a clear purpose, to be Principe of the clan. Sera's never had that. She doesn't know her place."

"I see what you mean. Life without purpose, far more immortality without purpose, is empty."

"Exactly. Byron strides through life with a clear purpose, to lead. She hasn't meant to do it, but Sera has been washed to the side in her wake," Michel said.

Bhal nodded. "She needs purpose."

"Yes, but purpose cannot be given. It must be sought and found."

Bhal got the feeling that Michel had some request hidden in this conversation. "Would you like me to do anything, Grand Principe?"

"Byron has had one other blessing bestowed on her." Michel pointed to her chest. "You, Bhaltair."

"I've always tried to be there for both of them, Michel."

"I know, but Byron was your priority as clan leader. It's only natural, it was your job, just as I was the priority when I was in Byron's position. But I want to ask you a favour."

"Anything."

"Leave Byron to the Duca and watch out for Sera. Make her your priority."

Little did he know, Sera had slowly become her priority for some time now.

"Of course, Grand Principe."

❖

Feeling alone in a roomful of people wasn't something Serenity Debrek had become aware of until recently. But here in the Debrek drawing room, surrounded by her clan and close family, she felt it keenly.

Sera gulped down a mouthful of whiskey and felt the pleasant burn. She turned around and took another sip of the liquid, hoping it would make some part of her mind duller. It didn't, not this anyway. Her parents were cooing over the seven months pregnant Amelia and Sera's sister, Byron.

They were even showering the prodigal vampire, Victoria—or Torija as she was now called—with praise. Sera had accepted Torija just as Byron wished—after all, Torija's blood bond was Daisy, one of Sera's good friends. If Daisy said she'd changed and been forgiven by her victims, then she trusted Daisy's judgement.

It simply galled Sera that Torija was fawned over and given important tasks and responsibilities, while she was constantly overlooked. But then, if she *was* given a chance, she would probably fail like the last time.

Byron had left her in charge of the home and their family, after repeated asking from Sera, while Byron was on a mission, and she'd messed up. She left their home and was taken on a wild goose chase, only to be taken hostage herself.

Sera had failed, but then surely she could do better. The thing was, Byron would never give her a chance now. She looked over at her father, who was now deep in conversation with Bhal.

She'd caught Bhal looking over a few times, no doubt her dad and Bhal discussing her failings. The whiskey she was drinking wasn't quietening her thoughts or the urge for something better to do the job. Sera had enough. She downed the rest of her whiskey in one gulp and slipped quietly out of the room then out the door without telling her guard, Henri.

Sera was going to the only place she could find that one better thing.

CHAPTER TWO

A few days after the successful party, Byron Debrek went back to work. She looked out over the London skyline. She always loved this view. Byron came into her office this morning, as she had a board meeting. The business had been sorely neglected by her recently because of the clan difficulties they had been facing.

Luckily she had an excellent staff around her that ran the business day by day and kept it ticking over. Some were humans who kept the Debrek vampire secret, from families that had always chosen to work for them. Some were turned vampires that pledged their immortal lives to the Debrek clan. And some, like her cousin Angelo Debrek, were family.

Angelo was in charge of the American and Canadian branch of the Debrek Bank and was going to join their meeting virtually. It was a comfort to Byron that if needed Angelo was there to help run things.

Byron turned and gazed at the picture of Amelia on her desk and felt her heart flutter—not something she would ever admit to. She sat down at her desk and picked up the picture frame.

Things could have been so different if her blood bond hadn't fallen in love with her. Byron's life had lit up with light and happiness, and she was going to be a parent. She'd never expected that. Byron always thought Sera would be the one to fall in love and provide the next generations of born vampire royalty.

But not Byron the eternal bachelor. That was until Amelia came along and stole her love, body and soul. She hoped that no matter their child's gender, they would be just like Amelia.

A buzz from the desk phone interrupted her thoughts. The first voice she heard surprised her. It was Sera.

"You don't need to announce me, Helen. I am half of the Debrek Banking Group."

Uh-oh. Sounded like trouble. Helen, her secretary, said, "Byron, it's Serenity to see you. Shall I send her—"

Sera was already bursting through the door. "It's okay, Helen."

Byron was worried when she saw the frustration, tension, and anger on Sera's face. She didn't look well either. She was very pale and drawn. "Is everything all right?"

"I'm fine."

Byron wasn't convinced. "Are you sure? If you weren't a vampire, I'd ask if you were ill."

"As I said, I'm fine. I just haven't fed this morning," Sera said.

Byron obviously wasn't going to get anything out of her. "We don't normally see you here at the office."

Sera started to pace in front of Byron's desk. "That's why I'm here."

"What?" She didn't know what Sera was talking about.

"Why don't I have an office on the top floor like you?"

Sera threw her hands up in the air, indicating the whole building. "This and the clan is half my legacy, as well as yours. Why wasn't I encouraged to go to university like you, so that I could work here?"

"You would have to ask Mother and Father, but it never seemed like something you were interested in. Is that what you wanted?"

"Not really, but it would have been nice to be encouraged. Instead it felt like all the family thought I was good for was sitting around a pool and shopping," Sera said.

Where on earth was all this coming from? Byron thought. "To be frank, that has been what you appeared to enjoy in life."

Sera slapped her hands down on the desk and leaned over it. "What about the clan? I'm a Debrek too. You might be clan leader, but I should be given some responsibility. Why haven't I?"

Byron sighed, got up, and looked out of the window, choosing her words.

Sera said angrily, "Why don't you let me help?"

Byron turned around, ready to tell Sera the truth. "You don't get responsibility because you are impulsive and have no common sense, and you are a danger to others. You nearly cost me my wife by sneaking her out to a club when the Dreds were looking for her. I could have lost her and my chance to have our child. Despite all that, I left you in charge while I went to France tracking Daisy and Torija. I gave you that second chance, and what happens? You acted impulsively, left Amelia, fell for a ruse cooked up by Anka, and put the whole clan in danger," Byron said firmly.

Sera looked like she had stuck a dagger in her heart, and Byron instantly regretted her honesty. Sera didn't say anything. She just sped out of the office and, no doubt, the building.

This wasn't the life-loving little sister she knew. Something was wrong, and Byron needed to find out what.

❖

Sera stopped running at top speed when she exited the Debrek building so that the humans didn't see one of her extraordinary skills.

She bent over, resting her hands on her thighs and breathing hard. The breathing wasn't because of the physical exertion—vampires were super fit—but it was because of the aching hole in her soul.

The feeling of deep gloom and emptiness had been coming on so slowly, creeping day by day, until she was overcome with it. Sera had always enjoyed her eternal life, drinking, dancing, sex, shopping, and had always made fun of Byron for not enjoying life and being too serious.

She'd been known to go to her favourite shops and buy every little thing she wanted, go to Harrods' champagne bar, wave her credit card, and buy the most expensive bottles for everyone there. She used to get a buzz out of it.

Sera had no idea about the business—she just always knew that her card was unlimited. Byron took care of all that. But the buzz she got felt meaningless now.

Sera stood up and tried to breathe. Having a fun eternal life wasn't fun any more—in fact, it brought misery. She should know about the business, the clan. She wanted to feel useful, a trusted member of the family. She wanted to dull the pain inside her, and lately there was only one thing that would numb the pain, and she was aching for it.

Sera waved down a taxi and got in. She gave the driver the address and they set off, but the traffic was heavy, and her need for oblivion was too great.

She held up her hands and they were shaking uncontrollably. "Can't you go any faster?"

"Love, the traffic is heavy. There's no way we can go any faster."

Anger fuelled by her need for the only thing that helped made her jump out of the car and run down the alley at the side of the Debrek building. If she kept to the spaces behind these great buildings, she could run at super speed without causing anyone to spot her, but if they did, at this point Sera didn't care.

Every fibre in her body was screaming out for what she could only buy at the underground club she was heading to. It didn't take long until she left the Debreks' high-powered business district and reached the earthy, run-down area where The No Such Place Club was.

Sera stopped running and fell to one knee, breathing hard. The withdrawal from the drug that had been anaesthetizing her life in the last six months was getting excruciating. She could hardly think of anything else.

Her family knew nothing of this, and it made her feel such shame. They would be horrified. *She* was horrified, which only added to the shame.

Sera looked up and saw the awful looking building. It was in an archway below a railway bridge that had once housed a car mechanic, and it looked derelict, but of course it wasn't. She walked up to the old wooden door and looked around for her way in.

A fly buzzed around her head. Instead of swatting it she said, "Sera Debrek. May I enter?"

The fly morphed into a tall, well-built bouncer. "Welcome, Ms. Debrek. You may enter."

The door opened, and Sera walked through on her way to find the only thing that dulled her pain.

❖

Deep in the basement of the Debrek London headquarters, Warrior Bhaltair stood before her trusted Celtic Samhain warriors in the large training room. Bhal led them in a series of practice sword routines.

The large room had mirrors on the walls and weapons of all kinds sitting in racks ready for use. There were training dummies and everything needed for a warrior to keep their skills as razor sharp as their swords.

Bhal and her people were an ancient clan of Celtic warriors, pledged to protect their people from evil spirits and gods who wished them harm. Samhain, the ancient word for Halloween, was their name, as it was at this festival that the veil between the worlds of the dead and the living was at its thinnest.

After their people were wiped out by the God Balor and his followers, they swore themselves to anyone who needed their protection from supernatural evil and evil in all its forms.

A long time ago, a debt of honour to the Debrek vampire clan made them pledge themselves to their service, but today and tomorrow were the one time when their traditional purpose was their goal.

In one corner of the room, Bhal's Samhain Chief garb sat on display, and another corner had an altar in praise of the other Celtic gods.

The warriors' set routine came to an end, and they stood, waiting for their chief to speak.

"Brothers and sisters, the evil that is Balor is stronger than he has been in many winters."

Wilder, one of her younger warriors, said, "We will defeat him."

Bhal put a hand on Wilder's shoulder and smiled.

"This Samhain is different. A long time ago, Balor destroyed our families, our lives, but then the other gods trapped him in the realm of oblivion. But now he is closer. We all feel it." The warriors murmured in agreement. "But what makes him all the more dangerous is that he now has help. The witch Anka."

Bhal had hypothesized that Anka had helped Balor's malevolent souls, called the Sluagh Horde, more easily leave the realm of oblivion and hunt down the souls of the dead. It was those souls that made Balor stronger.

"Balor's Horde is already ripping the unfortunates' souls from their bodies. The Sluagh will be plentiful and strong, and every innocent soul they bring Balor is an innocent soul lost to the void. Go and organize your team of vampires, begin your hunt by sunset. Anka and her alliance of witches, vampires, demons, shapeshifters, werewolves, and anyone else with evil in their souls will be helping to send those souls to eternal torment."

Alexis, the Debrek Duca, and some of her most trusted vampires walked into the room.

"Welcome, friends," Bhal told them.

"My vampire teams are ready for you, Bhal."

"Thank you for joining our cause. We all have a battle ahead of us, and even though we are smaller in number, our hearts are good and brave. The gods shall surely give us blessings in our cause."

Bhal pulled out her sword and hit the tip to the floor as she kneeled behind it. Her warriors followed suit, and they each bowed their head to the hilt of their sword, and repeated words of prayer together. "Danu, we beg you to bless us as we enter the battlefield to protect the innocent. If we fall, we accept death with gladness."

They stood, and Bhal shouted, "Head out."

"Aye, Chief," Wilder and the warriors replied.

Once she was alone, Bhal walked over to the small altar she had set up there and dropped to one knee. She closed her eyes to centre herself. In her mind she heard screams, not only of pain, but of the souls she couldn't save being dragged to a world of eternal misery.

It was Bhal's shame that she and her warriors couldn't save more people, but they were small in number. Suddenly Bhal felt a shiver, and goosebumps erupted all over her body, followed by the sound of a crow. That meant only one thing—she was in the presence of a Goddess.

She jumped up and turned around to find someone she hadn't seen in such a long, long time—Morrigan, the Celtic Goddess of war, battles, fate, and fertility.

"Hello, lover."

Morrigan had a cascade of long black hair framing a beautiful face. Everything about Morrigan was seductive—it was no wonder she had lured many to war. She wore tight-fitting black leather trousers, thigh-length black boots, and an equally tight-fitting black leather corset, which accentuated her generous breasts.

Around her neck a gold brooch in the shape of a crow held her black cape together.

"I am not your lover, Morrigan."

Morrigan stroked the tips of her black fingernails down Bhal's cheekbone. "You were once."

Bhal pulled away and walked a few steps from Morrigan. "Once, when I was at my lowest and most vulnerable."

Any time Morrigan and Bhal had crossed paths over the centuries, Morrigan tried to seduce her, but then sexuality was just one of the Goddess's tools of control. It was Bhal's shame that she had given in once.

"Yes, it was once, and it shows you just how much I care about you. Of all the countless lovers I've had, I always remember you the most fondly."

"Don't, Morrigan. I'm not one of the warlords who you manipulate so easily. You have a purpose here. What is it?"

Morrigan stalked around her. "I offered you everything when I came to you, Warrior. You wouldn't only have been Chief of the Samhain, but Warrior King of all the Celtic peoples. It would have brought peace and prosperity to the land."

"That's what you never understood about me, Morrigan. I was born to be a protector, not a king. I don't want people to cower at my boots."

"No one ever talked about cowering at your boots. You always misunderstood my goals. I am Goddess of war, fertility, and the land. I want to protect the people on the land."

"So you send them to their death to protect them?"

"War is sometimes what saves the lives of the people. Those warriors are all that stand between raiders, warlords, and evil, and their families at home. You should know that, Bhal. War is a natural consequence of life."

"That may be so, but you have always taken it too lightly. War is a last resort."

Morrigan brought her hand to her chest. "Well, excuse me, but it looks like you and the Debreks are at the beginning of a war, without any help from me."

"We are protecting the innocent."

"We are on the same page, then. I have information that can help you and your vampire friends," Morrigan said.

Bhal remained silent. She knew that Morrigan's favours always came with a price.

"You know I have premonitions—of what could be."

"*Could be* implies uncertainty."

"Of course there's uncertainty. You have free will," Morrigan said.

"In that case I think we would rather face whatever's out there on our own because your help comes at a price."

Morrigan gave Bhal an enigmatic smile. "Then perhaps I will go to the witch Anka."

"No, you won't. They serve Balor, and you despise him and have never been happier since he was trapped in the realm of oblivion."

Morrigan groaned in frustration. "Look, you are going to need my help. There are so many possible outcomes to what is coming, most of them worse than you could ever imagine."

"We will face whatever destiny throws at us."

She grasped Bhal's T-shirt. "Listen…"

Morrigan almost looked panicked and sincere in that moment. Bhal hadn't seen her like that before. This clearly mattered to her, but she had been fooled before. That was the problem—the Goddess was a contradiction.

She wasn't evil like Balor, but she thrived in the glory of battle. Morrigan could be in one moment untrustworthy, and the next sincere.

"Who are you talking to?"

Bhal snapped her head around and saw Sera standing at the doorway. She looked back to where Morrigan had been and saw she was gone.

"No one, I was just praying."

Bhal didn't want to explain Morrigan to Sera, and her history with her.

Sera seemed to buy her excuse and walked towards Bhal. She looked like a ghost, with pale skin and dark circles under her eyes. Something wasn't right, and worry started to niggle in her stomach.

"Have you fed yet? You don't look well."

"No, I was busy and forgot. Alexis says you're putting together some vampire teams to help with Samhain. I'd like to volunteer."

"What?"

"I'd like to volunteer," Sera repeated.

Bhal's reply was instantaneous. "No."

"What do you mean, no?"

This was all she needed tonight. She had pledged to look out for Sera, but on Samhain, humans had to come first. If Sera was there, Bhal knew she would put Sera first.

"I mean that Samhain is a solemn duty, where the eternal souls of good people are at risk. It is not a fun night out."

"I never thought it was. I'm offering to help those souls. Why can't I do that?"

The room dropped away, and all she could hear and see was a moment that haunted her, when Sera was held hostage by Anka. Bhal had felt true fear at that moment for the first time in millennia.

"Bhal? Bhal?" Sera shook her from her memory. "Why can't I join you tonight?"

"Because I can't be worried about you while I'm performing my duty," Bhal said.

"You wouldn't have to be worried about me. I'm perfectly capable of taking care of myself."

Bhal said nothing but determined she wasn't going to risk Sera's life again. When she'd thought she was losing Sera to Anka, Bhal finally admitted something to herself. She cared more about Sera than a mentor should. They had butted heads for hundreds of years, and here she was, realizing she cared about her, not like a sister, not like an elder, but something very different that Bhal didn't want to work through at the moment.

But that was something she would have to keep to herself. Sera's much older mentor, a servant to the Debreks, was who she had to be.

"Bhal, I want to do something useful. Please?" Sera said.

"No, okay? I said no." Bhal pushed past Sera.

"You're just like Byron, like my mother and father—no one has any faith in me. I'm a liability to this clan apparently." Anger and frustration seemed to fuel Sera's anger.

Bhal reached out to touch Sera's arm, but she jerked it back.

"Go and feed, Sera."

Sera zoomed to the side of the room, picked a sword off the wall, and ran at Bhal. Bhal pulled her sword from her back scabbard and met Sera's blow before it hit her.

"What are you playing at?"

Sera swung the sword around again and brought it down on Bhal's.

"Sera, don't do this."

But Sera wasn't listening. She crashed down one blow after another on Bhal's sword, but Bhal took the offensive and pushed Sera over to the wall at the other side of the room, then knocked the sword from Sera's hand.

Sera stood looking defeated, with Bhal's sword across her throat. "You've bested me, as usual. Are you happy now?"

"I never want to best you, Sera. I want you to be better. Every teacher wants that."

"I don't believe you."

Bhal gazed into Sera's eyes, full of hurt and pain. "I want only for you to be happy, Sera."

"Do I look happy?"

Sera had completely given up. Her body was limp. Bhal dropped her sword, and Sera reached out to touch her face.

"I need…"

Bhal took her hand and with her heart hammering whispered, "What do you need?"

Sera blinked a few times, then her body became rigid again. She pushed Bhal back and sped off out of the room.

Bhal picked up her sword, ran over to one the mannequins they used for practice, and roared as she sliced it in two.

CHAPTER THREE

Anka walked into Gilbert's bedroom and stood silently watching Gilbert enjoy the woman he was with. He was wearing a strap-on and thrusting into the witch on all fours in front of him.

Anka, on their God Balor's orders, had opened a portal to the underworld so that Gilbert Dred's spirit could be reborn in the body of the former Dred second in command—Drasas.

Since then, Gilbert had been enjoying the pleasures of the flesh at every opportunity.

It was exciting to watch but even more exciting to be part of it, as she had been only a few hours earlier. They had shared their bodies many times, together and with others. Anka touched her lips as she let her mind tune in to the witch Gilbert was having sex with. She could feel the heat start to penetrate her body and stimulate her sex, as if Gilbert was thrusting into her and not her witch. But as Anka touched her fingers to her cheek, cold water was poured over her ardour.

The scar that had been left after Daisy pressed her hand to Anka's cheek, in defence. Daisy's hand burned like acid, deep into her skin. It made Anka feel weaker than she had in millennia.

She had been through many things, but nothing had disfigured her like this. Beauty was part of her power, and Anka saw this as chipping away at her power. She would kill that woman Daisy, slowly and painfully.

Gilbert groaned louder and louder until he bit into the witch's neck and came inside her.

Once Gilbert was finished with the witch and regained his breath, he pulled on some trousers and walked over to Anka, while his bed partner slipped away, with serious injuries to her neck.

"Who knew a female body could be so pleasurable."

"I'm glad you are enjoying it, emissary, but try to leave my witches in working order."

Gilbert walked across to the drinks decanters and poured out two whiskeys. He brought one back to Anka and handed it to her.

"I'll try, but I cannot tell you how liberating it is to be myself again, broken from the blood bond of my wife. The feeling of confusion and madness has lifted like a fog. I haven't felt so alive in generations, and I have you to thank for it, Madam Anka."

"You are welcome. It was a pleasure to serve our God Balor."

Gilbert flopped down on an armchair, and Anka's eyes caressed his naked torso, his female body.

When Drasas inhabited that body, all Anka saw was weakness and handed out her sexual favours with her just to keep her compliant, but Gilbert inhabited Drasas's body like the superhuman vampire he was. Drasas's body seemed taller, bigger, more powerful, and intoxicating.

"Last night couldn't have gone better, could it?" Gilbert said.

"No indeed. The streets of Paris ran with blood, this Samhain. Our vampires, shifters, and witches were let loose on the streets last night as we planned. The bodies piled up and their souls were sent to feed our God Balor."

"And the famous Samhain warriors? Protecting the innocent from our evil ways?" Gilbert asked sarcastically.

"They had a bad night. The number of warriors Bhaltair has around the world cannot compete with our God. With every soul that goes to Balor, the stronger he becomes." Anka smiled.

Gilbert laughed and lifted his glass in a toast. "And the weaker every paranormal not on our side becomes. I'll drink to that."

"Bhaltair and her warriors once helped imprison me in a magical hex, a daisy wheel. I was impotent and imprisoned there for so long I lost count how long it was. It gave me time to picture how I would kill her and her band of half-breeds and humans."

Gilbert stood and stroked Anka's face. "And you will get that chance, Anka. I promise you."

Their lips came together softly. Both moaned at the touch. As individuals they had different needs and wants, but when they came together, they became one with the power of their God. It was their way to commune with him since Balor couldn't physically be here or talk to them.

Their kiss was becoming deeper when Anka's witch Asha walked into the room. "Madam? Emissary? You wanted to see me?"

Their kiss broke, and Gilbert roared. "Pick your timing better, witch."

Anka could feel Asha's jealousy. Asha had been hers for such a long, long time and was used to her full attention.

"Asha, we must ramp up production. The paranormal community needs to be under control if we are not to be stopped from reaching our goal."

"I have acquired a new production space. It will increase our product by twenty percent."

"Make it more, witch," Gilbert shouted.

Anka stroked Gilbert's shoulder to calm him. "Asha, I know you always do your best, and I trust you to get this job done."

"Of course, madam."

It wasn't only the Debreks and their allies that they were going after. The paranormal community needed to be controlled, and if they didn't join them, then they must be neutralized. Anka had come up with the answer, and the wealth of the Dreds and other contributors had made production and distribution of it possible. There were many paranormals that joined last night to kill who wouldn't normally take part in this kind of violence. Her plan was working.

"Thank you, Asha. Send a sacrifice for us."

Asha bowed and said, "Immediately."

After Asha left, Gilbert said, "You felt it too?"

"Yes, Balor wants our presence."

"Let's go."

❖

Bhaltair let the water from the tap gush over her bloodied hands. As soon as she and her group of warriors and vampires returned to base, and they debriefed, Bhal retreated to her room to clean up. As the water turned pink from blood, her hands trembled.

In all her ancient life, Bhal hadn't ever faced a Samhain quite like this one, apart from her first. Vampires, fae, shifters, and werewolves were all out taking lives. Then their souls were not given the dignity of passing over to the other side, to be with their families, friends, and those that loved them.

Instead, most of them, apart from those that Bhal and her warriors could get to in time, were ripped from their bodies and taken by Balor's Sluagh army, evil spirits who dragged innocents back to Balor's realm, to live forever in torment, giving Balor power.

A Druid priest had once promised Bhal that she would get the opportunity to battle Balor and release all the tortured souls from the ages, but that day never seemed to come.

All around the world, the scene had been the same. Her warriors in each region of the world were overwhelmed. She had the power to induct new members, like their last one, Wilder, but there were very few people suitable or willing to give their lives to service others.

They were so few compared to the population that Bhal wondered if there was any point any more. Did their calling matter?

There was a knock at her bedroom door. "Aye?" Bhal shouted.

"Bhal?"

It was Katie.

"The Principe has asked if you'll come down to the meeting room in an hour."

"Aye. I will do, Katie."

Bhal looked up to the mirror and saw blood splattered across her face. The blood was a sign of her own weakness. She couldn't save many of the humans, and their souls from attack.

Bhal kneeled on the lane in a back alley. She closed her eyes and tried to sense where she was needed next. A dead body of a man lay next to her, one of many she had encountered tonight.

She had been too late for him. His soul had already been dragged to the realm of oblivion. Bhal made a promise to him, to try to kill Balor one day and release him.

Bhal heard a woman's screams and ran, following her instincts to where she could find her. She ran down the back alley, past four buildings, then jumped a wall.

She found two vampires feasting on a woman who was either dead or close to it. Bhal pulled out her already bloody sword and ran at them. They hissed at her and stood up to fight.

They were two fairly new turned vampires with no sense of battle, combat training, or experience facing someone as powerful as Bhal.

In one sweep Bhal took off their heads, and their bodies fell like lead to the floor. Bhal sheathed her sword and quickly kneeled by the woman's side. She placed her hand on her face and felt the cold seeping in.

If Bhal was going to help her, it would have to be quick. She got her silver hip flask out of her pocket. One of the gifts of a Samhain warrior was to be able to revive someone from the point of death, after the dying person drank water from the warrior's hands.

Before Bhal got the top off the flask, she heard a growing sound of screeching, a blood-curdling sound that could terrify even the bravest warriors. Before she could place the flask down, the screeching became ear-piercing, and an empty area of sky, without stars or light—an absence of light—appeared above them.

It was similar to a black hole in space, the way it sucked in anything that was in its path. Bhal saw the woman's soul start to be pulled from her body.

She swung her sword, and the Sluagh dodged and dived at her. Bhal jumped over it and thrust her sword deep into it. A flash of light entered the entity, and it gave out a shriek of pain before dissipating into air.

Without missing a beat, Bhal dropped her sword and grasped the flask. She poured water into her cupped hand before pouring it into the woman's mouth. Her kind called it the water of life, and it could cure all injuries or diseases but had to be used with care.

Bhal poured some more into her mouth and then lifted the woman into her lap. She started to squirm and move.

"Bhal?" Alexis shouted as she ran towards her.

Alexis's vampires were helping every way they could, fighting off other paranormals and leaving the warriors to deal with the Sluagh Horde.

Alexis dropped down beside her. "Is she okay?"

"She will be. Can you get one of your vampires to take her to hospital?"

"Yes, let me take her off you."

Alexis lifted the woman into her arms. She would be safe now, but the after-effects of nearly having your soul pulled from your body were rough—cold shivers, sometimes high temperatures, and terrible headaches. The doctors wouldn't know how the woman got this way, but they could help with the symptoms.

Once Alexis left, Bhal heard the same blood-curdling screams again. It seemed like this night would never end.

And it didn't, until the wee hours of the morning. The number of paranormals rampaging—it was unprecedented. The numbers weren't just made up of the usual nefarious fae, shifters, werewolves, and vampires.

There were paranormals she recognized and knew had never posed a problem to humans. They had a glazed, hungry look in their eyes, and it was driving them to kill. What was causing it, she had no idea.

❖

Anka and Gilbert waited until Asha informed them that the sacrifice was ready, then descended to the temple to Balor that Anka had created below the Dred castle.

As they descended the final steps into the cavern, the smell of blood and smoke filled the air, as well as the cries of their latest victim.

In front of them was a stone sacrificial altar, with the dark stains of blood of the many sacrifices that had been made there.

Anka was surprised when Gilbert grasped her wrist. "I want to see my daughter Victorija on that altar. I want to take her head and her heart, but not before she watches the female she chose over her clan feel all kinds of pain."

"You will, Gilbert. You will when we smoke out the Debreks' ragtag following and separate them. We can't attack them now."

"Soon?" Gilbert lifted his hand.

Anka took it and kneeled with Gilbert at the altar. "Soon."

The cries of the male human became louder and more panicked. "Please, please, don't, please?"

Anka nodded, and Asha slit his throat. The blood dripped down the corners of the altar and collected in gold goblets. Both Anka and Gilbert took sips of the blood.

Anka said, "Balor, we come to you humbly, for your guidance."

They experienced what felt like a fist thrust inside their gut. It was painful, but soon they drifted into a place where time had no meaning.

CHAPTER FOUR

Daisy paid for her coffee at Starbucks and moved along to the pickup counter. She gathered some sugar and spoons while she waited, and then her gaze wandered to the glass windows of the shop. There standing against the glass was one of the most dangerous vampires in the world—and she loved her.

Torija, her deceased father Gilbert, and the Debreks were considered vampire royalty by the turned vampires, as they were descended from the original vampires who stalked the earth. They were stronger, faster, and virtually unkillable. Even turned vampires could be killed, but not the born vampires.

This time last year, to say she would have been shocked to hear that she would be in love with Victorija, one of the most dangerous vampires in existence, was an overstatement. But with Daisy's help, Victorija had become Torija and sought forgiveness from those she had killed and received it. But that wasn't enough. Daisy was constantly helping Torija steer her path of goodness, because doing the right thing didn't always come easy.

Daisy chuckled to herself as someone approached Torija with a tablet, clearly trying to sell her something. Daisy couldn't see or hear Torija's reply but laughed when she saw the salesperson's face go chalk white, as they hurried away. Daisy had to admit, she was attracted to the powerful vampire that was Torija and the muted bad side that was left in her.

"MacDougall and Debrek," the Starbucks barista shouted over the loud shop.

"That's me," Daisy replied.

She picked up the cups and started to navigate her way out of the busy shop. MacDougall and Debrek? Daisy thought. Made them sound like a nineties TV buddy cop show. Although the parallels were there.

Daisy started as a colleague to Amelia, her boss, in Amelia's uncle's tailor's shop. Amelia was a designer and Daisy fresh out of art college. They quickly became work friends, and then best friends outside of work, as their paranormal lives started to intertwine.

Amelia was wife of Byron Debrek, the most powerful vampire in the world, and Daisy had used her special powers to try to prove the paranormal world was real, with her friends the Monster Hunters.

When their paths crossed and it was revealed that she and Amelia were crucial to protect the world from the evil that was coming, they became like sisters. That's where she was off to this morning, the Debrek London house. Every morning both she and Torija left their flat to travel to the Debreks' so that Daisy and Amelia could work on their bond.

Daisy left the shop, and Torija immediately took the cups from her. "Such a polite vampire."

Torija gave her a head bow, her shoulder-length blond-highlighted brown hair flopping down, and said, "It's all part of the vampire royalty charm."

Daisy shivered a little at Torija's soft French accent. She felt its honey tones could talk you into anything. It wasn't just the voice—it was the powerful way Torija held herself, the way she dressed, like someone who had lived through many generations of style. But today she was wearing black leather trousers and a flamboyant ruffled white shirt, with a black suit jacket.

Torija's power and charm made Daisy hungry for her, and that was before their blood bond. Now touching, kissing, making love with Torija felt more essential than water or food.

Torija leaned in and whispered, "I know what you are thinking, cherie."

Daisy shivered yet again. It was sometimes annoying that you couldn't have one private feeling to yourself with a blood bond, but only mildly annoying. She treasured the feeling of sharing and becoming so close she felt like her love was one with the other's.

She decided to change the subject. "So who was it that you made turn white with fear? Haven't I told you not to scare people?"

"He was trying to sell me new home insurance. What on earth is home insurance good for?"

"Spoken like a true eight hundred-year-old vampire. Don't worry, I take care of that kind of thing. Just don't scare people."

"Cherie, you've made me get forgiveness from those I have hurt, and I've turned myself away from evil, but you can't expect me not to enjoy a little scare once in a while."

"You're right. I do like a bad girl."

As they walked along Daisy spotted a charity collector, with a Save the Children bib on. "Torija, get your wallet out."

Torija frowned and looked ahead. "Another one?"

Daisy didn't let her pass a charity collector without prodding her to give. "Yes, another, and it's a good one, Save the Children. You've got a lot of bad karma to make up for, and we're doing it one charity at a time."

Torija sighed, handed her the drinks, and took her wallet out as they walked along. "It's lucky I have plenty of money, or I'd be in trouble."

"Yeah, thank goodness the Dreds didn't get access to it. Who knows what harm they could have done with it," Daisy said.

"I never trusted anyone in my clan to know where I kept my money. Once you and I settled here, I felt safe enough to contact my bank and access the accounts kept for me in Switzerland. Now that the money is transferred to the Debrek bank, I am free to use it for us and the many charities you prod me to support."

Daisy smiled and watched her pull out a hundred pounds in notes and drop it into the bucket.

"Wow, thank you," the collector said.

Daisy laughed when the woman tried to put a sticker on Torija's jacket.

"Do not put that on me. This is couture."

Daisy stepped in quickly before the woman got any more frightened. "I'll take it, thanks."

Torija took the drinks back and started to walk. Daisy looped her arm through Torija's.

"You need to learn when to just smile and not be so scary."

"I can't see that working. Let's get going, cherie."

❖

Amelia was in her meditation room in her home, the Debrek mansion. Amelia came here every day, sometimes twice a day, to practice her magical witch powers.

When she found out that she was adopted, and her mother was in fact a witch, and that she was the new matriarch to the Debrek clan, it astonished her. But even more so when she found out she and Daisy were the descendants, the two prophesied to save the world from the evil that was coming.

To go from no knowledge about magic to saving the world seemed impossible, but Amelia's powers were building every day with practice, and now that she had Daisy alongside her, Amelia felt less alone in this almighty task.

Daisy joined her each day to build the bond that Magda, their teacher, told them they would need. Amelia always started early and tried to get tuned into the power of her ancestors before Daisy came.

They'd had a preview of the power they could produce together when they saved Torija at Stonehenge. The portal to the afterlife had been closing quickly as Anka and her group left the site. But together Daisy and Amelia had created enough power to hold open the portal and let Torija escape.

As she sat in the casting circle on the floor, the ancestors' voices were loud and confusing at first, but she soon tuned in and heard their collective voice. She had become quicker and quicker as the months passed and now was able to access her powers in seconds, but she had to get even faster.

They were facing one of the most feared witches of all time—Anka, and whatever she was playing at, opening the portal to the other side, they didn't know, but it couldn't be good, so they had to be ready.

Amelia gasped when the voice of the ancestors said, "Go to the river."

Almost immediately Amelia was in a place she had grown familiar with. She was standing by a river, a passive observer. She had dreamed of this scene for the last month, but never had she seen it in her communion with the ancestors.

It felt different from her dream. Sounds and smells were more real. The splashing of the clear river was so calming, and the sounds of the birds in the trees made this place feel alive.

Amelia heard singing coming from somewhere. She took some steps closer to the river and saw the most beautiful young woman bathing in the river. She was in up to her waist, and on top only wore a piece of cloth covering her breasts.

She had long dark brown hair down to her waist, and Amelia felt familiar with her in a weird way.

Amelia could hear rustling and turned around to see a young man in the trees watching the woman in the river. That was creepy.

He was wearing ancient warrior's attire. He had a sword just a little shorter than Bhal's, a dagger at his side. This situation could be seen as threatening to the woman, but somehow Amelia didn't feel danger.

Finally the warrior stepped out of the trees and walked down to the bank of the river. The woman in the river gasped and used her hands to cover the simple garment over her chest.

The man lifted his hands and said, "Please, my lady, I mean no harm." He walked closer to the water's edge and said, "I've listened to your beautiful singing for many days, but I was afraid to make myself known to you. My name is Raymond, Raymond of Poitou. May I know your name?"

The woman smiled for the first time and said, "Melusine, my lord."

"What a beautiful name."

Amelia had lost herself in the scene before her. It was like stepping into someone's memory.

Raymond took a step and kneeled on one knee on the grass. "May I meet you properly, my lady?"

"If you come back on Wednesday, I will be glad to share a picnic with you, my lord."

Raymond couldn't have looked happier. He placed his hand on his heart. "Thank you, and call me Raymond, my lady."

Amelia watched as he walked away. Once he was out of sight, Melusine didn't stand up to come out of the water to clothe herself—she ducked under the water and was gone. She didn't come up for breath. Melusine was just gone.

Amelia walked down to the water's edge but heard a voice calling for her.

"Amelia! Amelia!"

Amelia was pulled from the scene back into her practice room. She gasped for breath.

"Amelia? Are you okay?" Daisy rushed to her side.

"Yes, yes. I'm fine. I was just having a vivid vision. I think it was a vision, anyway. I've been having the same dream too."

Daisy helped her up onto her feet. "Let's talk about it. I brought Starbucks."

Amelia's heart was still beating fast. "Okay. I could use a time out before we start practice."

They both sat on the two seater couch, and Daisy handed Amelia her drink. "Decaf latte with hazelnut syrup, and a mocha with an extra shot for me."

Amelia rubbed her baby bump. "I can't wait to be able to have caffeine in my coffee again. It's not the same."

Daisy thought about that for a second and said, "Would caffeine affect you and the baby badly? You know, with the blood bond and with the Grand Duchess's ring?"

As it had for Lucia, the ring both protected Amelia and projected the life force that was now Amelia's role.

Amelia looked down at the ring on her wedding finger. "I suppose not, but I'd rather not take the chance."

Amelia had explained to Daisy that this ring had been made for Byron's great-great-grandmother because she was a witch and mortal and not like her husband Cosmo, an immortal vampire. It would protect her from injury, and allow her to heal immediately and live on even if her bonded vampire's life was ended.

It was also a conduit to the rest of the Debrek family to allow them to use Amelia's life force to procreate, something Daisy had thought about a lot.

"Amelia, can I ask you something?"

"Uh-huh." Amelia reached over and squeezed her leg. "Anything."

"Do you really think Torija is a Debrek now?"

Amelia looked quite surprised. "Of course she is. You know that Byron and the whole clan think that. Especially after she was forgiven on the other side, and she was willing to die for you, for this clan."

"I know, I know, but you know this matriarch, vamp baby thing? Well, if Torija is a Debrek, can she…*you know*?"

Amelia laughed. "Yes, you don't have to worry. I'm sure you'll be able to have children too."

That wasn't what Daisy was worried about. "The thing is, I'm still young and I'm not ready for that, and I'm not sure if I even want that. I don't want it to catch me by surprise…*us* by surprise, if you get what I mean."

Amelia smiled. "Yeah, I do. Don't worry, you both have to truly wish for a baby in that special moment between you both. It'll come at the right time—if you want it."

"Phew. I suppose *young* doesn't make sense when you'll live as your vampire's partner, but I still feel young inside, and we've got a lot of battles ahead."

"Very true. How is Torija this morning?"

"Her usual lovable and annoying self. She and Alexis were circling each other like wolves downstairs. I know nothing could make up for Torija ordering the killing of Alexis's girlfriend, but I hoped since she had been forgiven by her on the other side, they'd come to a truce. But it's really difficult for them working together now."

Amelia knew Alexis's pain only too well. Over a century ago, Victorija, as she then was, ordered an attack on the Debrek London mansion, and Alexis's girlfriend Anna was killed.

It had destroyed Alexis. She held that grief, never having another relationship for decades, before falling in love with the Debrek housekeeper, Katie. But when Torija went willingly to death through the portal the witch Anka had opened, she faced those whom she'd killed, and Anna's spirit forgave her.

"It's going to take time, Daisy. Just having Torija here in this house is going to be hard. Give it time."

Daisy raised her eyebrows. "I suppose that time is something we all have here."

"True." Amelia smiled.

"So where were you when I came in?" Daisy asked. "With the ancestors?"

"No. That's what I want to talk to you about. I've started having these vivid dreams, but this was the first time one broke into my waking life."

Daisy took a sip of her coffee. "What happened?"

"Well, I was connecting to the ancestors, but it was as if I was hijacked," Amelia said. "I was pulled into what felt like a memory. It was more real than the dreams. I felt the wind blowing my hair, the sun warming my skin. It was incredible."

"It sounds like when my ancestor's diary pulled me into Torija's memories," Daisy said.

Daisy's relative, generations ago, had fallen in love with the young Victorija, before she was a born vampire, before her father Gilbert's abuse and the murder of Daisy's relative broke her heart and turned her towards destruction. Daisy was able to experience these events through her relative's diary. From that she knew that Victorija could be redeemed.

"Yes, something like that. The dreams and this experience are the same. I'm on the edge of a forest. I look around and there's a river—"

Daisy interrupted her. "With a beautiful woman washing in the river?"

Amelia couldn't believe it. "You too?"

"Yup. This guy Raymond comes along and thinks, *Whoa, she's gorgeous*. Then they fix up a date."

Amelia was so surprised. "You think this is to do with our bond?"

"Must be. It's trying to tell us something. Why can't the other side just tell us what this all means? It would all be a lot easier."

"I asked Magda that. She said that they can get knowledge of what might or should come to pass, but it's all in flux. We have free will and…it's like a multiverse, there are different outcomes to different decisions."

"Oh, now you're talking my language." Daisy was immediately full of enthusiasm. "Did you know aliens pop in and out of our universe—that's why UFO sightings are so quick. They're here and then they are gone."

Amelia laughed and held up her hands. "I have enough trouble getting my head around this paranormal world, so don't bring aliens into it too."

Daisy sighed and picked up her coffee. "I suppose."

Something about Daisy's cup caught her eye, something that had always been there, but seeing it now, after recounting her vision, it seemed clear as day. Clearer, in fact. It was as if the magical realm put a big shining spotlight on the Starbucks brand symbol.

"That's her, Daisy." Amelia pointed to the cup.

Daisy looked confused. "What? Where?"

"Here. On the cup."

When Daisy looked at it properly, she said, "Oh shit. It is. It's Melusine." Daisy pulled out her phone and started to search.

"What does it say?" Amelia said.

"Wait a sec." Daisy stood up and started to pace and began to read. "Many people think the Starbucks logo is a mermaid, but it is in fact a Melusine."

Daisy began to bounce excitedly on her tiptoes. "A Melusine is a thing. We're onto something."

Amelia got up as quickly as she could. "Tell me, tell me."

"There's so much information here to study—would you mind if I asked my friend Skye to help us?"

Skye was a part of Daisy's paranormal research group, Monster Hunters, along with her friends Zane and Pierce. Since Zane was killed by Anka's witches, and Daisy was now part of the paranormal world,

Monster Hunters had been put on an extended break. But Daisy was still close with Skye and Pierce.

"She knows about our world now and has kept her promise to not expose our world. Skye was the research expert in Monster Hunters."

"If you think she can help, absolutely."

Daisy nodded and dialled her phone. "Skye, I need some help."

❖

Bhal had cleaned up and made her way down to the basement of the Debrek mansion. The blood room where the vampires fed on blood servants was down here, the training room where they practised combat, a holding area, a cellar with blood packs for travelling, and finally the meeting room.

She passed vampires and warriors who nodded to her on the way. When she entered the meeting, she found a tense situation. Torija was sitting casually with her feet on the table, and Alexis was looking everywhere but at Torija.

Bhal couldn't imagine going from despising the vampire that gave the order to kill your former girlfriend, to her being part of the clan. It had been a big adjustment for all of them, but Bhal thought Alexis was doing the best she could.

"Ah, Bhal, finally someone to save me from this sparkling conversation."

Alexis spit out, "You are lucky I let you breathe."

"Both of you, just calm down. We have enough people to fight at the moment—let's not fight each other," Bhal said.

Byron swept into the room. "Take a seat, Bhal."

She stood at the end of the table, pressed the touch-screen controls on the large TV on the wall, and selected the twenty-four hour news. A reporter stood on a London street while a chyron moved along the bottom of the screen saying: *Multiple unexplained deaths on London's streets.*

"This is what the public is seeing. Bhal, how was it in the streets last night?"

"Unprecedented. We lost many lives and souls, and my warriors spread through cities all over the world say the same. It was a bloodbath. Balor has gained so much strength."

"I'm sorry, Bhal," Byron said.

Alexis added, "Whatever Anka was trying to do, opening up that portal to the other side, it worked."

"Torija?" Byron said. "What do you think?"

"When I was on the other side, Drasas's soul was pulled, kicking and screaming, to the underworld, so when you told me her body came back, and Anka and her people took it with them, I was surprised. Whatever came back from the other side was an empty vessel."

Byron replied, "That empty vessel is giving Anka and her so-called God Balor strength. Bhal has always said that Balor pledged he would return to conquer the earth after he was trapped in his prison. He seems to be closer than ever."

"That is a terrifying prospect. I have been through it once, and he took everything I loved," Bhal said.

Byron walked around and put her hand on Bhal's shoulder. "It will not happen again."

"I pray you are right, Principe. We threw every kind of magic from our Druid priests, and bloody combat at him, and it wasn't enough."

"How was he defeated?" Alexis asked.

"A portal opened up. Two portals. One bright blinding light, the other a void of nothingness. I can't describe it any other way. Whatever it was, it terrified him. A light blasted him and sent him kicking and screaming into it."

"Was there any indication who sent him there?" Byron asked.

"Our priests said it was the gods. They cast him into a Ceal realm, a void that would save humanity from him. Only his Sluagh army of lost souls have ever been able to leave and return on Samhain, when the veil is thin. But never as many as I saw last night."

"What does Ceal mean?" Alexis asked.

"Absence. It is a void of nothing."

"This is a very dangerous situation," Byron said. "We not only have to stop this, but protect our paranormal world from association with this looming evil. For the moment you can see that the news channels are not reporting the scale of murder or the cause of the deaths, by vampire bite or shifter mauling. But I had a call from Daisy's grandmother, Margaret Brassard. She was representing the department."

The department was a secret branch of the state that knew and kept tabs on the paranormal world. They had in fact requested paranormal help during World War II, and Byron, along with her vampires, had worked in intelligence for the secret service. Daisy's mother and grandmother worked for the department, so they were closer than ever.

"Margaret Brassard wanted to know if we knew anything about this or not and told me that their government have taken control of the bodies, post-mortems, and release of information to the public. We have always cooperated with the department. I told her what I knew at that stage and promised that we would protect Daisy."

Torija suddenly sat up straight and said fiercely, "No one will get past me to harm my Daisy."

"We will put an iron ring around those we love," Byron said, "but as Amelia and Daisy are the descendants, they will be targets, and at the same time they are prophesied to stop a great evil overcoming the world."

"By this God Balor, I take it," Torija said.

Byron walked back to the top of the table. "Yes. Margaret Brassard works for the humans and their interests but now has a granddaughter involved in our world. She is getting pressure from those above her already. We need to try to take the lead in this situation and bring about a quick end to these problems."

"What's the plan?" Alexis asked.

"I want you, Duca, and Torija to put together a small team for a reconnaissance mission to France and the Dred castle. That's where they were last seen by our contacts."

Alexis looked at Byron in disbelief and then across to Torija. "I don't need her help, Principe. I will set up a team—"

"Frightened a born vampire will outshine a turned vampire, Duca?"

Byron brought her hand down on the table with a smack. "Enough. Torija has been accepted as a Debrek, and we will use her abilities as I see fit, Duca. I'm Principe here. If they still base their operations at the Dred castle, there is no better person to have with us for recon. Do you understand me, Alexis?"

"Yes, Principe."

"What about me, Principe," Bhal asked.

"I have a separate mission for you." Byron looked at Alexis and Torija. "Go now."

Alexis sped off at top vampire speed and was gone in a flash.

Torija, on the other hand, sauntered towards the meeting room door. Byron caught her attention before she left.

"Torija?"

Torija turned around.

"Behave."

"Oui, Principe," Torija said with a mischievous smile and flourished a bow.

Once she was gone, Byron sat next to Bhal. "Well, my friend. How are you really?"

Bhal looked at her hands, which not too long ago were covered in blood, and said, "I feel like this is the closest I've been to the endgame since a millennium ago, and I'm afraid for all the blood that will have to be spilled along the way."

Bhal's Druid priest told her that once Balor had been finally defeated, she would be given the choice to give up her eternal life and to rest on the other side. That had always been her intention. Maybe her rest was coming sooner rather than later.

"A wise old warrior once told me that it was good to feel scared because then you know how much you have to protect the ones you love."

Bhal smiled. "Old? Me?"

Byron laughed. "You'll forever be that eighteen-year-old warrior, with time sailing past you."

"A nice way to put it. What is this other mission you wanted me to do?"

"Sera hasn't been looking well these days, and yesterday she came to see me, angry, about why she wasn't given the same kinds of opportunities as I've had."

"That doesn't sound like her," Bhal said.

"No. It sounded like she had been reassessing her life and was unhappy with it. Anyway, she wouldn't let it go, and I told her some home truths."

"About not being responsible? Pursuing fun before responsibility?" Bhal asked.

Byron nodded.

Bhal sighed. "I used to tell her the same thing when I was training her, before she became a born vampire. I don't think she's liked me since."

"I'm sorry to say we argued, and she ran off. She hasn't been home," Byron said.

"Sera did come home briefly. She wanted to volunteer for my Samhain team. I expressed similar worries as you. I told her that I couldn't do my job if I was worrying about her."

Byron shook her head. "So she's had two lots of home truths. I wouldn't normally be worried about Sera not coming home. She's a big girl and has been known to go out partying for a week before now, but this time is different. Not only is there a danger out there to us, but she hasn't been herself. I have a bad feeling. Can you try to find her? I would go with you, but I really don't want to leave Amelia just now. She is so vulnerable at the moment."

Bhal didn't tell Byron that her father had asked the same thing. Just like Michel had requested, Bhal would make Sera her priority. The way things were, it wasn't safe out there, not even for a born vampire.

"Leave Sera to me, Byron. She will be my responsibility."

Byron clapped Bhal on the arm. "Thank you, old friend."

Bhal stood. "I'll start with her usual haunts, and report in."

CHAPTER FIVE

Bhal made her way down the street that led to The Sanctuary, with growing concern for Sera. Bhal had always been concerned for Sera, as she had for Byron. But as firstborn, Byron had been stronger and faster than any other born vampire before her and, apart from one brief incident when she had lost control as a newly born Vampire, had followed the rules.

Sera hadn't liked rules. She lived to break them, was stubborn, and hated to take instruction. It had been infuriating trying to teach Sera hand-to-hand fighting and combat fighting, but also, now looking back, being with Sera had made Bhal feel most alive.

Feeling alive might seem silly to someone who had an eternal life, but the longer Bhal lived, the less colourful and exciting life became. Not with Sera around. Feeling angry and aggravated made Bhal feel so alive, and she would let nothing ever harm Sera.

As Bhal approached the club, she saw more security people than usual at the front door. She recognized the were and shifter bouncers on tonight. They looked jumpy.

"Claud? Everything all right tonight?"

The tall, muscle-bound shifter offered his hand to Bhal. "Bhal, good to see you. We're just being a bit cautious after last night's events."

"I don't blame you. Has Sera Debrek been in?"

"Not since I came on shift at five, but she could have been before that. Do you want me to radio and ask Slaine?"

"That's okay. I'll go in and speak to her and have a drink," Bhal said.

A conversation with Slaine, the bar manager, would be better face to face. She walked down a few steps, and the door was opened for her. A low, heavy dance beat met Bhal as she walked into the darkened club.

Bhal was known by most in the community, but she seldom drank here, unless Byron was spending an evening here, which she hadn't much since she married Amelia.

Heads turned when Bhal moved past each table, and the customers leaned into each other to whisper. They were all here—witches, vampires, fae, shifters, werewolves.

The Sanctuary had a dark, sultry atmosphere, but tonight Bhal could feel tension. Probably because of last night. Something had been building up in the community since Anka turned up to cause trouble.

This was a place where both sides of the paranormal community could come and drink in peace. The peace was ably kept by Slaine, who she could see drying glasses behind the bar.

Slaine was half shifter, half fae, and six foot eight of solid muscle, with a heart of gold. There was no better custodian of the club.

There was one thing Bhal noticed as she reached the edge of the dance floor and saw the tables further into the club. It was quieter than Bhal had ever seen it.

"Bhal, good to see you," Slaine shouted from the bar.

Bhal made her way over to the bar and shook Slaine's hand. "How are you, Slaine?"

"Not bad. Could be busier. Drink?"

"I'll take a Wulver single malt," Bhal said. Slaine poured out the drink and handed it to Bhal. She took a sip and the liquid burned pleasantly. "I noticed it was quieter."

"Yeah, business has been down for a few months. Nights like yesterday evening don't help. Everyone's jumpy. The community is getting divided. Your warriors must have had a difficult Samhain."

Bhal swirled the whiskey around in her glass. "Aye, it was…" She had a flashback of the many humans screaming for help as she rushed from street to street, and being too late to save most. She should have saved more, but at the end of the night, her warriors only rescued a few. "Aye, it was a difficult night. It feels like the evil is closing in around us."

"You know," Slaine said, "if you need me for what might be coming, I'll stand with you shoulder to shoulder."

"Thank you, Slaine. We appreciate it. Has Sera been in? I'm looking for her."

Slaine shook her head. "Sera hasn't been in for a long time."

That surprised Bhal. "Really? But she's been out most nights. Sera always comes here."

Slaine shook her head. "Not any more. Sera has gone the way of some of my other customers. There's a new bar, so people tell me. Once a customer goes there, they don't come back."

"Where is it?" Bhal asked.

"I've no idea, but I've heard whispers that they serve more than drinks—if you know what I mean."

"Chemicals?" Bhal said.

"Drugs, yeah. You know I don't allow anything like that in my club," Slaine said.

Bhal's stomach started to twist with worry. Sera's pale face, dark eyes, and ill countenance could be symptoms of chemical use.

For most paranormals their own special abilities were enough, but there were always those who wanted to push it a little bit further. Luckily no chemical substances had really taken hold in the community, but why would Sera want to get involved with that?

Bhal needed to find her and quick.

"Do you have any idea where it is, or what it's called?"

"No idea, but you could try asking him." Slaine pointed to a table in the corner of the room.

"Who is he?" Slaine asked.

"A necromancer for hire, and someone who always knows what's going on. He's called Idris."

"Thanks, Slaine. What's he drinking?"

"Straight vodka."

"Can you give me another whiskey and your best vodka for our friend over there."

"I'll just be a minute."

As Bhal waited, she studied the man, who looked as if he was minding his own business, but he was actually scanning the room. He had long, black hair and wore a black fedora hat and a long belted leather coat. He couldn't look more like a dark magic paranormal if he tried.

Necromancers could communicate with the dead by summoning their spirits as apparitions or visions and, darker than that, reanimate the dead, to use the dead as a weapon or slave. A necromancer's power was malevolent, and she had a feeling he suited that reputation.

Slaine gave her the drinks and said, "Good luck."

Bhal walked over and stood by his table. He didn't look up. "Idris?"

He looked up slowly and said nothing.

"My name is Bhaltair."

Idris sat back and crossed his legs. "Bhaltair, Chief of the Samhain warriors, bodyguard to the Debrek clan, and left on this earth to fight all evil on solstice night."

Bhal sat down and pushed the vodka over to him. "You know who I am. Good, then you know it's probably a good idea to help me."

"I am available at the right price," Idris said.

"I wasn't planning on paying for your services. I simply want some information I think you might have."

Idris finished his drink then lifted the one Bhal brought him. He gave her a look of complete innocence.

"Oh? What information could I possibly have that the great chief would want?"

Idris was clearly an arrogant arsehole as far as Bhal was concerned, but she'd play along.

"I'm looking for a new bar or club that's become popular in the community."

"No Such Place," Idris replied.

Bhal sighed. "Funny. Slaine seems to think there is."

"I just told you— it's called *No Such Place*. I think the owner was trying to be amusing."

"No Such Place." Bhal rolled her eyes. "Can you tell me where it is?"

"I could." Idris drummed his fingers on the table. "But what is it worth? I need payment for my services."

Bhal's anger was starting to rise. Sera was out there, and Bhal was sure she needed her. She could feel it.

"Your payment is me not pulling my sword from my back and not running you through," Bhal said menacingly.

Idris gave her a half smile. "And I thought you and the Debreks were full of goodness and light."

Bhal leaned forward. "Not when people we care about are in danger."

Idris sighed and took out a notebook. He scribbled something down and ripped out the paper. Bhal snatched it from his fingers. It was an address. She got up quickly.

Idris said, "You are in my debt, Warrior."

Bhal ignored him and walked out of the club.

❖

Gilbert was lost in the Ceal void, as he and Anka communed with the God Balor. His senses meant nothing as they floated in terror. This was a nothingness that felt all-consuming and terrifying.

Gilbert had been here once before, when Balor tore his soul from the underworld and offered him a deal to get back to the land of the living as his emissary. That was just as frightening as now.

Of course Gilbert took that deal straight away. Existence in the underworld, the pain and the horror, made his anger towards his daughter Victorija all the worse. He'd thought and thought about how he would like to make her suffer, and make the Debreks suffer.

Gilbert had grabbed the chance to live again, help Balor, and destroy his daughter. It made him sick to find out she had gone back to the Debreks and blood bonded with a human.

Shrieks and screams of Balor's lost souls permeated the void.

"Anka? Are you here?"

"Yes. I'm with you."

But Gilbert could see nothing.

They waited and waited, Gilbert's anxiety building with every minute. Then his mind was seized, and he was only a spectator.

❖

Anka saw a flash of red in the void. Two red eyes permeated the nothingness. Her breathing became more laboured as her anxiety rose.

As the eyes got closer, a spotlight came over Gilbert. Balor was within him. Before now Balor had only shared thoughts with her as she prayed, and this was as close as she'd ever been to him.

"Balor?"

He lifted his hand and stroked her hair. She felt a buzz of power radiate through her body.

"My ever faithful Anka. We meet at last." Gilbert's voice was deep and booming.

"Balor, it has been my dream to meet you."

"Here I am in the body of my emissary. I am as strong as I have been since I was trapped in here by my people, thanks to you and the souls you are sending me," Balor said.

"Soon will you be strong enough to return to the earth?" Anka asked.

"I will, but the power that keeps me here is stronger than the portal you opened to the other side. We will need the keys, and I need you to find the isle of Lochlan."

"What and where is Lochlan?" Anka asked.

"It's a point on the earth where all the different realms of existence converge. I came to earth that way, but the location has been changed since then. It's only there that the portal can be opened, and only with the correct keys."

"What keys?"

"I came to this existence using a stone of the Anu. It took me a long, long time to find it, but when I did, it opened up the earth to me, and I knew I could rule it—and I will, with you and my emissary by my side. Your people—witches, vampires, shifters—they will not have to hide any more, I promise you."

"Where can we find the stone?" Anka said.

"Those that protected the stone of Anu came just as my dream of controlling this earth was coming into being and used it to send me here. All I know is they broke up the stone to hide it. What it became is something you and Gilbert will have to find out."

Gilbert cupped her face firmly, and Anka saw fury in his fiery red eyes. "I have been here a long, long time, and I need to get out of here. I gave you the knowledge to make your power even greater than any other witch all those centuries ago, when you needed it, and now it's time to repay the debt."

Balor was frightening, even to Anka, who had seen some of the most terrifying monsters.

"I will not be disappointed, Anka."

"I promise, Balor. I will find the keys to open up the portal out of here."

He loosened his grip. "I know you will. When I get out of here, my body will return from the very earth beneath our feet. But you must find the descendants. It was foretold to me a long time ago that only my human kin could kill me. They must be killed. They are the last two lines. All the others have been hunted down and killed."

"Yes, Balor. We will get them. One is well protected, and we are still trying to find out who the other is, but we will get them."

Balor pulled Anka to him and gave her a passionate kiss, making her moan. Then he dropped to his knees.

Balor was gone.

Gilbert was breathing heavily on the floor, and then suddenly they were both back at the altar. Anka turned and caressed Gilbert's face.

"I spoke to Balor." She was overawed by his touch, his power.

Asha rushed to them. "Thank the gods, Madam Anka. You were gone for hours."

It felt like only minutes had passed.

"Hours?" Anka said.

Asha nodded.

"Anka, I heard it all," Gilbert said. "We will bring about a new dawn on earth." Gilbert looked down at his shaking hands. "I can still feel his power. It's—"

Anka stood and took his hand. "Come with me."

Bhal stood in a small industrial area of the East End of London. It was a run-down area. Old sandstone housing on the other side of the road had boarded up windows and doors, and under the bridge, the arches that once held businesses looked abandoned.

One archway had a mechanic's sign, and another a taxi firm's, the perfect place to hide in plain sight. Bhal could feel the buzz of magic in the air.

She followed her instinct and walked to the former mechanic's boarded-up door. The buzz in the air was strong, but a hidden club like this must have security.

"Hidden security," Bhal said.

She touched the door and found herself thrown back onto the ground six feet away. "God's blood." Bhal bolted up onto her feet and brushed herself down.

She strode over to the door again. Bhal was having one more look before her sword took down the door. Her sword—forged by the Druid priests, and set with a powerful emerald gemstone—could break magic and destroy the spirits of the dead.

Above, a train rolled by, and a bird sat on the top of the bridge. She could feel that it was a paranormal creature, more than likely a shifter.

She stared at it and shouted, "You've got ten seconds to show yourself, or I break down this door."

The bird lifted off and flew down, transforming as it went into a human form. By the time it landed, it was a huge man, around eight feet tall, with a big bushy beard and tattoos. He stood in front of the door with his arms folded defensively.

"I wouldn't go making threats if you want entry."

Bhal took a step towards him. "It isn't a threat, it's a promise. I am Bhaltair, Chief of the Samhain warriors, and I'm not going to ask nicely again."

He narrowed his eyes, then took a step to the side. He waved his hand and the door opened. "Have a nice time, Bhaltair of the Samhain warriors."

Once she took a step inside, the run-down appearance fell away, and Bhal found she had entered a highly modern club with a black and silver interior and neon signage.

Nicely hidden. But who owned this place?

The clientele were sitting on couches with small tables in front, either kissing, having sex, drinking blood from each other, manically laughing, or staring into space.

The customers had drinks, but waiters were walking around with glass vials on their trays. When they dropped them at the tables, the customers grabbed at them, biting off the tops and guzzling the liquid inside.

This is not good. Bhal's worry was starting to reach panic levels now. Surely Sera wasn't involved in this?

Bhal grabbed one of the servers as they passed. "Has Sera Debrek been in?"

The young server hesitated but looked intimidated by Bhal's appearance. "In the last private room at the back exit to the club."

Bhal hurried as fast as she could without drawing attention to herself. Nearer the back of the club it was busier, so she could move unnoticed. Bhal came to a corridor with a set of four black doors.

She checked the first three rooms quickly. Two had guests clearly enjoying each other's company, and one was empty. When she tried the fourth door, it was locked. She took a few steps back and rammed it with her shoulder.

Her heart stopped at the sight waiting for her. Sera was stretched unconscious on the couch with her blouse ripped open, a female vampire kissing and touching her.

Bhal didn't think twice about it. She pulled the vampire from Sera and threw her against the wall, so hard that the vampire was embedded in the wall.

"Don't ever touch her," Bhal roared.

The vampire shook her head and recovered her senses. She snarled and bared her teeth. "Sera's mine, my little Debrek plaything."

Bhal felt pure fury and saw red. They launched at each other and fought hand to hand.

"I'm going to rip your throat out for disturbing me."

Bhal flipped her over her head, so that the vampire was facing the other way, pulled her sword from the scabbard on her back, and swiped the vampire's head clean off. It rolled on the floor and came to a stop, with a shocked look left on the vampire's face.

Bhal threw her sword on the table and fell to her knees beside Sera. "Please be all right, please."

Her hands trembled as she touched Sera's face. It was hot and clammy, but she was breathing normally. Bhal saw glass vials of whatever they were ingesting out front on the table.

"I have to get her out of here."

Bhal buttoned up Sera's blouse and stuffed a couple full bottles of the chemical into her pocket, put her sword in her scabbard, and lifted Sera into her arms.

"It will be all right, Sera. I'll take care of you." Bhal had to admit she felt scared, not something she was used to feeling.

Bhal carried her to the door and peeked out, making sure she wasn't about to be jumped by club security. Everyone was too involved in what they were doing. The back door to the club was right next to this private room. So Bhal pushed her way out of the back door, and into the gloom of early evening.

Sera moaned in pain.

"You're safe, you're safe now."

If Sera didn't need her so much, Bhal would have gone back into the club to kill whoever was responsible for this. But as much as she wanted to respond to the fury she was feeling, Sera came first.

Her first instinct was to head home, but Sera would hate Byron to see her like this. Sera was obviously going through some difficulties at the moment, after her argument with Byron yesterday. Bhal wanted to give her a chance to recover first.

There was one person who could help Sera and check what was going on in there—Magda. Magda was a powerful witch who was close to the clan since tutoring Amelia, the Principessa.

She set off, taking the back alleys and climbing from roof to roof, so they wouldn't be spotted by humans.

❖

Amelia nodded to the vampires she passed as she walked to Byron's meeting room. The door was shut but she didn't hear Byron talking, so she must be alone.

She opened the door and walked in. Byron was sitting at the table. Her hands were clasped, and she leaned her head upon them, deep in thought.

"Byron? Are you okay?"

Byron looked up at her and smiled. "I am now you are here."

Amelia joined her partner at the table, sitting next to Byron. Byron took her hand and kissed it.

"You looked deep in thought, sweetheart," Amelia said.

"Hmm. Everything is starting to happen. The humans are starting to notice. Daisy's grandmother called me. I fear we are going to have more nights like last night."

"We must do all we can to protect them," Amelia said.

"I think it will affect us all, paranormal and human. Witches, vampires, shifters, and the rest are becoming more confident. The humans starting to notice is just the beginning. This could be the dark time that was prophesied."

"If it is, we can come together and defend ourselves. Magda says my magic is coming by leaps and bounds."

Byron reached over and touched Amelia's baby bump. "You hold our future."

"I will be fine. Everything happens for a reason, and it was meant to be that I was pregnant."

"Hmm. How was practice with Daisy today?" Byron asked.

"Good. That's what I was coming to talk to you about. You know those dreams I've been having?"

"The one with the woman in the river?"

"Yes," Amelia said, "Daisy's been having them too. It must mean something."

"To do with your connection, as the descendants?" Byron asked.

"Yes. We've asked Daisy's friend Skye to investigate it. She used to do the research for Daisy's Monster Hunter YouTube channel, and Skye already knows about our world."

"Hopefully she can help, then," Byron said. "I'm sending Alexis and Torija to Paris on reconnaissance. We need to find out what is happening with Anka. She's become more powerful. Why else would she attack humans so blatantly."

"Are you sure Alexis and Torija will be the best team? Alexis barely tolerates her most of the time."

"Maybe, maybe not, but Torija knows the area like the back of her hand, and Alexis is my Duca."

Amelia narrowed her eyes. She could feel Byron's hunger for blood growing. "You're hungry."

"Come here." Byron pulled her over to sit on her knee.

Amelia could see her eyes were red, and her teeth erupted. "Wait." She locked the meeting room door and came back to Byron. She slipped off her jeans and underwear and sat on Byron's knee.

Byron kissed her, and Amelia teased her by running her tongue around Byron's pointed teeth and sucked on her tongue.

Byron moaned and said, "What do you want, mia cara?"

Amelia was always overwhelmed with the depth of their connection. As it had from the start, Byron could disarm and make Amelia beg for her touch with a look. When Byron did touch her, she hungered for more and more.

Byron sucked her earlobe while her fingers found Amelia's wet centre. Amelia held Byron's head with her hands. "Yes."

Amelia trembled when Byron's teeth grazed her neck, and she teased her wet entrance with her fingers.

She kissed Byron and gasped into her mouth as Byron pushed two fingers inside her. Amelia moved her hips the tiniest bit, backwards and forwards, savouring the feeling.

"My beautiful Principessa. Do you feel how much I love you?"

"Yes," Amelia gasped. "But I want more."

Byron eased her fingers out of Amelia's wetness. "Show me, mia cara."

Amelia smiled and reached between them to undo Byron's belt. "I want all of you inside me."

Amelia pulled the strap-on that Byron always wore free from her underwear. Until fairly recent history, both Byron and Alexis had to present as male to be taken seriously in the banking and business worlds. But Byron very much identified with her masculine side and continued to dress masc and wear a strap-on. It was an integral part of her dominant energy, and Amelia loved it.

Byron held the base firmly and allowed her wife to lower herself onto it, a bit at a time. She loved to be inside Amelia when she drank from her. There was nothing closer.

"Ah, good girl," Byron said as she was fully inside her.

She kissed Amelia and held on to her hips as Amelia started to lift them up and down on her. Byron thrust along with her, the pressure and pleasure building beneath the base of her strap-on.

Byron was hungry for her wife's blood, but it tasted all the sweeter if she held off as long as possible. Her hips thrust in time with Amelia until her wife leaned her body back, becoming overwhelmed with the building pleasure in her body.

Byron ran her hand up from Amelia's chest until she clasped her hand softly around Amelia's neck.

"Yes, sweetheart, yes."

Byron was always mindful to be careful with her wife, now that she was pregnant, and their lovemaking was a lot gentler now, but still as intense.

"I'm going to come, bite me now," Amelia shouted. Amelia leaned forward so Byron could bite her neck and shouted, "Now, now."

Byron's teeth pierced her neck, and she drank in her lover's sweet blood. As it hit her tongue, her own orgasm exploded from her sex and rushed all over her body, as her hunger was sated.

Amelia went stiff and cried out, holding Byron tightly around her neck as they lost themselves in each other.

CHAPTER SIX

B hal awkwardly pressed the bell at the back door to Magda's shop. It wasn't easy to do while holding Sera. Magda's shop sold tarot cards, crystals for any reason you could want, trinkets, incense, books on magic. Mostly it was for humans, but she did have some items for the paranormal community, hidden from human gaze.

She heard Magda shout, "Coming," then Magda opened the door while saying, "You're two hours late—" She looked both of them up and down.

Bhal said, "I need your help, Magda."

"Come in, come in."

Bhal was ushered in the door, and Magda called to her granddaughter, "Piper, shut the shop up and come upstairs." She then turned to Bhal. "We have the flat upstairs. I'll show you to the spare bedroom."

"Thank you."

Magda showed them to a bedroom and Bhal laid Sera carefully down on the bed.

"Let me see her," Magda said.

Bhal stepped back, pulled her long coat off, and started to pace. "I found her unconscious like this at an underground club for paranormals. I didn't want to take her home like this. Sera and Byron had quarrelled and—"

"You're welcome here, Warrior." Magda placed her hands on Sera's head and chest. "Her blood is poisoned with something."

Bhal rummaged in the pocket of her black utility trousers and took out the glass vials she'd picked up at the club. "They were all taking this."

Magda took the vials in her hand and her eyes went wide. "This feels like malevolent magic, not a human drug. May I take these and test them out?"

"Yes, please. Do you think it's safe to revive her?" Bhal asked.

Just then Piper popped her head in the door. "Is everything okay? What's wrong with Sera?"

Piper had been against helping a vampire clan when the Debreks first came in contact with Magda and her granddaughter, but since had come to see that the Debreks were on the good side.

"Piper, we have some potion to analyse. Bhal, I'm sure it's safe to revive her."

Once they left, Bhal got out her hip flask of water. Sera murmured and struggled in her unconscious state.

"It'll be all right soon, Sera. I promise."

Then Bhal realized her flask was near empty. "God's blood." She rushed to the bathroom sink to fill up her flask. The magic was in her hands, not the water. She had revived Katie from near death not long ago, when a newly turned vampire had attacked her, and those few humans she had got to on time on Samhain. The gift was powerful.

But now Bhal was frightened. Even though logically she knew it would work, the drug was an unknown quantity and the thought of losing Sera terrified her.

Bhal poured some water into her hands and then dripped it into Sera's mouth. Each second felt like a lifetime. Sera started to squirm, and Bhal took her hands in hers.

"You're okay. Come on, Serenity Debrek, waken up. I…" Bhal couldn't find the words to explain how she felt. "I need you."

Sera gasped and then her eyes sprang wide open. "What—?"

"Just catch your breath."

She could see how Bhal was holding her hands, and so Bhal moved away. "I gave you water to revive you."

"Where are we? Does Byron know?"

Sera turned on her side. Her head was full of mush and hurt like hell.

"Byron did ask me to find you, but she doesn't know where I found you. I came to Magda's to help you, and I hope she might be able to tell me about the stuff you've taken."

"Byron's going to kill me."

"Byron doesn't have to know where I found you. That's your call," Bhal said.

Sera was taken aback at Bhal's answer. "You'd keep something back from Byron? About me fucking up?" Ripples of pain and sickness ran through her, and she started to groan. "It hurts all over."

"When was the last time you fed?" Bhal asked.

"Can't remember."

Piper walked in with a bottle of water. "Here's some water for Sera. If you need anything, shout, okay?"

"Thank you."

Bhal held out her arm, covered with Celtic tattoos, and offered her wrist. The thought of stomaching blood at the moment was awful—not a reaction Sera had ever experienced in her life. "No, I feel too sick."

Bhal sighed. "What's the last thing you remember?"

Sera tried to make sense of her memories. They were there, but she felt like she was swimming underwater and then slowly sinking to the gloom of the deep. That's what she liked about this new drug, the nothingness she felt, but then as she slowly climbed back to consciousness, the shame loomed and then shrouded her.

"I walked in, took a seat, and the Malum was bought to me, and then I don't remember anything till wakening up here," Sera said.

"Malum?"

Sera didn't want to admit to her biggest critic what she had done. "It doesn't matter." She started to shiver. "Just leave me alone, Bhal. Just give me a chance to feel better, and we can go home."

"Sera—"

"Just go!" Anger and frustration erupted from her. "Go now. You'll soon have your chance to show Byron the Debrek that fucked up."

Sera saw hurt in Bhal's eyes. Not something she would expect to see.

Bhal got up and left her.

Sera wrapped her arms around her head and began rocking. The hunger for the drug had been increasing and increasing over the last few weeks. It was fun at first, the intense high and then the plummet into the gloom, but then the high slowly faded through time.

The hunger for a high that never was replaced with oblivion. She thought of what her family would think of her behaviour all the time. Her mother and father would be so shocked to see how far she had fallen.

Help, please, Sera pleaded silently, but who was going to help her? She was not going to admit to her family that she needed help. No.

❖

"I'm going to miss you so much," Daisy said. "I can't imagine a day without you."

Daisy was saying goodbye to Torija in the drawing room before she left for France.

"Who wouldn't miss me?" Torija grinned.

"Same old arrogant vamp." Daisy smiled.

Torija put her arms around Daisy's waist. "I know I turned my life around for good, but you wouldn't want me to be too good, would you?"

Daisy smiled, leaned in to Torija, and grasped her chin lightly. "That would be very boring. I like a bit of devil in my vamp."

"And am I your vamp?"

"You know it. It's written across my heart."

Torija pressed her lips to Daisy's. She grasped her lip with her teeth and released it slowly, making Daisy moan.

Daisy wrapped her hands around Torija's neck. "Are you sure you don't have more time?"

"We only said goodbye an hour ago, and what a goodbye it was," Torija said.

Daisy sighed. "This is the first mission you're going on without me. I feel worried."

"I'm an immortal born vampire with my blood bond's strong blood coursing through my body—I'm unstoppable."

Daisy put her hand on Torija's chest. "Have you got enough blood bags?"

To any non-paranormal couple, such a question would sound sick, but Daisy made it sound like a wife making sure her partner had packed her lunch.

Torija lost her bravado and looked down at the floor.

"What's wrong?" Daisy asked.

"You know I don't like having to use your blood bags."

Born vampires who weren't bonded and turned vampires could drink from anyone, but a bonded born vampire could only drink from their bond, or they would starve and eventually slip into madness and death.

So separations meant carrying blood bags. Amelia had to do this for Byron as well. Both Daisy and Amelia donated blood to store in blood bags, and they were kept medically refrigerated in the cellar.

Torija wouldn't go with Daisy to watch while she gave blood. "My father kept my mother drugged and locked up as a blood donor.

To think of you draining the blood from your body, for me…I hate it. I don't want to ever be like him."

Daisy cupped both her cheeks. "The difference is you don't take. I offer it to you because I love you. I know the pain your father put you through never really leaves you, but you have to know I do this with love. Besides, do you ever think that I would let you take anything from me?"

Torija smiled. "No, you are the bravest human I have ever laid eyes on. The first time I met you, *you* bit *me*. A human, bite Victorija Dred? I knew then you were going to be a thorn in my side."

Daisy laughed. "And I was, Torija. Come on, let's go before I don't let you leave."

They started to walk to the door when Torija stopped and chuckled.

"What is it?" Daisy asked.

"It's Katie. She's telling Alexis, *Try and work together. It's what Byron wants.* Giving Alexis her orders."

Daisy poked Torija with her finger and said sternly, "I'm telling you the same. Play nice, we want you to be accepted in this clan, and Alexis has suffered more than most by Victorija's hand."

Torija held up her hands. "All right, all right. I know that. It's simply amusing to see Alexis told to behave."

"Well, you've been warned too, so go."

Torija turned and gave Daisy her trademark flourishing bow. "Your wish is my command, Madam."

"I'm *Madam* now? Married, are we?"

"Oui, in the vampire world we are. You can't get rid of me now," Torija said.

"As if I'd want to."

Torija took her hand. "Remember what I told you too—stay close to Byron and this house. Don't go home to the flat on your own. Anka and her legion of hell would like nothing better than to get hold of you, when they find out who you really are."

"Don't worry. You know Byron won't let Amelia and me out of her sight."

"Good."

They walked out to the reception hall hand in hand. Alexis was holding Katie in her arms.

Alexis kissed Katie on her head and said, "Be careful."

Katie nodded and wiped away a tear.

A team of vampires waited by the main entrance, trying to give the Duca privacy.

"You ready to go, Alexis?" Daisy asked.

Alexis let Katie go. "Yes, we are ready."

Torija bowed once again. "Goodbye, Debreks all. I'll look after her for you, Katie."

In a low voice Alexis said, "I don't need your help for anything. Let's go."

Daisy stepped beside Katie.

Katie said, "I hope they can work together."

"I hope they both come back without taking each other's heads off."

That broke the tension and they both chuckled.

❖

Bhal watched as Piper handed Magda a bottle of green liquid and poured it into a glass beaker. Witches' potions looked more like chemistry these days.

Magda had taken the vial from the club to her potion room and was testing it to try to learn about it.

"Magda, Sera called it Malum."

Magda lifted up the beaker and swirled it round. It had turned deep green. "I thought as much. Malum translates as death, but witches tend to call it slow death. It's malevolent magic that only the most accomplished witch could make."

The word *death* associated with Sera was not something Bhal had ever had to think about. She was a born vampire, immortal. But this was dark magic.

I can't lose her. Her steady heartbeat. "What effects does it have? My power will keep her alive and safe, won't it?"

"Bhal, your power is like nothing I've ever known. It's an ancient power, and coupled with the fact that she is a born vampire, she'll be safe with you, but the withdrawal, if that's what she wants, will be hard. Sera's going to need you."

"Magda, on Samhain, the rampaging paranormals had a glazed look in their eyes, could that be connected?" Bhal asked.

"Yes, that fits perfectly. In humans this would kill immediately. To people from our community, it is a slow painful death, physically and mentally. Like any human drug, it starts off with such a high, and then the user sinks into oblivion. Over time, the high wanes, and oblivion is all they get, the more detached they become from themselves. So they look dazed, and even those paranormals who wouldn't dream of injuring anyone lose their sense of conscience and follow their basest instincts. You can imagine werewolves, vampires, shifters, following their instincts without any clear judgement. They will kill, and then eventually die themselves."

"Anka is weakening the community's ability to fight back against her, isn't she?"

Magda nodded sadly. "And causing mayhem for humans in the meantime."

"How do we fight it, Grandma?" Piper asked.

Just then they heard a crash and a howl of pain.

"Sera," Bhal said.

She ran from the room and burst through the bedroom door. Sera was lying hunched on the floor, a pool of blood beside her and blood all around her mouth. She wasn't keeping blood down.

"It's the withdrawal, Bhal," Magda said behind her.

Bhal scooped her up and placed her on the bed. "Magda, could you get me a washcloth and warm water, please?"

"Of course."

Bhal took some water from her flask and poured it into her hands. "Open your mouth, Sera."

Sera shook her head. "I feel…sick."

"I know, but this will make you feel better. I promise."

Sera slowly opened her lips, and Bhal poured the water in. Sera smacked her lips together and her shaking started to calm.

Bhal stroked her blond hair from her brow and whispered, "Take deep breaths. You'll feel better soon."

After a minute, Sera's eyes flickered open and she gazed deeply into Bhal's eyes.

Bhal smiled at her. "Do you feel better?"

"My head's clearer, and the pain in my stomach and all over my body is calming."

"Good."

Magda arrived with the cloth and water.

"Thank you, Magda."

"Anything else you need, let me know."

Bhal dipped the cloth in the water and began to dab it against Sera's mouth.

"What are you doing?" Sera asked. Her voice was strained.

"Taking care of you."

The look in Sera's eyes was surprise. "Why?"

"Because I care. Is there room in your life for someone who cares?"

Sera was taken aback by the kindness and gentleness Bhal was showing her. "I…I didn't think you cared."

"I always have."

Sera didn't answer that. She didn't have the words. This was the person who bossed her around her whole life and pointed out her failings.

Bhal finished wiping Sera's mouth and stretched out her arm. "Drink from me. The blood will make you feel even better. You must be so hungry."

She was, ravenous. Now that Bhal had made the withdrawal symptoms fade, the hunger was coming racing back. Sera eyed Bhal's wrist greedily, and then she looked up at Bhal's eyes.

Now that she could think much more clearly, Sera realized that the softer look in Bhal's eyes had been there for a while now. Since she had been taken hostage by Anka, Bhal had been constantly checking up on her, but Sera pushed her away. But what did it mean?

Whatever it meant, Sera sensed that once she tasted Bhal's blood, nothing would be the same.

"Come on, Sera. My blood is rich."

No sooner than Bhal had said it, Sera's teeth bit deep into Bhal's wrist. Sera moaned as Bhal's rich blood washed over her mouth. No one had ever tasted like this.

When the intensity of her hunger started to calm, Sera looked up at Bhal. She was watching her feed, her lips parted, and her breathing was short and breathy. It felt like they were taking part in this together.

Sera experienced a warmth racing all over her body, an energy that tingled her fingers and toes and awoke every nerve ending in her body that had been dulled since her path spiralled downward, especially her sex. She pulled her teeth away from Bhal's wrist.

That feeling was…just *no*. Sera had experienced a less intense version of this when they had fought on Samhain night. Sera couldn't think about it. There was too much going on in her head as it was.

"Do you feel better?"

"Yes, thank you."

"The colour is coming back to your cheeks."

"Thank you, Bhal, for taking care of me."

Bhal took her hand. "I always have, but maybe you didn't realize it."

This conversation was getting too intense—for the way she was feeling, anyway.

"What are we going to do? About going home, about Byron."

"I think you should sleep here tonight to recover, and we can go back in the morning."

Sera nodded. "But what do I tell Byron? What do *you* tell her?"

"What do you want, Sera? Do you want to break away from this drug? Truly?" Bhal asked.

"I was looking to escape from my life. I felt useless to my family, to my clan, and an eternity of those feelings stretched ahead of me. Then when someone introduced me to Malum at The Sanctuary, I got this huge high, then oblivion. Oblivion was what I wanted. I didn't want to live my life with these feelings. Then when Slaine kicked out the dealer, I followed him to No Such Place, and I sank deeper and deeper, but I can't see a way out. I'm lost."

"But do you want to get better?" Bhal asked.

"Yes, I don't want to feel lost from my family and see their disappointment. I want to get better and see if I can live life again."

"Then if you allow me, I'll help you get through this. My rejuvenation power can get you through withdrawal."

"Like methadone does humans?" Sera asked.

"Magda seems to think so. Like I said to you earlier, it's up to you what you tell Byron. But if you want to keep it between us, why don't we tell her you were on the lead of this new drug, and tell her what you've found out about it?"

"You'd really do that?" Sera asked.

Bhal took out her phone and started to text Byron. "I'm telling the Principe that I found you and that I'm helping you follow a lead."

Bhal's loyalty to Byron was unshakable, but she was offering a greater loyalty to Sera in this moment. Sera didn't know what to make of it. She lay back, feeling tired after the rush of Bhal's blood. "I'm tired."

Bhal pulled a blanket over her.

"You won't leave me, will you?"

Bhal shook her head. "I'll stay right here." She sat on the floor, leaning her back against the back of the bed.

As tired as Sera was, her mind was still busy with so many thoughts. "Bhal, can you tell me a story? One from your people's legends, maybe?"

"I'm not a bard, but I'll try my best. Umm..." Bhal was silent for a few seconds then said, "Yes. This is a good tale. Long ago, before even the Celtic peoples populated the lands of Scotland, Ireland, and France, a tribe of people with godlike powers came to our land. They were called the Tuatha De Danann, or the tribe of Danu. They were said to come from a mystical place in the cold north."

Bhal's lilting of the old tongue was so relaxing to listen to. In Sera's mind she pictured these godlike people from the tale, and her thoughts were calming.

"It is said that ships of the sky surrounded by dark clouds brought them to our land. They were tall with red or blond hair, and the most amazing blue eyes. They invaded the isles of Ireland and conquered them with power unknown to the peoples there. Their king lost an arm in the battle, and the doctor replaced it with an arm of silver, and over time it grew skin and was as good as it had been before."

"That sounds like a robot arm," Sera piped up.

"You're supposed to be sleeping. Just listen."

Sera sighed. "Okay. It's interesting, that's all."

"It's a story as old as time. My mathair told me this tale since before I can remember."

"Who is your mathair?" Sera asked.

"My mother."

Bhal said the word *mother* with such sadness, such longing. She had never seen this side of Bhal. She was the stoic warrior—do this, do that, discipline—but a mention of her mother who was long, long dead, and a hint of the emotion underneath came out.

Tonight had been full of new sides of Bhal, but she was too tired to think about it too deeply. She put her hands under her head and closed her eyes. "Tell me more."

Bhal smiled. "The Tuatha De Danann brought us the belief in the Goddess Danu that the Celtic tribes worshiped. They conquered and subdued the land with a magical sword that glowed white, a spear that shot balls of fire, an axe that..."

Sera drifted off with Bhal's voice creating peace in her mind.

CHAPTER SEVEN

Amelia and Daisy walked downstairs to the drawing room. Skye had been in touch to say that she could give them some information. Byron had promised to meet them shortly, so she could hear what Skye had found.

Amelia put the iPad on the coffee table and shared the screen with the TV above the fireplace.

"I've texted Skye to say we'll be ready in a few minutes," Daisy said.

"Good. How are your friends coping with finding out about our paranormal world?"

"Skye and Pierce are cool with it. Like me, they've always believed in this world. That's why we started Monster Hunters—to find out the truth. It's still a shock when you do get the whole truth. I still get overwhelmed sometimes when I wake up in the morning and find I'm sharing a bed with a vampire, but then my brain and my heart click into gear, and I remember all that has happened," Daisy said.

"Yes, me too sometimes. This descendant thing and fighting what's coming worries me. I try not to say that to Byron because she worries too much about me as it is."

"Yeah, is it like a fist fight?" Daisy joked, "'Cause if it is, I don't think we are the best candidates to fist-fight a God."

Amelia laughed and rubbed her growing baby bump. "Very true."

The drawing room door opened, and Byron entered. "Bhal has texted me. She's found Sera, and all is well."

"I told you she'd be fine," Amelia said. "Sera can look after herself."

Byron sat down on the couch beside them. "It was that last argument we had. She wasn't like herself—in fact she hasn't been herself for a while. But Bhal says she's working on a lead about Anka, and Bhal's helping her."

"Bhal has got a lot of love for Sera," Amelia said. "I wonder if they could work it out."

"You think?" Byron asked.

"Yeah," Daisy agreed, "her eyes follow her about the room."

"You don't have reservations about Bhal's interest in her?" Amelia asked.

"Bhal's never had a relationship in all the time I've known her. She's maybe not the best thing for Sera—besides, they've always fought like cat and dog. No, I can't see it. Right—is your friend ready?"

Byron shut down their talk. She obviously wasn't comfortable with the conversation.

"Yeah, I'll call her now," Daisy said.

Daisy connected the call, and Skye appeared on the TV. "Hi, Skye."

When Skye saw who was in the room, she tensed up. "Hi."

Daisy said, "This is Amelia, and this is Byron, the head of the Debrek clan."

"Good evening, Skye," Byron said.

Skye waved and said nervously, "Hi, everyone."

"Daisy says you've got some information for us on Melusine?" Amelia asked.

"Yeah, lots. Should I go ahead with what I've found?"

"Go, Skye," Daisy said.

"Okay." Skye tapped her pen on the notebook in front of her. "Melusine is part of a myth in many European countries, which started in the late 1300s."

"Wow, okay. Tell us more," Amelia said.

"The story goes that one day the King of Albany, which is an ancient name for Scotland, went hunting and came across a beautiful lady in the forest."

Amelia thought, *That's got to be what I'm seeing in my vision. Melusine.*

"She was a faerie called Pressyne."

Amelia looked at Daisy who said, "Not Melusine?"

"No, I'll get to her. The king wanted to marry her, and she said she would if he made a promise. In these tales there's always some sort of condition to a mortal and faerie marrying. The promise was that he wouldn't enter her chamber when she bathed or gave birth. So, she gave birth to triplet girls—Melusine, Melior, and Palatyne—but her husband violated that promise and saw her in her full fae form. So she took her babies and was exiled and travelled to the lost isle of Avalon."

"You're kidding," Daisy said.

"Nope, not kidding," Skye replied, "this myth has it all, doesn't it?"

Amelia looked at Byron and then Daisy, before saying to Skye, "Like King Arthur kind of Avalon?"

"Yes, totally, but there's so much more. When the three sisters get to fifteen years old, they feel so angry for the way their mother was treated that they punish their father by trapping him and his wealth in a mountain. Their mother was so angry at the way they had disrespected their father that she cursed each of them. Melusine was cursed with becoming a serpent from the waist down."

"Like a mermaid?" Byron asked.

This was the first time Byron had asked Skye a question, and she became a bit ruffled. Amelia smiled. She knew what Byron's powerful presence did to people.

"Um…no…uh…not a mermaid. Mythical experts appear to agree it was a different thing. A Melusine was a thing in its own right. Like the woman on the Starbucks cup was a Melusine."

Daisy jumped in, "That's what Amelia thought when she looked at her coffee cup. Skye, we saw a vision of a woman called Melusine in a river, meeting a guy named Raymond. Is that what happened?"

"Yeah, similar to her mother, King Raymond wanted to marry her, and she agreed as long as he promised not to enter her chambers on a Saturday."

"Sounds familiar," Amelia said. "Let me guess, he didn't keep his word?"

"He did for a long time. Time enough for them to have ten sons, and Melusine to use her magical power to expand Raymond's territory and construct huge castles to consolidate his power as king. Here comes the *but*—a courtier who didn't like the queen convinces him that she sees another man on Saturdays. So he barges in, sees what he describes to the court as a hideous serpent. Melusine turns into a dragon and flies off."

Daisy's eyes went wide. "I didn't see the dragon thing coming. Was she ever seen again?"

"Well, she did come back only in order to feed her two youngest sons. The stories talk this up to say that she really was a good Christian woman who couldn't help her own lineage. The writer did this, it's said, to give her this Christian makeover because the royal houses of Europe wanted to claim their lineage from her and her ten sons, making them ethereal and above the population."

"Wow," Daisy said.

"Did you learn anything else, Skye? Any connection to Amelia and Daisy?"

"No, sorry. That's as far as my research went," Skye said.

Amelia said, "Don't be sorry. That's an amazing amount of information. Thank you so much."

"Yes, thank you," Byron added.

Skye blushed. "You're welcome. Take care of yourself, Daisy, and keep in touch."

"I will. Thanks, Skye."

Skye signed off and they were left alone. The three of them were silent until Amelia said, "I don't know where to start. It's like a fairy tale you'd read as a child. Why are we seeing this, Daisy?"

"I don't know. There's, like, so much information to take in. We've got a darkness coming—"

"Bhal says that Anka devotes her life to the so-called God Balor. A Celtic God," Byron added.

Amelia rubbed her forehead. "Darkness, Balor, and a fairy tale. We need help, but who can help us?"

"Sybil, maybe?"

Sybil was a witch from the coven called the cunning folk, based in the New Forest in the south of England. She had protected Amelia's birth mother from Anka's forces and made sure baby Amelia was safe after her mum died.

"I wish I could speak to the Grand Duchess at will," Amelia said. "She would be able to help."

The Grand Duchess, the former great matriarch of the Debrek clan, had spoken to her before when Amelia tuned in to the ancestors, but only at the Grand Duchess's will.

"I could ask my granny to contact Sybil," Daisy said. "They are good friends. Maybe with her and Magda we could get some answers to some questions."

"Good idea," Amelia said. Daisy hissed as if in pain, all of a sudden. "Are you okay?" Amelia asked.

Daisy screwed her eyes shut. "It's okay. Torija is hungry. I can feel it."

Byron reached over and took her hand. "She will be all right, Daisy."

"I know. It just hurts being apart from her."

"She'll be back before you know it," Amelia said.

❖

Alexis, Torija, and their team found a deserted area in a container storage area next to the ferry port in Calais.

They thought it would be easier to get in and out of France by ship, rather than the Debrek plane. Less scrutiny on their forged documents. Also the Dred clan would be looking out for the Debrek plane landing at an airport.

It was around ten o'clock, dark, and while standing between containers, out of the way of the security cameras, Torija took out a blood bag from her rucksack. She watched Alexis and the others do the same.

Torija looked at the bag with a knot of worry inside her. She hated to drink Daisy's blood this way. It went against everything she and Daisy had together. When she fed from Daisy, it was special, a loving, bonding act.

This reminded her of when she was still Victorija, before Daisy saved her soul. She remembered with shame taking humans with her to feed on whenever she chose. Torija had even refereed to one woman as a portable lunch box.

The guilt ate away at her—she supposed it always would. When she felt like this, Daisy always told her that what was important was what she did from now. She couldn't change the past. It was all about the good she could do in the world.

She looked up at Alexis, who had just finished with her blood bag. Her eyes were red and a trickle of blood ran down her chin.

"It's not the same, is it?"

Alexis narrowed her eyes and said, "Hurry up. We need to move out," then just walked away from her.

"This is going to be fun." Torija drank the blood she needed and took up her position at the front with Alexis. There were two turned vampires with them—Malk and Harris. Calais to Paris was a three-and-a-half-hour drive but with vampire speed not long at all.

So she was surprised to see Alexis heading for the hire car place at the front of the ferry terminal.

"We're driving? We could be there in no time," Torija said.

Alexis looked at her stony-faced. "We don't want to be noticed, and we could be if we ran there. Wait here."

Alexis went into the car hire place, and Torija said to Malk and Harris, "Is she usually this awkward?"

"The Duca is a great leader," Malk said.

Great. Fully paid-up members of the Alexis fan club.

Alexis came out of the car hire and waved them over to a car park. They came to a black Mercedes SUV.

"At least we'll be riding in style," Torija said.

"It's nothing to do with style—it's for practicality." Alexis got in the driver's seat. She patted the passenger seat and said, "You in here, where I can keep an eye on you."

Torija sighed and had to restrain the anger inside her. She got in and said, "Why on earth would I double-cross you, or the clan? The woman I love, my blood bond, is back there in the Debrek clan, under Byron's protection."

Alexis didn't answer. She started the car and drove off.

The group were soon on their way. But the car ride was taken in silence. It got to be too much for Torija, and she switched on the radio. Two seconds later Alexis switched it off again.

Although Torija had turned her life around, she was an alpha vampire, and this sort of provocative behaviour made her want to slam Alexis against a hard stone wall. But she remembered Daisy's advice. *Behave and try and build trust in the clan.*

So she used every fibre in her being to bite her tongue and look out the window. How was she ever going to be able to live in peace in the Debrek clan with Alexis? How could she make up for killing Alexis's first love, Anna?

Torija hadn't killed her in person, but she had ordered the attack on the Debrek house, at her father's instruction. But she still was responsible. All she could do was try to keep doing good. Like this mission to the Dred castle.

It was strange and horrifying going back to her former home. So much pain had happened there, not all inflicted by her. Her mother had been kept a prisoner in the dungeon for her blood, and Torija wasn't allowed to see her.

It damaged her, even more so when she managed to sneak in to see her and saw the pain she was in. It damaged Torija beyond measure, but that didn't excuse the killing that she became a part of.

Torija honestly wished she could raze the whole castle to the ground.

Alexis stopped the car at the side of the road fifteen minutes away from the castle. "I'll travel on foot from here with Malk. Torija and Harris, you wait here as backup."

"Wait, what?" Torija said.

"You heard my orders." Alexis stepped out of the car, and Torija followed her.

"I'm going. I was sent by the Principe because I owned this place. I've lived here all my life."

Alexis looked as if she was trying to find a reason not to change her mind. "Fine. Malk, stay here with Harris. I'll call you if we need backup."

"Yes, Duca," both vampires said.

"Let's go," Alexis said. She shot off and didn't even wait for Torija.

They ran till they hit the edge of the forest surrounding the castle. Alexis stopped on a rocky outcropping with a high drop.

Behind them was a small cave. Torija walked over and touched the rock. "I used to come here as a child to hide."

"Please spare us the all our yesterday's bit."

"Excuse me?" Torija asked.

"The I was an abused child, so I grew up to be a murderous arsehole bit. I've heard you."

Torija's anger was close to boiling over. "Listen, I have not used that as an excuse. I've also been on my knees before all who I've killed and begged for forgiveness, not with the hope of life. I thought I was going to die anyway. Even Anna forgave me."

Alexis strode over to her and shoved her in the chest. "Don't you say her name."

Torija hit her hand away. "Do not touch me."

"Why did you have to come to *my* clan, *my* family? Wasn't it enough that you turned me from a human without any thought to my wishes"—Alexis was shouting in her face, her eyes red and her fangs erupted from her gums—"and killed my first love? That wasn't enough for you. You had to come and become part of my clan?"

Torija pushed her back. Her own fangs erupted, ready for a fight. "Get out of my face, Alexis."

Alexis picked her up and threw her against the back of the cave wall, stone crumbling around her. Torija lost her restraint and ran at Alexis, toppling her to the ground.

They fought back and forth until Torija held Alexis on her back, her hand around her throat. Torija was a born vampire, so stronger than Alexis.

Torija hissed, ready to rip Alexis's throat, but then Daisy's face floated into her mind, and she started to calm.

Be the best vampire you can be, Torija.

Torija loosened her grip but kept hold of Alexis so she had her full attention.

"I don't expect your forgiveness, Alexis. I do expect you to believe that we have the same goals. You have your clan and the woman you love, as do I, and nothing will distract me from those goals. We are of one mind, and I will do everything to help protect her and the clan from Anka and whatever she has in store for Daisy and Amelia. Can you at least believe that?" Torija stood and offered her hand to Alexis. "Come on, my new wife told me to behave on this trip."

Alexis hesitated and raised an eyebrow and said, "Mine too. I'll never hear the end of it if this mission is a failure because of us."

She took Torija's hand and pulled herself up.

Torija and Alexis brushed themselves down. Torija said, "That's one thing we can agree on. Eternity is a long time with an angry spouse."

"So," Alexis said, "where is the best place to enter the castle?"

"There is a secret passageway from my old bedroom to the upper balcony in the great hall. We could observe in hiding there. Most things that are important happen around the great hall."

"Okay, lead the way." Alexis ushered Torija in front with her hand.

Torija walked on. Hopefully things would go smoothly from here, depending on what they found in the castle.

Torija and Alexis sat on the perimeter wall of the castle, waiting for their chance to get past the patrols. Security was tight. The number of Anka's people on patrol was way more than Torija used to have.

They weren't all vampires either. She could sense werewolves and shifters, as well as vampires, something she would never have allowed. This was going to be difficult.

The vampires would hear anything they said, so she and Alexis used hand signals. Eventually there was a break, and this side of the castle was clear, but they had to move quickly.

Alexis pointed to the gap and used her fingers to count down from five. Alexis was in the middle of jumping when Torija spotted a vampire coming around the corner. She grabbed Alexis by the collar and pulled her back up on the wall.

When Alexis saw why, she held up her hand in thanks. Soon enough they had the break they were looking for, and Torija led them up the castle wall, climbing from windowsill to balcony until they got up to the turret.

Torija held her hand up when they arrived at the windowsill to her old bedroom. She put her finger to her lips, hearing there was someone in there. Torija jumped as quietly as she could onto the stone balustrade. She perched there, flat against the wall, and inched along until she could look around the corner into the room.

She couldn't believe her eyes when she saw who was in the bedroom. Drasas, her former Duca, was standing by the bed in a state of undress kissing Anka. It couldn't be. When Torija had been on the other side, she'd seen Drasas's soul dragged kicking and screaming to the underworld. Byron told her that Drasas's body was sent back through the portal that Anka had opened, but it should have been an empty shell.

She kept as quiet as she possibly could, closed her eyes, and concentrated on the voices from within the bedroom.

"Get dressed. Tomorrow, we start our search," Anka said.

"Where do we start?"

"The keys that came to this world will appear in oral history and legends. I know some historians and ancient artifact dealers who don't come by them in the traditional way. With what Balor has told us, we can narrow it down."

"I can't wait to see the Debreks' faces, and my daughter's face when we destroy her new clan and Balor returns. We will crush them."

"Then, Gilbert Dred, we will stand on each side of Balor and run this world the right way."

The name hit Torija's ears like a hammer, and her legs turned to jelly, and all she could feel was falling.

❖

Alexis saw Torija fall and reached out to try to catch her but she was gone, down to the ground. "Fuck."

She climbed down as quickly as she could. If the patrols found her broken body, they would be in a lot of trouble. Alexis had heard what was said in the room. In that one conversation, their task got a whole lot harder.

Anka and her quest for Balor was bad enough—now they had the most evil vampire in history back in a healthy body.

She dropped down next to Torija. Her legs were facing the wrong way, she had double fractures, her arms were broken, and her skull was caved in at the side. Her body would repair, but not instantly from such a bad state.

Alexis patted her cheek. "Come on, Torija, heal fast. We need to get out of here." She heard voices around the corner. "Torija, you better heal fucking fast. We are in a bad situation here."

Her head injury was knitting back together, but the patrols were upon them. "Shit."

Alexis had to protect her.

She ran into the mob of guards and began hand-to-hand combat. She was up against five vampires, one with a gun pointed right at her. She broke the necks of two, grabbed the gun, and threw it behind her. The odds were looking a bit better until they healed, but no doubt there would be more guards upon them soon.

Alexis grabbed one of them and threw him through the air. He landed on an ornamental fence around a garden area. A black spike from the metal fence went right through his heart.

"Now would be a good time to heal, Torija."

She had a quick look behind her and saw Torija's legs looking straight again. One of the female vampires used Alexis's distracted state to punch her, and the force threw her in the air. She landed next to Torija.

"Come on, Torija. I need you."

All of a sudden Torija took a huge intake of breath and jumped to her feet.

"Glad you could join me at last."

Torija's eyes were red with utter fury. Alexis watched Torija dispatch the last few vampires with ease. She had to admit, a born vampire was a good person to have on your side.

Torija had blood dripping down her chin and was breathing heavily. "Did you hear?"

"Yes," Alexis said, "we can think about that later. Now we just have to get out of here."

Just as they were about to run, two feet slammed into the dirt next to them. Alexis turned around and Drasas, or Gilbert as he now was, was standing in front of them, smiling.

"My dear daughter. Daddy is back."

The blood Torija had just drunk looked to have drained from her face. "You can't be."

"Oh, I am, my dear. Do you like my new look? Drasas didn't really make good use of this body, but I am."

Alexis looked from one to the other. This was not going to end well. She reached into her pocket and covertly called Malk and Harris. They knew a call was for help.

Gilbert started to prowl around. "You see, my precious daughter, who I loved and cared for, usurped me, took my head and my heart, then my clan. I needed a new body, and Anka was kind enough to oblige."

"You never loved and cared for me. You beat me, destroyed my mother, made her life a living hell, and killed the girl I loved."

To Alexis, Torija appeared as if she had lost control, but the one good thing was the more they talked, the more time Malk and Harris had to get here.

"Love?" Gilbert laughed. "You were always weak, just like your mother. She loved me, and I thought that I loved her when we had you, but the longer we were together, the more I realized how pathetic she was, and that love was a weakness."

"I will kill you."

But in the next instant Gilbert held Torija by the throat with one hand, the other hand on the side of her head.

"I watched you from the other side," Gilbert spat. "You betrayed your clan, chose a woman over—" Gilbert stopped and then said, "It's *her*. I can see inside your pathetic mind. Your blood bond is the other descendant. Thank you for telling me."

Torija suddenly broke free, grabbed the gun that was lying on the ground, and filled Gilbert's chest full of holes. He fell to the ground. "You will not touch a hair on her head."

Gilbert was on his knees, and despite the holes in his body, he looked strong and fierce. "You do not deserve the name Dred."

Malk and Harris appeared by Alexis's side. The vampires she had killed were starting to moan as their injuries healed.

"Torija, come on—we need to get out of here."

Torija nodded, then said with passion, "I am not a Dred, I am a Debrek."

"Torija, let's move," Alexis shouted again. She could see the bullet holes in Gilbert healing fast. Alexis grabbed Torija's arm. "Let's go."

Gilbert got up onto one leg, and as they started to run, Gilbert shouted, "That's right, Victorija, run like the weak little mouse you are. I will kill you and everything you love for usurping my rule. Everything. Do you hear me, Victorija?"

CHAPTER EIGHT

Sera had the best sleep in she didn't know how long. The water that Bhal had given her had allowed her to finally rest, without the pull of the drug dragging her to the club to buy more.

She couldn't even put a figure on how much she'd spent. With a Debrek bank account, money was not something she ever had to worry about. Sera sat up on the bed and saw Bhal wasn't there. She was disappointed.

She shivered with cold. The withdrawal was kicking in again. The addiction was starting to claw at her insides, made worse by her hunger for blood.

She had a surge of excitement, remembering her taste of Bhal's blood last night. Sera closed her eyes and remembered the very first taste. It was as if she had been suffocating her whole life and then burst through the surface to breathe at long last.

It must be because of Bhal's rich blood, Sera thought. During the time Byron was without Amelia and going mad with blood sickness, Bhal's was the only blood that could keep her from the edge of insanity.

That will be why.

Piper knocked on the door and came in. "Hi, Grandma thought you might like a cup of tea."

"Thanks." Sera would welcome some heat now. "Do you know where Bhal is?"

"She's just on her way up," Piper said.

"Thank you."

Sera took a sip of hot tea, but it was her hands around the warm cup that felt the best. It was then she remembered her dream from last night—or maybe it actually happened, and her unconscious was letting her see it. Bhal had her in her arms and was carrying her out of the club. She thanked her lucky stars that Bhal found her. That was the worst blackout she'd had. Anything could have happened to her.

She could hear Bhal's heavy booted footsteps coming up the stairs and her rarely beating heart thudded.

Then there she was, the solidly built warrior that had always been in her life but now looked different. Nothing had changed about her. She was like a Viking warrior, blond-streaked brown hair shaved at the sides, one thin plait down the side, and Celtic tattoos on both arms.

"How are you? Withdrawal symptoms back?"

Sera nodded and held out her shaking hands. "Have you contacted Byron yet?"

"I told you I wouldn't. We agreed last night," Bhal said.

"I didn't know if you meant it. You're so loyal to my sister," Sera said.

Bhal went down on one knee in front of her. "I'm loyal to you too. I always have been. You just haven't recognized it."

Sera felt frustration rise inside her, made more intense by her hunger for blood and her drugs. "You mean while you were criticizing me my whole life, that was you being loyal?"

Bhal sighed, took out her hip flask of water, and unscrewed the top. "That was instruction, not criticism. It's the way I was taught, and the way I taught Byron."

"No, it wasn't."

Bhal poured the water into her hand and said nothing. In a way Sera wanted her to. She was so full of frustration, pain, and hunger that she wanted to fight.

She lifted up her hands and said, "Drink."

Sera placed her hands under Bhal's and raised them like a cup to her lips. She gulped the water down and felt its extraordinary effects.

A warm glow travelled down her throat. When it reached her chest, Sera experienced a ball of warm heat in her sternum, which then travelled all around her body, to the tips of her fingers, to the end of her toes.

Sera's body had gone from chattering, anxious, and cold, to calm warmth.

"Feeling better?" Bhal asked.

"Yes. Thank you."

Bhal extended her arm. "Now feed, and then we can get you back home. I know I'm not your favourite person to drink from, but it's just to make you feel better. Then the blood servants can take over."

If only Bhal knew Sera was salivating at the thought of drinking from her again. Maybe this time, when she was calmer, Bhal's blood wouldn't taste quite as good. She didn't want it to be good.

Her brain was confused enough about the way she was looking at Bhal today.

Sera sank her teeth into Bhal's wrist. It was good, it was exquisite. No blood servant's offering had ever tasted like this.

She hummed with pleasure as her tongue lapped up the warrior's rich blood. When her blood hunger calmed, she found herself licking Bhal's wrist with the tip of her tongue, while her teeth were still deep inside her wrist.

Sera's head fell forward onto Bhal's chest, and she felt Bhal stroking her hair.

Then suddenly Bhal went stiff and said, "Is that enough now?"

Sera was shaken out of her blood lust and pulled back. "Yeah, of course."

Bhal moved to the other side of the room, looking flustered. They'd shared a moment that didn't altogether make sense to Sera.

"I'm sorry if I drank too long."

"No, no. I heal quickly, look." Bhal held out her arm, and the injury was already healing itself. She looked ruffled. Sera didn't think she'd ever seen the warrior ruffled.

"So, we agree what we'll say to Byron when I get you home? You were following a lead about the drug, I found you, and then we investigated together. You tell Byron what you've discovered. The Principe will be pleased."

"Not if she knew how I'd really learned about it," Sera said.

"You deserve a chance to beat this, and I will help you. Byron doesn't have to know."

"What do I do when the withdrawal is too much?" Sera asked.

"Just text me, and I'll come to your room. You'll get through this, Sera."

"Will I?"

Bhal smiled at her. "I have every faith in you."

❖

Byron, Amelia, and Daisy were in the breakfast room of the Debrek house. While Amelia and Daisy ate, Byron watched the TV screen on the wall with concern. There were more murders overnight, murders that the authorities were struggling to make excuses for.

Murders were one thing, but murders with bites to the neck and bodies ravaged by animal bites were another.

Byron rubbed her temple. The pressure was building and building, and Byron knew this could blow the lid off their own paranormal world.

"Byron," Amelia said, "this is bad, isn't it?"

She didn't want to worry Amelia, but she couldn't lie to her.

"It is worrying. I spoke to Cousin Angelo this morning, and the same thing is spreading across the US, and I've had similar reports from all over the world. Not to the extent it is here, but the chaos is slowly building."

"Can Anka have recruited that many paranormals to her cause?" Amelia asked.

"That's what I don't understand. No, she wouldn't have the numbers—yet. Something else is driving this."

Daisy put down her cup of tea on the table, and her hand shook slightly. She hadn't slept well. She felt something was wrong with Torija. Through their bond, Daisy could feel her tension, her stress. She just wanted her home.

Seemingly reading her tension, Amelia said, "She'll be home soon, Daisy."

Daisy nodded. "It'll only be so long until someone talks to a journalist or to a group like mine. There are countless groups like the Monster Hunters all over the world."

"You're right," Byron said.

Amelia sighed. "What do we do now?"

Byron got up and walked over to the screen. "We can't protect all humans all over the world. We need to find out why so many fellow paranormals are behaving this way, and defeat Anka. That's the only way we can protect our fellows and the humans."

The door opened and in walked Serenity and Bhal.

❖

Bhal stood by Sera's chair being as supportive as she could without putting her arm around her shoulders. Sera was telling her story, the one they'd agreed on. Keeping things back from Byron was the last thing she wanted to do, but she had to give Sera the chance to get over this addiction with as little stress as possible.

Sera had always hero-worshiped Byron, and to have Byron disappointed in her would destroy Sera.

But if she was honest, she had the urge, deep down in her soul, to protect Sera against anything or anybody. Even if that person was Byron, her Principe.

"That sounds as if this drug is being mass-produced," Byron said.

"And could be behind the murders," Amelia added. "You did say there was something else driving these murders."

Byron nodded. "How did you find out about the drug?"

Sera hesitated and looked up at Bhal with pleading eyes.

Bhal answered for her. "Wasn't it at The Sanctuary, you said, Sera?"

"Oh…yes. Um…I was out at The Sanctuary, and this man offered me something to make my evening more enjoyable, he said. I asked Slaine about it, and she said that she had kicked out people for trying to sell this new drug. I followed the lead and found the club."

"No Such Place, eh?" Byron said. "I don't want you to do something like that again on your own, but well done."

Sera smiled nervously. "Thanks."

"I found her, Principe," Bhal said firmly.

Byron frowned. "I know you did, Bhal, but anything could have happened to her before that."

The thing was, it had. If Byron knew how Bhal had found Sera, Byron would be at that club just now ripping it, and the people in it, apart. It was best to let Sera breathe while she attempted to beat this drug.

Daisy suddenly had an intake of breath. "Tor."

Then she ran out into the entrance hall. They all followed her, and as Bhal and Sera entered the hallway, Alexis, Torija, and their team came through the front door.

To Bhal, Torija looked as if she had a storm raging inside her. Torija took one look at them and ran upstairs at super speed.

Daisy ran after her. "Tor, what's wrong?"

"Alexis?" Byron said.

"Principe, we need to talk," Alexis said ominously.

❖

Daisy's heart was hammering as she followed Torija upstairs. She could feel through her connection to Torija that she was confused, in emotional pain, and scared.

She opened the bedroom door and found Torija sitting on a chair, bent over, her head in her hands.

"Tor?"

Torija didn't even acknowledge her. Daisy went to her and kneeled. "Tor? What happened?"

Torija rubbed her face and then grasped her hair tightly. "He's back."

"Who's back?" Daisy asked. When Torija didn't answer, Daisy asked again, more forcefully this time. "Tor, who?"

Torija stood quickly and stormed over to the window. "My father—Gilbert Dred is back. Is that plain enough for you?"

Daisy felt like she had been hit with a ton of bricks. "No, that can't be."

"Really? That's all right then. I must have been fighting with someone else."

Daisy got up and joined Torija at the window. She placed her hand on Torija's back. "Tell me. He can't be back."

"He is. Remember that whole thing, Anka needs a born vampire to open a portal to the other side?"

"Yeah, you swapped yourself with Sera. Saved her and were forgiven by the people who you hurt."

"That's the one. Well it was a ruse to send a vampire's soul to hell, and give Gilbert their body," Torija said.

"Gilbert is in Drasas's body?"

"Yes. Something to do with this God Balor that Anka worships. We were listening to Anka and who I thought was Drasas's conversation, then when Anka unmasked him, I fell off the castle. If it hadn't been for Alexis, we would all be there as prisoners, at best."

Daisy gasped. "You fell and died?" It was still taking time to get used to the fact that the woman she loved was immortal. The thought of Torija dying made her feel sick.

"You know I can't die. I just needed time to heal."

Daisy gulped. "What happened then?"

"No sooner I was back on my feet than my father jumped down from the bedroom window to where I was standing. I don't care what body he is in—I can still tell those sick, evil eyes."

"It's okay, Tor. You're home now."

"When he is in front of me"—Torija's eyes started to fill with tears—"he still has the ability to make me feel like a frightened sixteen-year-old."

"That's all right. Let yourself feel." Daisy used her thumb to wipe away a tear on her face.

Torija pulled away from her and roared, "I can't. He knows who you are. He read my mind and found that my blood bond was the other descendant. One of the descendants that Anka wants—and now he wants—to kill. He vowed to destroy everything I loved. He vowed to kill you."

"Torija, Amelia and I are working out this descendant thing. It's going to be okay."

Torija laughed. "A pregnant witch just learning about her powers and a young woman who doesn't know what her powers are are not going stop Gilbert Dred, Anka, and this God Balor."

Daisy felt a stab of hurt to her chest. She knew Torija was lashing out because she was scared, but it still hurt.

"This *young woman* faced up a whole castle of Dreds and turned the infamous and universally feared Victorija Dred."

Torija walked over to Daisy and cupped her face. The emotions of pain and fear were eating away at Torija. "Gilbert killed my mother, killed your ancestor Angele. I'm afraid I'm going to have to become Victorija again to protect you, and you'll hate me for it."

"No, you won't," Daisy said firmly. "We will fight him and whoever else together. You are a different person now, Tor."

Torija rested her forehead against Daisy's. "I wish I had your faith in me."

She started to kiss Daisy's cheeks then neck. Daisy knew that Torija was so scarred from her father's violence. It made her feel weak and out of control. Only the love that they shared soothed Torija's pain.

Torija kissed her lips demandingly and passionately. "I need you."

Daisy took off her T-shirt. "You've always got me."

Torija kissed her while Daisy pulled Torija's T-shirt off. They then struggled with each other's jeans and underwear.

Daisy got onto the bed and said, "I want you to come. Just come."

Torija's eyes were dark red, and her teeth were bared. She got onto the bed and without foreplay parted Daisy's legs, and Torija pushed her sex against Daisy's.

Daisy felt in her heart that Torija needed to feel powerful and strong, and that was why she allowed Torija to be so demanding.

Torija began to thrust against Daisy. Daisy was wet. She loved Torija's powerful side because they both knew it was Daisy that allowed it. Torija thrust fast and hard, with no attempt to make it last long.

"I love you, Tor. You are strong, powerful—make us both come."

Daisy wrapped her legs around Torija's hips and enjoyed every movement. She would come soon, but this wasn't about her. It was about her lover.

Torija's breaths got louder and her thrusts faster until she went still as a board and shouted out a howl of painful pleasure. Torija's body was released from all her pent-up tension and fell onto Daisy.

"I love you, I love you, cherie," Torija said with tears coming down her face.

Daisy held her tightly till she calmed.

"I don't know what I'd do without your love," Torija said.

Daisy kissed her on the cheek. "You'll never have to find out."

Torija pushed herself up and stroked Daisy's face. "I will never let him hurt you."

"I know." Daisy gasped when Torija slid her fingers into her wetness. "Feed while I come."

When it came, Daisy's orgasm roared through her body, helped by the feel-good hormones that Torija's bite gave her.

"I'll love you forever," Daisy vowed.

CHAPTER NINE

C ould things get any worse today?" Amelia sighed.
       Byron took her hand. "Don't tempt fate."

They had moved from the breakfast room to the drawing room where Alexis joined them. Katie, Alexis's wife, joined them too.

Alexis held Katie's hand, keeping her close, and Bhal was standing behind Sera. Sera could feel her and feel her blood crying out for hers. She needed to feed soon. Hopefully when she fed on one of the blood servants, her hunger for Bhal would go.

"How is Torija?" Sera asked.

Alexis cleared her throat. "Shaken. In fact I never, ever thought I'd see her this emotional. She was her normal self, cracking bad jokes and trying to rile me, but when she realized Gilbert had been reborn in Drasas's body, her bravado just fell—as well as her body. Her legs went and she tumbled down, breaking nearly every bone in her body. Then, when she recovered and Gilbert confronted her, she looked genuinely scared. That is one emotion I have never seen in Victorija."

"On top of everything else, Gilbert Dred and an emotionally charged Torija are the last things we need," Byron said.

"What kind of artifacts are they looking for?" Katie asked Alexis.

"All we heard was artifacts or keys to open up a portal for this entity Balor."

"Bhal?" Alexis said, "What do you know about this?"

"Not a lot. One day when we were trying to fight him and his army, he was forced into this…portal, a void, how else can I describe it? An absence of space. He had attacked my village and others nearby. It was said he is a shapeshifter, but the day he attacked us, he was the size of a twenty-story building and had one eye. That is the form he has in the Celtic myth cycle. Our gods have a monstrous appearance, and it's my guess he appeared that way to match our myths, but how he would appear now could be very different."

Sera could feel anger mixed with guilt and pain from Bhal without even looking at her. It was strange.

"He gains power from collecting the spirits of the dead—that is why my clan exists. Our priest gave me and my warriors immortality to try to protect human souls from him."

Amelia sighed. "So we have Sera's information about the drug, Malum, Gilbert Dred returning to help Anka and Balor, artifacts or keys to open up a portal, Daisy and me somehow foretold to stop him, and some connection to a magical woman called Melusine. How do we even begin to deal with all this?"

Byron stood up and rested her hand against the mantelpiece. "Anka is clearly trying to soften resistance within the paranormal community and, by killing the humans, create distrust between us and those humans who know about us."

"Not to mention create a whole load of bloodthirsty paranormals," Sera said.

"It's too much to deal with," Amelia said.

"No, we take this one problem at a time. Magda is trying to contact Sybil to see if she can help with the Melusine angle. I'll try and talk to some of my contacts to see if they know anything about these artifacts. Alexis, try to find out where these drugs are being made. In the meantime it looks like I'll need to contact our allies. Ready them for what lies ahead, and I think I'll engage Brogan to keep an eye on Anka and Gilbert. See where they go when they leave the Dred castle."

Brogan Filtiaran was an artist who lived as a lone wolf in Paris, even though she was part of the Irish pack. As well as being an artist, she worked as a private investigator and tracker for hire and had been a useful ally to the Debreks before.

"Byron, I can look into the drug making. I have the contacts now," Sera said.

"No, I want you safe here with us."

Sera felt a rush of anger. "No matter what I do, you never give me a chance." She stormed out of the drawing room but stopped at the bottom of the stairs and brought her hand to her mouth. She was overcome with emotion.

"Sera?" Bhal had followed her out. "Are you okay?"

"No matter what I do, she will never see me as an adult woman, only as a twelve-year-old girl. We know how I came about this information, but Byron doesn't. Still, she won't let me help. I know who gave me the tip about No Such Place. I can find him again if anyone can."

"Why don't we do that tomorrow?" Bhal asked.

"You mean go against Byron's instructions?"

Sera saw Bhal's jaw tighten. "I suppose I am."

"You seriously disagree with your Principe?"

"On this occasion, yes. As long as I am with you."

Sera looked at Bhal, trying to work her out. She was changing in front of her eyes. Since Bhal found her—no, that wasn't right. Since Anka ransomed her, Bhal's attitude had changed. Now she was willing to go against Byron's instructions. That was unheard of.

She would see how long it lasted. By tomorrow Bhal's mind could revert back.

"We can check out my lead in the morning, then."

Bhal nodded. "Do you need…"

Sera's withdrawal wasn't too bad at the moment, and besides, she wanted some time alone to think.

"Not at the moment. I just need to go down to the blood room to feed," Sera said.

"I can feed you if you want," Bhal offered.

"You don't need to bother. It's okay."

"Let me know when you need me later," Bhal said, offering her the water that would control her symptoms.

"I will. Thanks, and thanks for last night."

"No trouble."

Sera walked away towards the basement stairs and felt something pull inside her gut. She looked back and saw Bhal standing in the same place, watching her walk away. The pull was more intense. *You need to feed.* Sera kept on walking and took her phone out to call a blood servant. The Debreks had an app that they used to call blood servants. They might be age-old vampires, but the Debrek clan did not live in the past.

Once she fed, this ache would go away.

When Sera arrived at the blood room, she opened the door and looked inside. She couldn't help but feel disappointed. One of their blood servants, Jonas, was waiting for her.

"Ms. Debrek. I'm honoured to serve you."

"Thank you, Jonas."

Sera liked Jonas. He was a good person and she'd fed from him many times, but today Sera felt he wasn't what she needed. But she doubted anyone would be after the rich blood that Bhal gave her.

"Where do you wish me to feed from, Jonas?" Sera asked.

Consent was the main tenet of the Debrek clan. They only fed on those that consented and where on the body they would allow it.

"Neck or wrist, Ms. Debrek." Some of the blood servants were too tall for Serenity to feed at their neck, but Jonas was around her height.

"I'll feed at your neck then."

He took off his black T-shirt and stood still. Sera stood behind him, and her sharp teeth erupted from her gums. She could see the pulse point throb and invite her to bite.

"Do you consent?"

"Yes, I consent."

Sera sank her teeth in, closed her eyes, and saw Bhal standing by an old oak tree. She stopped feeding briefly. Why was she there?

Bhal then smiled and held out her hand.

"Is there something wrong?" Jonas asked.

Sera was brought right back down to earth. "No, sorry, Jonas."

As she bit the second time, Sera purposely tried not to think of Bhal. Instead, she saw herself, and a dark cloud started to envelop her. She experienced the beginnings of the gnawing ache for the Malum.

She broke off from Jonas. "Sorry, Jonas. I…just don't feel like it any more."

Sera ran from the room, no doubt leaving Jonas bewildered.

Byron entered the bedroom, carefully holding a plate of food requested by her wife.

"Oh, gimme, gimme." Amelia reached out her hands.

Byron raised an eyebrow. "Me or the beef?"

Amelia's baby craving was lightly seared Japanese Wagyu steak, and their chef Dane always kept some in the fridge for her.

"Sorry, sweetheart, the beef wins."

"Fine. I'm only good for fetching food now, am I?"

Amelia took the plate and rested it on her baby bump. "Don't sulk. It's what the baby wants."

Byron took off her suit jacket and hung it up on the hanger, ready to be taken into her dressing room.

"At least I'm good for something." Byron took off her tie and unbuttoned her shirt.

"Oh, you know you're good for many things, many things I enjoy." Amelia gave Byron a wink and Byron smiled.

"I emailed the home wolf packs and our other allies. We're having a Zoom call in the morning."

"Good. We're going to need all the help we can get."

Amelia put down her piece of meat and said, "Sweetheart, why did you not give Sera the chance to find out where the drug is getting made?"

"I saw she didn't take it well, but it's for her own good. I've been so worried about her, and all the time she was keeping this investigation from me. She was on her own. Anything could have happened to her."

Amelia sighed. "You just shut her down, Byron. I—It doesn't matter."

Byron walked to the bed and said, "What? Say it."

"It feels like you treat her like a teenage sister, not a few-hundred-year-old vampire."

"She might be old in human terms, but not in a vampire's timespan. You know what Sera is like. She always manages to get into trouble."

"You're going to push her away. We need a strong family unit, Byron. This is not the time to make her want to run. Besides, it looks like Bhal is watching over her."

Byron flopped down to sit on the bed. "I'm frightened of losing her, losing you. I feel like I'm out of control, like I can't protect you all."

"You can't wrap us in cotton wool. Let Sera take charge—if she takes Bhal with her, she'll be safe."

Byron rubbed her forehead. "Well, I suppose it's pointless pretending that her bodyguard Henri does any good whatsoever. I'll talk to Bhal in the morning."

"And Sera?"

"Yes, yes, and Sera."

❖

Bhal was lying on her bed, her arms behind her head. She was wearing only her boots, combat trousers, and white sleeveless T-shirt. Her sword and scabbard sat carefully on the stand next to her bed.

She'd cleaned and sharpened her sword as she did every evening, but that had not settled Bhal for the night.

She'd been unsettled all night—well, since she'd left Sera's company. No matter what she did to try to keep busy, the image of Sera going down to the blood room imposed itself on her brain. Worse than that, her mind was conjuring up imagined images of Sera sinking her teeth into the neck of one of the blood servants, and Bhal hated it.

As well as hating it, Bhal didn't understand it. She'd always kept an eye out for Sera and cared about her. But this was changing. Bhal felt jealousy, and about something she knew didn't mean anything.

A vampire who fed was performing a task to ensure their immortality. But the act of drinking blood became personal when it was someone you cared about, and Bhal did care, and did feel jealous.

Bhal jumped up and started to pace. "I have no right to feel this way."

"Oh? What way is that?"

Bhal turned around and found Morrigan lying seductively on her bed. "What are you doing here? Get up."

Morrigan disappeared and then appeared behind her back. "Is someone having confusing feelings about Serenity Debrek? What would her big sister, your Principe, say about that?"

Bhal was angry that she could read her so easily. "I told you before, Morrigan, keep out of my life."

Morrigan looked at her seriously. "I would if you and your band of humans could be trusted to keep your lives in order. You need my help. All of you need my help, but I have history with you, Bhal. So I come to you."

"We don't need your kind of help. It'll come with a price."

Morrigan grasped Bhal's T-shirt. "You have to listen to me."

Bhal pulled her arm away. "If it's important, then you go and fix it."

"I'm not allowed to interfere."

Bhal laughed. "Morrigan, Goddess of war, not interfere? You've interfered, influenced, and played with humanity for all of time."

"Influenced, helped, but only for the good of humans. But in this case I'm forbidden from interfering, but if you ask the right question…"

Bhal folded her arms. "Forbidden by whom?"

"From my fellow gods. You are supposed to have free will, but I don't want the worst to happen. I am fond of this planet."

"What question can I ask?"

Morrigan threw her arms in the air. "Just use your initiative."

"Whatever will be, will be," Bhal said.

Morrigan looked off to her side with a strange look on her face. "I have to go."

And with that she was gone.

Bhal had never seen Morrigan so worried before. There was something going on, but Bhal knew Morrigan's help came with a high price.

Bhal was hit suddenly with a blow to her gut. She bent over, breathing hard, and had a vision in her mind of Sera going down the stairs. If this was true, Bhal knew where she was going. She rushed out of her room and saw Sera approaching the stairs, looking as if she was trying to creep out of the house.

Her eyes were red but were surrounded by deep black circles. Sera's breathing was heavy, and she was clearly struggling.

"Don't do this."

"Just once more. Once more is all I need—then I can start from tomorrow. I promise."

Bhal took her hands. "You know that's not true."

Sera put her hand on her stomach. "It hurts too much... everywhere."

"Why didn't you text me? Let me know you needed help like I told you?"

Sera pressed her fingers into her temples. "I wanted to deal with it on my own. It's humiliating."

"Let's talk." Bhal led Sera back to Sera's bedroom and shut the door. "You don't have to feel that with me. We made a pact at Magda's that I wouldn't tell Byron and we'd get through this together. We're a team."

Sera sat on her bed and bowed her head.

"If you go back to that club, you'll regret it." Bhal went to Sera and kneeled down. "The way I found you there...I can't see you like that again. Please let me help?"

Sera nodded. Bhal took out her hip flask and asked Sera to fill her cupped hands. Sera put down the bottle and placed her hands under Bhal's and guided them to her mouth. Bhal's hands were warm and it transferred a warmth to Sera's body that calmed it right down.

"Thank you."

"Do you feel better?"

Sera nodded. "Starting to. Thanks for stopping me from going to the club."

Bhal touched the side of her mouth and wiped away a drop of water with such tenderness that she found herself grasping her wrist so she didn't take it away.

"I want to help. You can do this. You've got more strength in you than you give yourself credit for."

Sera was captivated by Bhal's green eyes. They reminded her of the forest. She was reminded of the vision she had when she drank from Bhal's wrist. Bhal was standing underneath a tree, with her hand outstretched. Was it outstretched to her?

She looked at Bhal's wrist still in her hand and her body reacted to it. Sera heard the rush of strong, powerful blood through Bhal's veins, and her heart pumping strongly to send it around her body.

Sera could remember the rich taste, and her mouth watered.

"Are you all right, Sera?" Bhal asked.

If Sera looked up at her, she would see the evidence of her need, blood hungry eyes and her vampire teeth that were aching to bite her.

She closed her eyes and let go of Bhal's wrist. "I'm just tired."

"Would you like—"

A knock at Sera's bedroom door made them both jump, and Sera regained control of her vampire.

"Shall I get it?" Bhal asked.

Sera nodded.

Bhal opened the door to find Byron standing there.

"Bhal?" Byron asked with surprise.

"Principe."

Byron looked between them suspiciously. "May I come in?"

Sera nodded. "Yes, we were just—"

"Talking about the evidence we found about the drugs," Bhal finished for her.

Bhal covered for her again. Sera was grateful and astonished that Bhal would protect her like this.

"I see," Byron said. "That's what I wanted to talk to you about."

Sera looked nervously to Bhal. Had Byron found out?

Stay calm. Everything will be all right.

What was that? Her mind talking? It could be Bhal. She had no powers of telepathy as far as she knew. It must be her own mind talking.

"What is it, Byron?"

"I'll go and let you both talk," Bhal said.

"No," Byron raised her hand. "This concerns you both."

"What is it?" Sera asked.

Byron put her hands in her pockets and looked a bit sheepish. "I want you both to continue with the drugs investigation. I was wrong to shoot you down and take the investigation off you."

"Wait," Sera said. "Who are you and what have you done with my sister?"

"Very funny. I had it pointed out to me that I wasn't being fair."

"Amelia?" Sera grinned.

"Might have been."

Sera rubbed her hands together. "I love having a sister-in-law."

"It's your task only if you partner with Bhal. Bhal, I want you to stay with Sera, help her with this investigation, and be her bodyguard for the time being, since my dear sister continually slips her guard's net. I will be fine with the Duca."

"Aye. I will, Principe."

Byron looked to Sera and said, "What? No arguments?"

What would Sera object to? She'd have Bhal by her side. Just what she wanted—only for recovery, of course.

"No, Bhal has been helpful to me." Sera looked at Bhal. "I'm grateful for her help."

"Hmm," Byron said.

Sera was sure she suspected something.

"Bhal, I have a video conference with the wolf packs and some others about our current problems in the morning. I'd like you to be there before you head out anywhere with Sera."

"Of course, Principe."

"I'll leave you to it then."

Byron finally left, and Sera let out a breath. "She suspects something."

"It'll be fine. Don't worry," Bhal said.

"You lied for me again."

"No, I wouldn't call it lying. I did come to you to talk about the drugs. Byron doesn't know it was because you were taking them. Now we'll be investigating, so we are doing what Byron has told us. Where did you find out about the No Such Place?"

"At The Sanctuary. A man in a long dark coat called Idris."

Bhal shook her head. "That's how I found you. He's a necromancer."

Sera hugged herself. She was still trembling inside. The water wasn't taking away all symptoms, just calming them.

"We can try to find him then. Sounds like he knows more than he's said," Sera said.

"Okay, I'll let you have your beauty sleep, not that you need it, unless you need anything else."

"What did you say?" Sera asked.

"Do you need anything else?"

"No, before that."

Bhal gulped with discomfort. "I…uh…said get your beauty sleep." Bhal looked down at her feet. "Not that you need it."

"You think I'm beautiful?" Sera asked sheepishly.

"You know you are. Glamour and beauty drip off you, but you know that already. But there's something that most people don't know—there is so much more under your surface."

Oh shit, I want her. The bane of my life, the instructor who drove me fucking crazy, and I want her. Shit, shit, shit.

Sera decided to change the subject. "You go on. I'm sure you've got stuff to do."

Bhal nodded. "Unless you haven't fed tonight. I can if you want?" Bhal offered.

"No," Sera said all too quickly. "Sorry, I mean I've already fed."

"Aye? That's fine. See you in the morning then if you don't need me before then."

"I'll message you if I do."

"Good enough. Remember, if you ever want to talk, I'm here. I can help with the symptoms, but you have to do the work mentally to get a grip on this addiction."

"I will. Thanks, Bhal."

"Goodnight." Bhal brought her fist to her chest and bowed her head.

"'Night."

Once Bhal finally left, Sera let out a breath. She scrambled over to the fridge in the corner of the room and brought out a blood bag.

No, she hadn't fed this evening. Sera had tried but it went even worse than this morning. She'd made a fool of herself again. She stuttered with her teeth, hurting her human host.

It was worse than her first time. Sera felt her body pull away physically from feeding. The drugs were having an outrageous effect on her. Magda had said the drug was a slow death, so maybe her body was trying to stop feeding, in order to kill her?

She sank her teeth into the blood bag. Sera didn't react as badly to the bag as she had to the woman blood servant. She was still fighting her body to keep drinking, like a human forcing themselves to drink some bad medicine, but it was easier than with a human.

When Bhal had offered her services, Sera's body screamed *yes, yes, yes*, but her brain actually shouted *no*. The two times she had drunk from Bhal had been the most intense feeds of her life. She couldn't afford to let herself experience that, especially now when she was struggling.

Her eyes closed softly, and she remembered Bhal's hot, rich blood flowing into her mouth. In her mind Sera saw Bhal pulling off her T-shirt. She stood before her with broad, muscular shoulders and chest and Celtic tattoos all over her body, then kneeled before Sera.

My body is yours, Sera.

Sera's eyes burst open and she threw her blood bag across the room. She clasped her head with her hands.

What was happening to her?

She went to her bathroom, wet a towel, and began to wipe the blood away.

Why was she feeling this way? Bhal had always been there, an older stoic warrior who didn't give her a fair chance, but now she was feeling very different. Byron once told her that Bhal's age was frozen in time at eighteen years old, much like Byron and herself, but Bhal's experience and the way she carried herself gave her natural authority and age.

Bhal had shown her a different side to her nature. She was caring, thinking only of Sera's needs, and putting aside her usual main priority of the clan. It was making her muddled-up mind more confused.

She looked at herself in the mirror and saw an extremely pale vampire, with dark shadows under her eyes, her whole body tremoring. Bhal had said she was beautiful. How could she think that?

CHAPTER TEN

Anka was led by a security officer into the archaeology department of the historic Sorbonne in Paris. The building itself gave her the feel of entering a place of excellence, a place where the best brains could help her find what she needed.

Asha, two vampires, and a shifter walked behind her. The security guard looked quite concerned at the look of their little band, but with a quick incantation, he was leading Anka right to the person she wanted to see.

He opened the double doors ahead of them. "This is the library. You will find Professor Beaufort in here."

The library was stunning. It had a high curved ceiling with gold and white plaster and cornices, and tall windows. Rows of dark wood tables lay in lines, and each space at the table had an ornamental glass lamp.

It wasn't too busy, and Anka quickly spotted the woman she was looking for, at the back of the room.

"Asha? Spread yourself and our guards around the room. I will speak to the professor myself."

"Yes, Madam."

Anka glided to the back and stood beside a woman in her late fifties. "Professor Beaufort?"

The woman looked around slowly and her eyes went wide. "You…"

"Yes, I'm Madam Anka. I see you remember me, Marie."

"How could I forget, Madam."

The last time she had dealings with Marie was when she was looking for the ring with the large stone, which now sat on her finger.

Balor had told her of the ring that could steal the power from any paranormal.

It had helped her open a portal to the other side so that she could retrieve Gilbert's soul, but opening the void that Balor had called his prison for millennia was an altogether different matter.

"I would like to talk to you, my good friend, Dr. Beaufort. As a professor of ancient history, I think you could give me the information I need."

Professor Beaufort shut her books and stood. "I'm sorry, I have a class to get to."

Anka put her hand on her shoulder and Professor Beaufort fell back to the seat. "I think it would be best if you sat and talked to me, Professor. If you look around, you'll see I have my people around the room. I think you should talk to me civilly—or we can do it the hard way."

"Yes, of course. Please sit down," Professor Beaufort said.

"Good answer, Marie."

Once Anka sat, she flourished her hand, and a shimmer surrounded them. "Now we can talk in private. No one will hear our conversation."

Marie looked pale and scared. "How can I help?"

"I'm looking for some artifacts, ancient artifacts, and I knew you could help me."

"What period are we talking about?" Maria asked.

"That is what I don't know. The information I have is that artifacts or keys were created from a stone of Anu?"

"Anu?" Marie asked.

Anka nodded. "Does that mean anything to you?"

"In Sumerian, Anu is the divine personification of the sky, king of the gods and father of the gods. It also refers to the Anunnaki, a pantheon of deities of Mesopotamia. In Europe Anu becomes Danu, an ancient Celtic Goddess, and in Hinduism she is the primordial Goddess."

"If Anu is a God or Goddess in many cultures, then surely there must be some truth to it?"

Marie wrung her hands nervously. "I would have said you were crazy, that it was shared culture, but now I know that a powerful witch exists, so who knows?"

Anka crossed her legs and smiled. "There is much more than me, Marie. I want you to study these myths, as humans have written them down, and find out anything that could be as I've described."

"Artifacts or keys that open a portal?"

"That's it, and where they could be now," Anka said.

"How will I contact you?"

Anka smiled. "We have your number, and your address. You'll be contacted regularly." She stood up and said, "Happy hunting, Dr. Beaufort, for your sake."

❖

Byron walked into the conference room at a fast pace, followed by Alexis, Torija, and some of her senior vampires.

She sat down and unlocked the tablet she was carrying. "Right, we have a busy day—our video conference and the visit to the department that I've been called to." Byron looked at her watch. "We have five minutes to the call. Now, Torija, I think it's best if you stay here with Amelia and Daisy today. The department might be a little too spooked if I turn up with the former Dred Principe."

"I'd rather stay close to Daisy and Amelia in any case," Torija said.

Byron could see Torija had lost some of her arrogant confidence since meeting her father again. She was scared of losing Daisy, just as she was with Amelia.

"Who has confirmed, Principe?" Alexis asked.

"The BaoBhan Sith, the Northern and Southern fae tribes, a representative of the some of the UK covens, and the shifters, plus the friendly packs from Britain and North America—the US based Wolfgangs, the English Ranwolfs, the Irish Filtiaran, the Welsh Blaidds."

"Let's hope that they are willing to help. We're going to need them," Alexis said.

"We will. Now Bhal is going to be with Sera for the time being, so I need you, Alexis, to liaise with Wilder and the Samhain warriors while she is with her."

"Yes, Principe."

Byron looked at her watch. "It's time."

She connected to the video call.

The screen populated with lots of different boxes. Some she knew well—most notably her cousin Angelo, Kenrick from the Scottish Wulver wolf pack, and Dante Wolfgang from the American wolf pack—some she had only made contact with recently.

"Good morning. Thank you for joining us. We in the paranormal world are facing more danger than we ever have before, and I wanted to bring you up to speed with what we know so far, and hopefully gain your support."

Kenrick put up her hand. "You will always have the Wulvers' support."

Then Dante Wolfgang followed up with, "And we will always support our Wulver cousins."

This was a good start, but then the leader of a fae tribe said, "Look, can we stop licking the vampire's arse and hear what she has to say?"

Now it's started. This was going to take all of her diplomacy.

The Sanctuary in the afternoon wasn't quite as atmospheric as night-time, but hopefully Bhal and Sera would be more able to talk to its patrons.

Bhal led Sera into the club, constantly scanning the area for anything that might cause Sera any problems. Now that they knew some of what Anka was planning, they knew she wouldn't hesitate to try to take a Debrek out of the fight.

Bhal turned around to check on Sera. She was worried about her health. Although they knew little about the effect of Anka's drug on a vampire, far less a born vampire, she'd expected her to be feeling better than she was. Sera had taken some water from Bhal this morning before going to feed, but Bhal could see the suffering in her eyes. They arrived at the bar, but Slaine wasn't there.

One of the female bar staff approached them. She bowed her head to Sera. "Ms. Debrek. How can I be of service?"

Bhal could tell she was a young turned vampire. Turned vampires looked up to the Debreks. They were considered royalty within the vampire community.

"We're looking for a necromancer. His name's Idris, he drinks in here a lot."

"No, I haven't seen him. Do you want me to check with Slaine?"

"That would be good, thanks."

When she went into the back office, both of them ordered a drink with one of the other servers.

Bhal watched Sera's hand tremor when she took a drink. "Are you all right?"

"I'm fine. Don't fuss, Bhal."

Bhal sighed. She couldn't seem to say the right thing today. She had thought they had an understanding, but since this morning, Bhal felt like she was pushing her away again.

Slaine came out and said, "Sera, Bhal, good to see you."

Bhal let Sera take the lead. "Hi, Slaine. We're looking for that guy Idris. Has he been in?"

Slaine came closer and said in a low voice, "No, I haven't seen him since Bhal spoke to him in here."

"I must have spooked him," Bhal said.

Slaine nodded. "I think he was purposely directing my customers to that No Such Place. I've heard bad things have gone on there."

Bhal saw Sera stiffen at the mention of the club.

Sera stood and said, "I'm going to the toilets."

Bhal made a move to follow her, but Slaine said, "Bhal, can I have a word?"

She had to let her go. "Aye."

"The word on the grapevine is that your Principe had a meeting of all the friendly packs, covens, and tribes."

Bhal trusted Slaine so she nodded. "Aye, she did. There's likely to be a battle ahead. A battle between good and evil, you could say."

"Madam Anka and her followers?"

"Aye, she wants to turn this world into one led by the so-called God she follows, kill or enslave the humans, and cause a civil war among the paranormals."

"I'd heard rumours, but I hoped it wasn't so serious. Please tell Byron that my family and I will stand shoulder to shoulder with you in the fight."

"I will. Thank you, Slaine." Bhal gave her a warrior's handshake.

Slaine went to serve another customer, and Bhal sipped her drink. She looked at her watch. Sera had been a long time.

She didn't want to suffocate Sera, but she needed to keep her safe. Bhal downed the last of her drink and walked towards the door that led down to the toilets. The stairs seemed to be a popular place to hang out, maybe because the lighting was low.

Bhal passed people talking and a couple kissing and enjoying each other's bodies. The music from upstairs pounded downstairs, giving the basement, along with its low lighting, a sensual feel.

In fact the area outside the communal toilets was filled with couples caught up in the feel of the place, even though it was only the afternoon. Down here was so cut off from the outside, it felt like it was two in the morning.

When she walked into the toilets, she saw Sera standing at the washbasins, staring into the mirrors, her body shaking.

"Sera?"

A woman came out of one of the other cubicles and went to wash her hands. When Bhal gave her an intense stare, she didn't stop to dry her hands and rushed out of the toilets. Bhal moved next to Sera.

"Sera, what's wrong?"

"Can't you see what's wrong? I look like a vampire who hasn't had a drop of blood in a year. Why do I still look so sick?"

Bhal knew that while Sera wouldn't be cured mentally of her addiction yet, she had hoped that she would at least look and feel better. "It's going to take time. We know virtually nothing about the effect of this drug on a born vampire. Give it more time."

Sera pushed her fingers into her scalp and pulled her hair. "It feels like rats are nibbling the ends of my nerves all over my body."

Bhal took Sera's hand. "Follow me." She pulled her into one of the toilet cubicles. "I'll give you more water."

While Bhal took out her hip flask Sera said, "What if I end up addicted to you—to your water? It makes me feel good."

"I know that won't happen. You'd have to spend all your time around me if that was the case, and I know you won't want to do that."

Sera put her hands under Bhal's palm. Bhal thought that she couldn't stand her, but that wasn't true. Sera had seen the warrior in a completely different light. She was kind, loyal, and caring. Sera supposed Bhal had always been like that, she'd just never taken the time to get to know her, which was a strange thing to say since Sera had been alive centuries.

Sera sipped the water from Bhal's hands and almost immediately felt the rush all over her body. It was like a clear, spring stream washing over the ends of her nerves, making them calm and renewing her energy.

"How does that feel?" Bhal asked her.

Sera experienced such a high, not an unnatural high like when using the Malum, but simply from feeling better.

She couldn't help grasping Bhal's cheeks. "It feels good." Sera heard the thump, thump of the music and had an idea. "Let's go and dance."

"What?"

She held Bhal's hand tightly and dragged her upstairs.

"I don't dance," Bhal said.

"Why do you always have to be joyless, Bhal? I'm dancing anyway."

She made her way onto the floor and left Bhal at the bar. The dance floor only had a few couples on it since it was only the afternoon. Sera didn't care. She felt better than she did ten minutes ago and wanted to enjoy it. She danced on her own, losing herself in the low, pounding beat. It wasn't long before a female werewolf joined her and started dancing with her.

The werewolf put her hands around Sera's waist, and they undulated together, losing themselves in the music. Sera smiled at the wolf. She was having fun, and she would enjoy every second before she felt ill again.

Sera saw the were's eyes turn yellow and she bared her teeth, then a second later she let Sera go and walked away. Bhal was beside her the next second.

"I will dance with you."

Sera was surprised. Bhal must have scared the werewolf away with a look.

"I don't dance. Teach me," Bhal said.

Sera did not expect her to say that. Before she changed her mind, Sera took Bhal's hands and placed them on her hips, then wrapped her arms around Bhal's neck.

"Now just move. Like me." Bhal was stiff at first. "Look in my eyes, not at my feet, and just relax."

She did as was asked and Sera was met with Bhal's green eyes. Sera saw and felt so much in those eyes. The pounding music faded, and she heard the unmistakable sounds of the forest. The sound of the birds singing, the smell of the fresh air, the smell of wood burning, and the crackle of the fire. Most of all she felt serenity, and all of that in one look into Bhal's eyes.

Sera shook her head and gulped hard as her body reacted. Those eyes had always been there, Bhal had always been there, but she had never taken the time to slow down her life and look at what was right in front of her.

Bhal's lips parted when Sera tenderly caressed her neck with her nails. Sera's mouth watered at the thought of sinking her teeth into her strong neck. It had been so long since she'd felt the satisfaction of feeding.

They hardly swayed now, but there was no gap between them. Their hips were pressing against each other, and both were bringing the faces closer together.

I need to kiss her. I need it, Sera thought.

To kiss her and taste her was everything that she needed in that moment. More than the drug she was addicted to, more than the life-giving water that Bhal gave her.

"Your eyes are red," Bhal said.

Of course they were red. Sera wanted her and wanted to feed on her. *No, no. This is too much.* Sera broke their embrace. "I need to feed. Can you take me home?"

"Yes, but I could feed you."

"No," Sera said a little too harshly.

She wasn't prepared to think about what that would mean. She had to get away.

Bhal stiffened and put on her stoic warrior face again.

"Let's go then."

CHAPTER ELEVEN

Amelia, Daisy, and a guard of four vampires waited in the entrance hall to the Debrek mansion, while Byron gave out the orders. Magda had been in touch, having had contact with Sybil.

Sybil was the leader of what was left of the cunning folk coven in the New Forest. She had also met and protected Amelia's mother. Now both Daisy and Amelia had questions about their origins and what being a descendant meant.

Magda had set up a meeting for them.

"Torija, I want a ring of steel around Amelia and Daisy while you are away."

"Do you think I would do any less?" Torija said.

Any reservations Byron might have had against Torija's sincerity went away as soon as she proved her love for Daisy. Now Daisy was so closely linked with Amelia, Byron knew that Torija would protect them with her life. Others in the clan were slower to trust her.

She turned to her vampires and pointed at them. "You follow every order Torija gives you, understand?"

"Yes, Principe," they said in unison.

"Don't worry, Byron," Amelia said, "we'll be fine."

"I wonder why she wants to meet in Highgate Cemetery?" Byron asked.

"I'm sure there'll be a good explanation. Now let us go, and you get off to your appointment."

While Amelia was meeting Sybil, Byron had been invited to the MI5 building, which housed the department, the section that monitored paranormals.

Amelia kissed Byron on the cheek. She understood Byron's fear, but she had to step out on her own if she was to reach her potential and stand against Anka.

"Let's go."

Amelia, Daisy, and Torija went into the back seat of the blacked-out people carrier waiting at the front door.

Torija turned around and said to the driver, "Stop at the first flower shop you see."

Amelia saw the driver hesitate, but Torija nodded yes to him in the driver's mirror.

"Yes, Torija."

"Why do you need flowers, Torija?" Amelia asked.

"For someone who is buried at Highgate cemetery."

"A friend," Daisy said to Amelia.

"No, not a friend," Torija said sharply, "someone who needs to be remembered."

Amelia saw Daisy turn and stare out the window. She wasn't happy with that reply. It wasn't long before they stopped at a flower shop.

When Torija got out, Amelia asked Daisy, "What is this about?"

"She found out that Alexis's Anna is buried there. Even though she was forgiven on the other side, she feels guilty about ordering the attack that killed her."

It must be a heavy burden to carry guilt like Torija did. It wasn't as easy as saying you wanted to turn your life around.

"How is she feeling now, about her father?" Amelia asked.

Daisy sighed. "Troubled. That man destroys her confidence. Knowing what he put her through, it's no surprise."

Daisy indicated that Torija was on her way back to the car, so they cut short their conversation.

There were soon on their way to Highgate Cemetery. The car door was opened for Amelia and she got out.

Highgate was a famous place in London, and not as gruesome as it sounded. This Victorian resting place was filled with gothic architecture and the resting places of many famous people, the most famous being Karl Marx. It was such an unusual cemetery that there were guided tours each day.

As they walked through the gate, Amelia grasped Daisy's hand. "I don't like cemeteries."

"Don't worry. There's nothing to be frightened of. I spent nights in places like this with my Monster Hunters."

"Did you ever catch anything on film?" Amelia asked.

"Flashes of light, noises. The dead didn't want to be found, I think, unless they were troubled."

"That doesn't make me feel much better, Daisy."

Once they were through the gates, they saw Sybil sitting on a bench with her eyes closed. "Sybil?" Amelia said.

"Amelia? Daisy? Wonderful to see you."

Daisy helped her stand and the three women kissed.

"How is baby Debrek?" Sybil touched her stomach.

"They are good, I think. Can you tell?"

Sybil smiled. "They are strong."

She turned and nodded her head to Torija. "Behaving yourself?"

Torija smiled. "As much as I can."

"Come with me, ladies. I have something to show you."

Sybil led them through a corridor of gothic Victorian vaults, like rows of mini stone houses.

"I've never seen a graveyard like this," Amelia said. "It's full of graves, but it's green with trees and plants snaking around the pillars."

"You haven't seen anything yet. This way," Sybil said.

They came to a tall archway with ivy and other plants cascading down over the top. It was carved in an Egyptian style to mimic some of the ancient Egyptian ruins.

"This is awesome," Daisy said.

"It looks very old," Sybil said, "but it is Victorian like the rest of it. It was built during what was called *Egyptomania* during the Victorian days. It is special. But we need to find the mausoleum at the end of this walkway."

They walked slowly through the Egyptian avenue and came out to be faced with a large mausoleum. The mausoleum was beautiful, as beautiful as a tomb could be. There were three sarcophagi in this space, beautifully carved and matching the white stone of the rest of the tomb.

The walls and ceilings held coloured friezes of different scenes. There were angels above women either planting or picking plants. Then there was one woman holding bowls to the lips of the ill. Could they be witches?

"Sybil? Are there witches buried here?" Amelia asked.

Sybil smiled. "Well done."

"It was the paintings."

"Yes. Those that made this mausoleum couldn't be too explicit about what they were, or they'd never have been allowed to bury them in a Christian graveyard."

Daisy took a step towards one of the sarcophagi and placed her hand on the top. She jumped back as if she had been burned.

Torija was beside her in seconds. "What happened?"

Daisy tried to get her breath back. "It was my spidey sense. Al these memories rushed at me, but there were too many all at once."

"Who's buried here?" Amelia asked.

To her surprise, Torija answered, "People who died because of my orders to attack the Debreks." Torija set her flowers down on the cold floor, propped up against one of the tombs.

Daisy held Torija's hand, trying to soothe her pain.

"Who are they?" Amelia asked.

"Three very important witches: the leader of the London coven, Rose—Daisy's mother, and your mother."

Suddenly all the strength from Amelia's legs disappeared, and she dropped to the floor.

When she came to and opened her eyes, she found herself in Torija's arms while Daisy was talking loudly and gesticulating wildly.

"Let me get you up," Torija said.

One of the guards helped, and Torija asked another to go and get a bottle of water from the car. Daisy joined them and put her arm around Amelia's waist. Amelia said, "I don't know what's happening."

Daisy's brain was overloaded with thoughts, feelings, and memories.

"Is the baby okay?"

"Yes, yes, it's fine. Did Sybil really say our mothers are here?" Amelia asked.

"Yeah, and it's not true. My mum was buried with my dad in Scotland. I went to visit their grave every Sunday with my granny."

"That's what you were supposed to think. It was very important that both your mothers and Rose were kept secret."

"Rose was Byron's lover, a long time ago," Amelia said.

Daisy detected sadness in her voice. It wouldn't be much fun to come face to face with your partner's ex. Torija didn't have relationships like that. She'd probably slept with half the Dreds, but it wasn't something that had come up.

"Rose came to visit my coven many years ago. She told us of her vision, that the daughters of two women would save us from the evil that threatened our world. Each was a descendant."

Daisy almost growled in frustration. "Would you just tell us once and for all what this is all about? I'm sick of riddles."

She felt Torija's reassuring presence behind her.

Sybil walked up to the tombs and said, "Rose told me that I must save your mother Bronte and that she and Daisy's mum must be buried together with Rose, because here you would finish your training, and you could only do that with the power of three."

Daisy and Amelia went to their mothers' tombs. Daisy saw no nameplates.

"Why are there no names on the tombs?" Daisy asked.

"Because we didn't want Anka's people to know where they were. Both of your mothers are crucial to the next stage in your powers, and how to control it. You do understand the power of three, don't you?"

"It's a magic number," Daisy said, "in witch lore, anyway."

Amelia looked around sharply. "What about when we are fighting Anka and Balor? We'll only be two."

Sybil walked over to her and placed her hand on her baby bump. "You will be three."

"What? My baby? No."

"She will be safe. She has great power within her, both witch and vampire."

"She?" Amelia asked.

They purposely hadn't wanted to know at their scan so it would be a big surprise, but now Amelia was glad to know.

Torija squeezed Daisy's waist. "I can just imagine Byron's reaction when she hears about this."

"Please don't worry," Sybil said, "and yes, you're having a little girl. It had to be. The women coming together are very powerful."

Amelia looked at Daisy, feeling emotional, and said, "Byron said she'd love a little girl."

"Come and let's start your final lesson," Sybil said.

Amelia looked unconvinced at Daisy and Torija. "Are you sure we should do this?"

"Sybil's not steered us wrong before, but it's up to you. I'll back you whatever you decide."

Amelia sighed. "Let's do it."

"Will we find out about these visions and dreams we've been having?" Amelia asked.

"Yes. Trust me. Now hold hands with Daisy."

Daisy reached for Amelia.

"Look into each other's eyes. Reach out to the other, then listen for the voices of the ancestors."

This they could do. Daisy and Amelia had practised this. They had come a long way. First they could only do it by closing their eyes to shut off any distractions, but not now.

Amelia said, "One voice."

It was their cue to drown out the many voices of their ancestors and tune in to one voice.

"Welcome. I am Rose. We have been waiting for you both."

"What do we do?" Amelia asked.

"See a ball of light inside yourself, and when you find it, send it to meet Daisy. Then say Open the other side. We wish to meet our ancestors.*"*

Amelia was better at this than Daisy as she wasn't a witch, but Daisy tried to follow their training. She found the ball of light in her chest and forced it down her arms. When her ball met Amelia's, a whirlwind engulfed them.

The sound was deafening, and bits of gravel and twigs from the mausoleum floor whizzed around them. It was hard to keep holding on to Amelia, but Daisy put everything she had in to not letting go.

"Are you ready, Daisy?"

"Yes, go."

"Open the other side. We wish to meet our ancestors," they said in unison.

"Again," Amelia shouted.

"Open the other side. We wish to meet our ancestors."

The light grew exponentially and swallowed them whole.

CHAPTER TWELVE

When Bhal and Sera arrived back at the house, Sera was ravenous for blood. She wanted to run upstairs for a blood bag, but Bhal had other ideas.

Bhal helped her into the house as Sera's own legs were weak and her body shaking. It was true that she hadn't been feeding properly, but being so close to Bhal and hungering for her and her blood made Sera feel worse.

"Put all your weight on me and I'll help you down to the blood room," Bhal said.

"No. I just want to go to bed."

"You need to feed. Do you see how unwell you look?"

"Thanks a lot. That's just what a girl needs to hear."

"You know what I mean. Come on."

Sera pushed away from Bhal. "No. Just leave me alone, okay? I can handle this myself."

"Clearly."

Sera stumbled her way upstairs. At the top she met Katie.

"Are you okay, Sera?"

"I would be if Bhal would stop hovering around me."

Katie took her arm. "I'll help you."

Sera looked back down at Bhal, who just walked away. She couldn't help but feel guilty. *I can't handle this.* Between the drugs craving, not tolerating blood, and her confusing feelings for Bhal, it was just too much.

Once Katie helped her into her bedroom, Sera sat on the bed. Katie crouched down in front of her and stroked a strand of hair from her face.

"What's going on with you, Sera? I hardly see you home any more, and you seem like you're in pain."

"Things are messed up. My head's messed up, and I just don't know what to do about it."

"Can you tell me what's messed up?" Katie asked.

Sera shook her head. "I can't, Katie. Not this time."

"Does Bhal know?"

Sera didn't answer.

Katie grasped her hand. "If she does, then let her help. She cares about you, Sera."

That was the problem. Bhal was all she could think about.

When the blinding light dissipated, Amelia found herself standing outside a wooden building with Daisy a few paces away.

"What is this place?"

People were busy walking by, some riding horses, some walking down to a busy market next to the wooden building.

"It looks like we've fallen into the Middle Ages," Daisy said.

The dirty, muddy dress of the people did point that way, apart from the one or two who were dressed better, with fine-looking swords and helmets.

She looked up at the sign on the wooden building and it said *The Tavern*.

"The local pub?" Amelia said.

"Looks like it. It feels like when I was watching Torija through the diary. We look so different, and nobody is noticing."

Daisy shivered.

"What is it?" Amelia asked.

"My spidey sense is saying we have to go inside."

Amelia raised her eyebrow. "Do we really have to?"

"I think so. Come on." Daisy took her hand, and they walked up the muddy path to the entrance. "Here goes."

They walked in and found wooden benches and tables, with rough and ready people drinking at them. Amelia looked down and saw straw on the floor.

Daisy scrunched up her nose. "It doesn't smell the best, does it?"

Amelia chuckled. "No, not the best. Where is your spidey sense leading us now?"

Daisy looked around and said, "Through to the back of the room."

On they walked, Amelia holding her hand over her bump protectively.

"Look," Daisy said.

In the corner of the room Amelia spotted a woman looking out of place in Victorian dress, and next to her was Lucia, the Grand Duchess, matriarch of the Debreks.

Amelia hurried over to the table, bringing Daisy with her. "Lucia?"

"You're here at last. At last." Lucia stood up with the aid of a stick and hugged Amelia, before placing her hand on Amelia's stomach. "She is strong."

"This is Daisy."

"We have met, haven't we, young lady?" Lucia said.

Daisy leaned in and gave her a kiss.

"Bless you, Daisy, for saving my Victorija. You are a brave woman taking on that troublesome vampire."

"I love her," Daisy said.

Amelia looked at the woman standing next to Lucia. She was looking at her bump and smiling.

"Can you introduce us, Lucia?" Amelia asked.

Lucia sat back down. "Of course Amelia, this is Rose."

Amelia sat down slowly. She didn't know how she should act meeting her vampire's ex, but her heart beat fast and her mouth dried up. She was also the woman who saved her mother, after acting on a premonition.

Rose presented much older than her and had a warm, open smile.

"It's wonderful to meet you at last, Amelia." Rose reached over and squeezed her hand. "Do not think of the past. Everyone is where they are supposed to be."

That relaxed Amelia. "Thank you. It's nice to meet you too. Byron talks of you warmly."

"I'm so glad she has found such happiness. I always told her she would lose her heart when she least expected it, and I was right."

"Hi, Rose," Daisy said.

"Daisy, the woman who tamed Victorija Dred."

"I'm sorry. I—"

Amelia could see Daisy was uncomfortable. It was Torija who had ordered Rose's death.

"Don't fret, Daisy. It was my destiny to die, as it was yours to save Victorija. We need her for the battle ahead."

"Thank you."

"Where are we?" Amelia asked.

Lucia smiled. "*We* are…on the other side, but *you* are seeing a world that happened a long, long time ago."

"Can we meet our mothers here?" Daisy said.

Rose smiled. "Yes, they've been waiting a long time to meet you."

❖

Byron and Alexis had been waiting at MI5 reception for thirty minutes already. Byron was a patient person, but with Amelia out on her own, she was anxious to get this over with.

"Principe, they are showing you disrespect. There is no way they weren't ready for you when we arrived."

Byron crossed her legs. "It's a power move. They are showing us that they will deal with us in their own time."

"They have short memories. What we did during the Second World War should be enough to show us respect."

"They are frightened, Alexis. The humans are losing control of the streets, and so many people are dying. We must make allowances."

Finally four grey-suited men approached them. The lead man said, "If you'd follow me please, Ms. Debrek."

When Alexis stood he held out his hand. "Ms. Debrek only."

"I go where my Principe goes," Alexis snarled.

This wasn't worth the fight, Byron knew. "I will be fine, Duca. You stay here."

"But, Principe—"

She locked eyes with Alexis and gave a straight order. "Stay, Duca. I will be back soon."

Byron followed the men over to the lifts and got in. It was lucky she wasn't claustrophobic, as she was surrounded. She also noted the guns below their suit jackets.

It amused Byron to see the weapons. They had no idea what a born vampire could do to them. She could have killed them all before the lift doors opened again, but if it made them feel safer, that was okay.

The lift was going down for quite a while longer than she expected. Byron hadn't met with the department in this building. During the war, she and Alexis were briefed of their missions in Churchill's war rooms, a bunker deep below London.

Finally the lift doors opened, and she was led down a deserted corridor. Then she was shown into what she could only describe as an interrogation room.

"Take a seat," one of the men said.

She sat down on the chair next to a table in the middle of the room. Byron had no doubt she was being watched. There would be disguised cameras everywhere. Byron sighed and sat back in her chair.

On the wall opposite was a mirror. Could this be any more clichéd?

The door opened and Daisy's grandmother, Margaret Brassard, came in. As far as Byron knew she worked in Edinburgh, at the Scottish section of the department.

Byron stood politely.

"Byron Debrek? We haven't been introduced, although my granddaughter has told me about you. I'm Margaret Brassard."

Byron shook her hand. "A pleasure, Ms. Brassard."

"Margaret, please. Do take a seat."

"I understood you worked in Edinburgh, Margaret," Byron said.

"I do normally, but with the murders and because Daisy is involved, I was called to London."

"Have you been sent to soften me up, before they"—Byron pointed at the mirror on the wall—"come in?"

"My superior will be here shortly. I just wanted to say that I'm glad Daisy is staying with you. I know she'll be safe under your protection."

"Of course she will."

Margaret stood quickly when the door opened. She stood off to the side and a man in his late thirties took charge and a seat. A younger woman was behind him holding an iPad.

"Thank you for coming, Ms. Debrek. My name is Josh and this is my deputy Chris."

Josh had an artificial air of civility, but Chris stared at her with anger in her eyes.

"I'm always happy to cooperate with the department."

"Hmm. Yes," Josh said.

He didn't sound convinced.

"You know, I take it, what's been going on up and down the country?"

"Yes. It is tragic," Byron said.

Chris handed Josh the iPad. "These are some of the pictures we have of the victims." Josh handed her the device, and she looked and scowled at the images. Josh continued, "People with bite wounds, their throats ripped out, and their bodies savaged. I want you to tell me exactly what has been going on in your community."

Did Byron tell them the exact truth or a watered-down version? Things were only going to worsen in the short term, before they defeated Anka, so they should be prepared for what's to come.

"There is a civil war breaking out in the paranormal community. Good versus evil, you might say."

Chris snorted. "Evil versus evil, more like."

Josh gave her a hard look, and she put her head down. "Tell me more."

"A malevolent witch called Anka is working with a group of renegade vampires, werewolves, and many others to achieve their goal."

Josh leaned forward on the table. "What is their goal?"

"To crush humans under their boots," Byron said with humour in her voice. Sometimes humour was the only way to deal with this kind of situation.

Josh looked shocked. "The murders?"

"Anka has let loose her people to kill and flooded the market with a drug aimed at addling the minds of those paranormals who wouldn't normally behave like that."

"She must be involved, sir," Chris said.

Byron laughed with disdain. "Chris, I was serving and killing for our country when your great-great-grandfather was in short trousers. I think I am owed a little more respect than that."

It seemed Margaret couldn't hold her tongue any longer. "Byron and her clan served with distinction, Byron in RAF intelligence. She did a lot of jobs for the country that were too dangerous for our soldiers, and only the prime minister and his close cabinet knew what they were."

Josh cleared his throat. "We do appreciate that, but you have to understand, some people in the department are straining at the leash to blame any paranormal. The deaths have been so horrific."

"You need us, Josh. The best thing for you and your *department* can do is to stay out of our way. Only paranormals on the side of good can win this civil war. Just pray to whatever God you believe in that we win, or the future of humans will be death and slavery."

"My Daisy is with them, sir, and I trust Byron with her."

Josh took out a mobile phone and called someone. If Byron was to guess, they were behind the mirror.

"Yes, sir…Of course. I will."

He hung up and said, "Very well, Byron. You may go."

Byron could only smile at these humans' arrogance. She could be out of this building in minutes, but she let them have their imaginary power over her.

"Thank you." Byron stood up.

"Margaret will be your liaison. Keep her up to date with what's happening."

"Very well. Goodbye."

❖

Lucia and Rose took them down to a path by the river.

"We'll leave you here. Just walk further up the path," Lucia said.

Daisy held Amelia's hand as they walked. They saw a bench, and two women were sitting on it.

"That's our mums, aren't they?" Daisy said.

"I think so. I'm nervous."

Daisy pulled her up towards the bench. Two women stood. The one with curly brown hair, a brown flying jacket, and jeans was Daisy's mum, Freya, and the other woman, petite with dark hair and a light flowery dress, was Amelia's mum, Bronte.

"Mum!" Daisy ran and fell into her mum's arms.

"You found us, sweetie," Freya said as she squeezed her.

But Amelia didn't run. She was so unsure. Daisy had at least known her mum, but Amelia had never met hers.

Bronte held out her hand to Amelia. "Hi, Amelia. I've waited so long to meet you."

Amelia couldn't hold back any more. She wrapped her arms around her mum, and they both started sobbing.

"Mum? I've missed you my whole life."

"I'm so sorry I couldn't be there for everything." Bronte stood back and studied every part of her. "I missed your first step, your first word—"

"You sacrificed yourself for me, Mum. That's the most noble thing anyone could ever do for their child."

Bronte touched her baby bump. "My granddaughter. Sounds strange when I look twenty-five, doesn't it?"

They both laughed and hugged again.

Then Bronte said, "This is my friend Freya—and she's Daisy's mum, but you know that."

Freya reached out to Amelia. "Come here, darlin'."

Amelia and Daisy hugged each other's mum, then sat on the bench.

Freya said, "I know there's a lot of questions you both will have, but we don't have much time. Take a look across there."

Amelia did and saw the beautiful woman from the river, sitting enjoying a picnic with the young man, Raymond.

"It's the woman in our dreams," Daisy said.

"And all our ancestor," Freya said. "They had ten sons, and each son had a family, and down every family line, the magic went with it."

Bronte added, "Pressyne, Melusine's mother, was Balor's sister, and he heard a premonition that his kin and only his kin could destroy him." She continued, "Balor had his people hunt down all of his family. All ten strands of his family—until us."

Freya said, "Bronte was running from people sent to kill her when Daisy's father and I met her. Your dad was killed trying to protect us." She rubbed Daisy's back. "Bronte and I both found out we were pregnant at the same time."

"Dad was a brave man," Daisy said.

"He was," Freya agreed.

"Who was my father, Mum?" Amelia asked.

"I don't know, Amelia. You just happened. I couldn't explain it."

Amelia might not have a father but she had a mum who gave her life for her, and that was all she needed.

Freya stood and looked to the side, at what Amelia couldn't see. "We don't have long, Bronte."

"Okay, listen, girls, the power you harnessed to come here—use that when the moment comes," Bronte said.

Daisy asked, "What moment?"

"The moment with Balor," Freya said. "Use the two of your and this baby girl's strength to stop his flesh from coming back to earth."

Bronte said, "We need to go now."

Freya and Bronte hugged both of them, and the next thing Amelia and Daisy knew, they had fallen to the marble floor of the mausoleum.

❖

Back at the house, Amelia and Daisy held court in the drawing room and told their story. It hardly seemed real as Daisy recounted meeting Lucia and Rose in the tavern, then meeting their mothers, and what had happened to them.

"Do you think you know now how to fight this Balor when he arrives?" Torija said.

Daisy looked at Amelia and shrugged. "We know what they told us, how to harness a great amount of power with three instead of two, but kill him?"

Daisy walked over to Torija and sat before she spoke. "Mum said the rest would know what to do. I don't know if she meant all of you guys, but she was rushed. They didn't have much time."

"There's something else," Amelia said, "but I need to talk to Byron about it on my own. Would you all mind?"

"No problem," Sera said, "I need to feed anyway."

Once everyone had left, Amelia walked to Byron and sat on her knee.

"Is it bad news? Tell me, mia cara."

"No, it's not bad. I wanted to talk to you about Rose, and something else."

"Ah. Was it awkward for you?"

"No, she made it comfortable. She's a nice woman. Rose said she was so happy you met me."

"She was a kind, lovely woman, and I cared about her, but I love you and will for eternity."

"I know." Amelia put Byron's hand on her baby bump. "I also found out that we're having a baby girl."

"A baby girl?" Byron's face lit up with joy.

Amelia smiled. "You're happy then?"

Byron held her close. "I couldn't be happier. My two girls. Who told you?"

"Lucia."

Byron laughed. "Of course she did. The Grand Duchess Lucia knows everything."

CHAPTER THIRTEEN

Two days had passed since Daisy and Amelia's news. Two days that had been awkward in the extreme for Sera. She needed Bhal to help with her addiction, but they'd exchanged few words since their argument when they got home from the club.

Sera was not feeling good. She was keeping some blood down but not much, and she hadn't ventured back to the blood room.

This evening Sera had her water fix from Bhal two hours ago, but the clawing inside was starting to come back. There was no way she was going to see Bhal again, so she put the light off and tried to get to sleep.

She wasn't tired. Sera tried to remember that Celtic myth story that Bhal told her. The race of beings that came in ships in the sky. The Tuatha De Danann with their magical weapons, the one that had soothed and sent her sleep.

The spear that shot fire-bolts, the shield that would repel any bow, the axe that—

Wait a second.

Sera sat bolt upright. Something niggled in her brain. Bhal had described the story as one her mother told her, but there was one her own mother had told her as a child. A folktale, one of the many from a book read to her about the other paranormal creatures that inhabited their land.

"The wolves."

Sera turned the light on and grabbed her iPad from the bedside cabinet. She first looked up the myth of the Tuatha De Danann. She read it all through as quickly as she could, then put her iPad down and went over to her cupboard.

She dropped to her knees and pulled out a box of childhood memories—toys, keepsakes, and books. Her dad had commissioned this one for Sera's birthday.

Sera flicked through the pages. It contained fables and stories handed down to each generation about vampires, witches, werewolves, shapeshifters, and the fae. She came to the page about the werewolf packs and traced her fingers over the gorgeous illustrations of wolves and their clan emblems.

Sera thought through all the swirling thoughts in her head. *Balor. The void. Melusine's mother was Balor's sister...*

"That's it, that's it!" Sera had a rush of excitement. She had to talk to Bhal. Before she did, Sera took a picture of the illustration in her book.

Sera didn't want to go to Byron if this was a stupid idea.

Her heart was racing fast. This could be the answer, and she had to get this out of her head. She couldn't remember being so excited or energized in a long, long, long time.

She left her room and walked along to Bhal's. Sera knocked at the door, and Bhal soon opened up. "Sera? Do you need more—"

"No, no—well, maybe—but can I talk to you about something?"

"Always. Come in," Bhal said.

Once Sera got in she started to feel nervous. What is this sounded ridiculous out loud? "Can you sit down and hear me out?"

Bhal took a seat in the armchair in front of her bed, and Sera started pacing.

"Are you sure there isn't something wrong, Sera? You seem worried."

Sera held up her hand. "No, I have a theory about something, and I wanted to run it by you before I talk to Byron about it."

"Okay, tell me."

"You know what Amelia and Daisy found out about being the daughters of Melusine? That Melusine's mother was sister of Balor?"

"Aye."

Sera was bouncing on her feet, so excited to share this information. "What if they were the Tuatha De Danann? The people you told me the story about? Maybe they were an advanced civilization from a different place, a different reality, who had control over opening up different places, realities, who knows—and that's what Anka wants open to let Balor out?"

Bhal wasn't laughing at her idea, so that was a good start. She narrowed her eyes and looked as if she was thinking deeply.

"Balor was trapped in his prison by something or someone, and it could be them," Bhal added.

Sera snapped her fingers. "Exactly, and what if the keys or artifacts were the weapons of the Tuatha De Danann. The light sword, the axe—all those weapons you told me about. Maybe they help open up the portal. Does that sound stupid?"

Bhal moved to take Sera's hand. "It does not sound stupid. I never made the connection, but it makes so much sense."

"There's one more thing."

"What?"

Sera took her phone out of her pocket and opened up a picture. "You see this? This is the shield that the Wolfgangs in America have to remind them where their pack comes from. The four packs of the UK and Ireland. Look what represents them."

Bhal's lips parted, and she shook her head in shock.

Sera continued, "A sword, a spear, a shield, and an axe."

Bhal smiled and threw her arms around Sera. She lifted her up and spun her around. "You are a genius!"

Sera laughed. "Put me down."

As she slid down Bhal's body, they came so close together and gazed into each other's eyes. Bhal cupped her cheek and whispered, "It was in front of us the whole time, and you found it. I told you that you could do anything. You're special."

"Do you use that line on all the girls, Warrior?" a voice behind them said.

They jumped apart, and Bhal took a defensive stance in front of Sera.

"Morrigan," Bhal said.

"Morrigan?" Sera said. "Like the Goddess Morrigan?"

Morrigan brought her hand to her chest and bowed her head. "Goddess of war, battle, protection, and"—Morrigan winked at Bhal as she said—"fertility."

Bhal felt discomfort that this was happening in front of Sera. It shouldn't matter, but she didn't want Sera to know how well she knew Morrigan.

She looked to Sera, who had crossed her arms defensively. She looked annoyed.

"Why are you here, Morrigan?"

"Because this vampire—"

"The vampire has a name," Sera said while pushing Bhal from in front of her.

Morrigan grinned and walked over to Sera. "My apologies, Serenity Debrek." Morrigan's eyes slowly scanned Sera's face. "You do know how to pick them, Warrior."

"We are not together," Sera said forcefully.

Sera's words punched Bhal in the stomach. Bhal wished she could shut the door on these feelings that were creeping out of her soul, but she couldn't. Sera obviously found the thought of them together ridiculous, and it was.

"So why are you here?" Bhal said again.

Morrigan kept looking into Sera's eyes for a moment, then moved away. "Because this Serenity Debrek has put all the pieces together. The information that I kept trying to get you to see when I visited you."

"She visits you?" Sera said.

She sounded surprised and annoyed.

No, no, this did not sound good at all. "She doesn't visit me, Sera. She drops in unannounced."

Morrigan laughed. "Listen to her flounder. We've been friends for a long time. Friends with benefits on both sides, eh, Warrior."

"Just say what you want to and go, Morrigan," Bhal growled.

"Very well. I have been bound by a non-interference policy by my people on this matter. I couldn't say anything until one of you put the pieces together." Morrigan inspected her perfectly manicured black nails. "Very annoying, but I am bound to it on this."

"It's never stopped you before," Bhal said.

No matter what this thing was between Morrigan and Bhal, Sera wanted to know exactly what was going on, and she had a good idea.

"You're one of the Tuatha De Danann, aren't you? All the Celtic Gods are?"

Morrigan smiled. "You're very clever. Balor is my brother. It pains me to call him brother after all that he has done."

"Balor's your brother? I should have seen it," Bhal said.

"You should have seen a lot of things. Some of us came here to learn about your world, and some of us grew fond of you and stayed, like my sister who fell in love in more ways than one."

"Melusine's mother?"

"Pressyne. She fell in love with the King of Scotland. Why she fell in love with a barbarian is hard for me to understand, but she paid a high price, and then her daughter went and did the same. What fools."

"So Daisy and Amelia are the daughters of your people," Sera said.

Morrigan snapped her fingers, and the chair from across the room shot over, allowing her to sit down. "Yes, the last of their kind. Balor has killed his kin because it was foretold that the only one who could defeat him was from his own family."

Sera's tension was making her ache for her drug. Her feelings for Bhal, meeting this Morrigan, were just getting too overwhelming. She closed her eyes and tried to focus on this moment and finding out exactly what they needed to know.

Bhal must have read her hunger because she tried to take Sera's hand, but Sera brushed her off.

"Why is he so determined to harm this world?" Sera asked.

"Jealousy, darkness—where we come from, he was nothing, and he hated it."

Sera folded her arms. "Here he can bully those he thinks are weaker?"

"Exactly. Bhal's warriors have helped keep him weak over time, but nobody counted on Anka. She's ruthless, clever, and would do anything for Balor."

"So what do we do? Get the weapons from the wolf packs?" Bhal asked.

Morrigan crossed her legs seductively. "Clever Warrior…and at the crossroads."

The way Morrigan was looking at Bhal was as someone who had known her intimately.

"Lochlan?" Bhal said.

Morrigan said nothing and disappeared.

The silence in the room was deafening.

Bhal closed the distance between them. "Sera, there was nothing between us," Bhal said with a hint of panic in her voice.

Sera lifted up her hands between them and tried to sound as nonchalant as possible. "It's none of my business. You can do what you like."

"Morrigan has just tormented me from time to time over the centuries."

"As I said, it doesn't matter." Sera had to get out of there and started walking away. "I need to give my sister this new information."

"You need some help, don't you? Have some water before you go," Bhal pleaded.

"No, I'm fine." She used her vampire speed to race out of the room and along the corridor.

She could hear Bhal shouting, "Fucking Morrigan."

❖

Professor Beaufort put her key in the front door and walked into the hallway of her flat. Her elderly father came out of the kitchen.

"Marie, there's two friends of yours in the living room. I'm making them coffee."

The door opened and she saw Anka. "Come in and talk to us, Marie."

She gulped and nodded. "Dad, go watch television in the family room. I'll get the coffee."

He nodded and walked off. She put her bag down and hung up her jacket. When Marie went into the living room, Anka was sitting on the couch, while a woman with dark hair was playing with her cat on the floor.

"Marie, let me introduce my associate, Gilbert Dred."

"Gilbert?"

"It's a long story," Anka said.

Gilbert was stroking the cat, but Marie felt an atmosphere of threat as she did. She had to get these people out of her house quickly.

"We came to see what progress you've made. Gilbert thought that we would have to show just how urgent your help was, but I said, Marie won't let us down. She hasn't let me down before." Her cat suddenly hissed at Gilbert and ran away. "I never liked cats. Maybe I should go and keep your father in the other room company, eh?"

The threat level just increased. But hopefully what she had would be enough for Anka.

"Wait, I have something." Marie frantically went through her bag, looking for papers. "Yes, this one."

She brought it over to Anka. On it was a hand-drawn picture and some notes.

"What is this?"

"Ancient in origin. It was found at a megalithic site in Ireland. The site is a series of mounds and tunnels, we believe connected to death and travelling from this world to the next, and served as an astrological calendar."

"How does that help us?" Anka said.

"The people carved stones and things like this urn. They tell stories of the ancient gods. The Tuatha De Danann, who came to Ireland in ships of the sky."

"Ships of the sky?" Gilbert said. "What does that mean?"

Anka waved at Gilbert to let Marie speak. "And what does the urn tell us?"

"From the picture I can see the term *Lochlan*, meaning a place in the north. That is where the ancient people believed their gods came from, and they brought many items that the ancient peoples thought magical. It sounds like something similar to what you're looking for. Ancient artifacts, and the place you need to find. If you can get me this urn…"

"Where is it? What museum?" Gilbert asked.

"It's not in a museum. Not long after it was discovered, it went into private ownership. It's lost," Marie said.

Anka stood. "Not for long. I have contacts. We will be back with it for you to decipher. Good work, Marie."

As they walked out of her house, Marie let out a long breath of relief.

But she would be back.

CHAPTER FOURTEEN

B hal was cursing her luck. Just as she and Sera were getting closer, Morrigan had turned up. She had helped them become clearer about what Sera had discovered, but now Sera thought there was something between her and Morrigan.

Sera did appear to be annoyed by that fact. Did she care?

Bhal saw Amelia as she walked downstairs. "Principessa."

"Bhal, are you coming for dinner? I've had the kitchen put on a buffet for us, so we can all talk while we eat."

"Aye, that would be nice. Has Sera joined you yet?"

"No, she said she was on her way. Is everything all right with Sera, Bhal?" Amelia asked.

"As far as I know, Principessa."

"You two have been spending a lot of time together. If there was anything…"

Bhal didn't want to outright lie to Amelia. "She had felt a bit useless in the clan, but since Byron gave her some responsibility, it's helped."

"That's what I told Byron. She needed to feel more a part of the clan. Are you coming in to dinner?"

"I'll just have to check with Wilder about something. I won't be long."

Sera couldn't have told Byron about her discovery yet, or Amelia would have known. Why hadn't she? Bhal had a bad feeling. She closed her eyes and tried to focus on Sera, in the same way she sensed souls in torment on Samhain night. Bhal heard the patter of rain, the rustle of leaves in the wind. The garden.

Bhal hurried out to the back of the Debrek house. The patrols were walking the perimeter.

"Has anyone seen Sera?"

"No, Bhal."

Bhal's attention was drawn to a flash across her vision, down at the bottom of the garden. It was next to an old shed the gardener used for tools and supplies. She ran down and opened the door.

There in front of her was Sera with a rucksack. "How did you find me?"

"I'll always find you. What do you think you're doing? I thought you were going to tell Byron and Amelia what you found out?"

"I changed my mind. I'm going myself. I'm going to collect the artifacts. If I tell her, she'll send Alexis and Torija. You saw what she did about the drug investigation."

"She changed her mind and sent us. This has to be done right, Sera. It's too important. Trust her, trust me. I'll speak up for you, for us going as a team."

"Let's go and do this together if you insist. My first stop is the English pack—the Ranwulfs."

Despite what Bhal had said, there was more than a chance that Byron would send somebody else.

"Do you think they are just going to hand over their weapons without Byron arranging this?"

"We can call her once we are on our way. I know I'm supposed to do this."

Bhal was silent. What was she going to do? Her loyalty to Byron was so strong, and there was a chance Byron would never forgive her.

"I'm going the minute you turn your back, Bhal. You're either with me or not."

Bhal remembered what the Grand Principe had asked of her. Put Sera first. But would he really mean *this*?

There was only one answer. "I'll come with you, as long as we give Byron all the information before we get to the Ranwulfs. Deal?"

"Deal. Let's go." Sera held up a car fob for one of the Debrek vehicles.

"I need a few minutes to pack a bag."

"You're going to tell Byron, aren't you?" Sera said.

Bhal grasped her by the shoulders and looked deeply into her eyes. "I swear to you, on my word of honour, that I am not."

Sera looked at her carefully. "I know what your word of honour means. Don't let me down."

"Please be here when I get back," Bhal said.

"I promise. I am going to need you for the withdrawal symptoms."

"Five minutes."

True to her word, Bhal came back with a bag. They jumped the wall at the back of the garden. One of the black Jeeps waited for them.

"I'll drive," Bhal said.

"I think not. I'm in charge here. Get in."

Sera held open the passenger door. Bhal took her sword from her back and got in, cradling it between her legs.

When Sera joined her. Bhal pulled out her hip flask. "Do you need some help?"

"Not right now. I just want to get going."

As they started to drive, Sera smiled and said, "First lying for me, now this?"

"Byron will take my head from my shoulders," Bhal said.

Sera laughed. "Who wants to live forever anyway?"

Bhal couldn't help but smile. Sera made her smile.

❖

Byron paced around the drawing room, positively furious. "Where are they?" Amelia tried to take her hand, but Byron pulled away. "Sera I can believe disappearing into the night when we're about engage in full-on war, but Bhal?"

Torija, Daisy, Katie, Amelia, and Alexis had been eating dinner when Bhal and Sera never turned up. Byron asked one of the staff to find them, but when they returned without finding them, she sent Alexis.

"There must be a reason, Byron," Amelia said.

"The reason is Sera is reckless. When I get her back, she is not leaving this house," Byron shouted.

Amelia raised her voice. "Byron, you need to calm down. Sera is an adult. She's not three years old."

The rest of the room held their breath. No one was used to anyone taking that tone with the Principe, but Amelia was her equal and kept her eyes firmly on Byron.

A few seconds passed with tension filling the room before Byron walked over and took Amelia's hand and kissed it.

"Forgive me, Principessa. It is fear talking."

"We will work this out, sweetheart."

Alexis, Torija, and Wilder entered the room, and Alexis said, "There's no sign of them, and one of the cars is gone."

Byron pulled out her phone and dialled Sera yet again.

"What can they be doing?" Katie asked.

Torija came and flopped down next to Daisy and took her hand. "Do you think she and Bhal have found out about these artifacts? The keys?"

"How could they? They only know what we know," Daisy said.

Byron threw her phone down on the coffee table. "No answer."

Amelia joined Byron at the fireplace. "They'll call us. Trust in them."

Byron slipped her arm around Amelia and pulled her closer. "Looks like we don't have much choice."

❖

Anka's car pulled up beside the fence of a gated property. Anka turned to Gilbert and said, "Let me handle this. My contact Pascal has been very useful to me over the years, and I'd like him to remain intact."

Gilbert lifted her hand and kissed it. "You are no fun, Madam. Let's hope he behaves himself."

Anka got out of the car. Underneath a lamppost stood Pascal. He was short and bookish and combed his few strands of hair over his bald head, in the vain hope of looking like he still had his hair.

"Pascal."

Pascal bowed his head. "Madam, pleasure to meet you again."

"Pascal, this is the Principe of the Dred clan, and my close associate, Gilbert Dred."

Pascal's smile faltered. He obviously had heard of the Dred clan and was confused about the apparent female in front of him, but still he bravely offered his hand.

"Pleased to meet you, Gilbert."

Gilbert looked at his hand disdainfully. "That remains to be seen."

"The collector lives here, Pascal?" Anka asked.

"Yes, he wasn't keen on meeting you. To say he is a private collector is to put it mildly, but I said you had something very interesting to sell. It will get you in the door to negotiate."

"We are good at negotiating." Gilbert grinned as he said that.

Anka ignored him. This was serious. "How did your contact gain possession of the urn in the first place?"

"A man called Sir Thomas Molyneux visited Knowth in Ireland in 1713 and found the urn with charred bone in it. After that it was lost and sold into private hands. I don't know when Mr. Darvel got hold of it, but he's a big collector of ancient artifacts, including those of the ancient peoples of Britain and Ireland."

"Let's go," Gilbert said impatiently. "We need to get this thing and get it back to your Professor Beaufort."

Anka nodded to Pascal, and he led them to a large security gate. "He has security guards, just to make you aware."

Pascal pressed a button and a stern voice said, "*State your business.*"

"My name is Pascal. Mr. Darvel is expecting me and my associates."

There was a moment's silence, and then the gate started to open.

Gilbert leaned close to Anka and said, "I could have been in and out by now."

"Just play along. Mr. Darvel may have more information we can use."

"Fine."

As they approached the door, it was opened by a member of staff. The man was not welcoming and never smiled.

"Follow me. Mr. Darvel will see you in his Egyptian room."

That jolted Anka. The mention of her birth country made her mind flood with memories, both good and bad.

They were led into a huge room groaning with artifacts, artifacts better than any museum could boast. It was almost like walking into a tomb adorned with grave goods. It made Anka feel angry that they were so far from home, and in the hands of this man sitting in his wheelchair in the corner.

"Mr. Darvel, your guests are here."

He turned around and appeared suspicious of those Pascal had brought with him.

"Pascal? Who are they?"

"This is Anka and her friend Gilbert."

"Anka?" Mr. Darvel said.

"Yes, I am from Egypt originally."

"I thought as much. Come and see this." It was a statue of a cat. "Taken from the tomb of Tutankhamen. It's exquisite, don't you agree?"

Anka felt alive. She had been coming here to her brother's library for weeks now. Her stepbrother Kheti was the pharaoh's priest and used his knowledge of magic to keep and maintain his position.

Anka wanted to know everything about magic, but Kheti jealously guarded that knowledge. It was only in the last few weeks that she'd found his library with spells and incantations on scrolls all over the room.

She was learning how to create fire in her hands from nothing when her brother burst in with guards, and her life changed forever.

She was now in a jail cell. Her face was beaten to a pulp, bloodstains were all over her clothes, and her ribs were broken.

Kheti stood at the cell door. "You are nothing, Anka, just like your mother. My father was a fool to lie with that bitch. Magic is not for a woman, and you disgrace the gods trying to learn about it. Tomorrow you will die, and the world will never remember you."

Once he left. Anka lay in agony, wishing that her death would come sooner. She felt weak and alone. Fury and anger screamed inside her.

Then in the darkness she heard, "Anka, do you want to be powerful?"

She couldn't even jump in fright because of her Injuries.

"I can help you become strong, so strong that your brother will tremble at your feet."

"Who are you?" Anka mumbled.

"Balor. The God who will make the world tremble, just like your brother said. Join me."

"Anka?" Gilbert shook her shoulder.

She took a huge breath and returned from her memory. The next morning every person in the palace was dead at her feet, and her brother Kheti did beg, but she made him suffer a long time before she gave him the release of death.

She had been reminded of why she was doing this. No one would ever be able to make her feel as weak as she did then.

She handed the statue back.

"I understand you have something to sell me?" Mr. Darvel said.

"No, we want something," Gilbert butted in.

Anka held up her hand to him. "We want to buy something off you."

"I don't sell. Pascal, you have deceived me. You said they wanted to sell. My butler will show you out."

"Please, hear us out." Anka was sure a man of his knowledge

might have clues about the keys they were looking for, so she wanted to keep him onside.

"You have five minutes."

"I understand you have a keen interest in the ancient Celtic myths and stories."

"I do," Mr. Darvel said.

"We believe you may have a bowl or urn that was found by Sir Thomas Molyneux?" Anka asked.

"I don't know how you found that out, but yes, I do."

"It's said to be a map to the land of Lochlan. Is that correct?"

"So they say. Why do you have an interest?"

"I'm fascinated by the myth of the Tuatha De Danann. They are said to have brought it here, is that right?"

"Yes, it's the pride of my Ancient Celtic collection."

"May we see it?" Anka asked.

Mr. Darvel was quiet for a time. "Only with my security guards present. You may look, but I am not selling— at any price."

"As you wish."

While Mr. Darvel called for his guards, Anka looked at Gilbert and inclined her head as if to ask him to keep calm.

Gilbert was struggling to control his impatience. If it was up to him, Darvel and everyone in this house would be long dead. But while he was hot-headed, Anka was cool, and he knew it could pay to let her lead this one.

One of the guards pushed Darvel in his wheelchair while they followed behind. The other guard opened two big double doors.

They walked into a room staged with green lighting that bounced off glass cases holding many artifacts.

"This is a beautiful display, Mr. Darvel."

"It is my favourite collection. The urn is over here."

A glass case in the centre of the room was filled with a large urn. It had lines and runes carved around the outside.

"May I hold it?" Anka asked.

"No, not this one. It's too precious, and just in case you're wondering, it's alarmed, and if set off the alarm would alert the police immediately."

This human was really pushing it. He was lucky he still breathed. Anka tried a different tack. "Have you ever heard any stories about items that were connected to the Tuatha De Danann?"

"As a matter of fact I have, and it connects to Egypt," Mr. Darvel said.

"Princess Scota?"

"You know of her?"

"Oh yes, she took half the Egyptian treasury and founded her tribes in Ireland, England, Wales, and Scotland." The wolf packs.

"That's her. Wolves were her emblem. In that treasury were magical items left in safekeeping with the royal family, by the ancient gods. I've always wanted to find the weapons if they are real. The closest I got was this picture."

He pointed to a picture on the wall to the side of them. It was a shield with a howling wolf in the middle, and four quarters containing weapons. A sword, a shield, a spear, and an axe.

Anka smacked herself on the head. "Of course. Why didn't I make the connection before?"

"What is it?" Gilbert asked.

"Princess Scota and her people were werewolves. That's why they were sent from Egypt. She set up the British packs, and they each have a weapon as their emblem."

"Werewolves? What are you talking about?" Mr. Darvel asked, suddenly seeming confused.

She marched over to the picture and said, "He is no longer useful, Gilbert. Kill them."

Gilbert didn't need to be asked twice. He ripped the throat out of Mr. Darvel while his guards shot him. His other vampire took care of them and the rest.

❖

Sera's initial excitement about going on this adventure was waning. Not because she didn't believe this was the right thing to do, but because her new sense of purpose wasn't glossing over her addiction any more.

Everything was worse because of her low level of blood consumption. What was hunger for blood and what was addiction were becoming difficult to differentiate.

"Sera? Do you need a break?"

It went against everything in her to admit weakness, especially to Bhal, but she had no choice.

"Yeah, I need some water."

"Pull into the next service station, and you can get refreshed."

Five minutes later they were looking for a parking space. Sera tried to find one furthest away from the main doors to give them some privacy.

Bhal took out her hip flask. "Have you got any bottles of water in your rucksack? I'll need a top-up after this."

"Yes, I've got everything. Water, blood bags, change of clothes."

The Debreks kept a big stock of rucksacks that kept blood bags cool, for a travelling supply of blood, and Sera had grabbed one before leaving.

Sera cupped the underside of Bhal's hands and drank the reviving water, then sighed as it calmed her body.

"Thanks, Bhal. Thanks for doing this for me."

"I'll do anything for you, Sera."

The sincerity with which she said that hit Sera in the chest. "Thank you."

They gazed into each other's eyes, before Bhal looked away. Sera could get lost in those eyes. Why hadn't she noticed them before?

"I was thinking," Bhal said, "we'll arrive quite late at the Ranwulf pack lands if we keep going. Why don't we stay overnight here, and we can send Byron the information you found. Then tomorrow we can arrive in Northampton at a reasonable time."

"You mean stay in the car?"

"No, there's a budget hotel attached to this service station. Look." Bhal pointed at a dull brick building with a sign saying *Rooms available*.

"I'm not a budget girl," Sera joked.

"Beggars can't be choosers. Come on, it'll give Byron a chance to contact the Ranwulf Alpha," Bhal said.

"Or give Byron time to send people after us?"

"She won't. Give her a chance. Please?"

Sera sighed. "Fine, but if she reacts badly, I'm leaving tonight."

"Fair enough."

Bhal got out and got Sera's bag. Sera led them over to the hotel reception, where they got the usual strange looks. Humans never knew what to make of Bhal or her gender—she was so far removed from a human self-imposed standard. Plus her natural authority tended to scare humans.

Bhal didn't help by giving the reception boy the hardest of stares. Sera got the key card for their room and said to Bhal, "Come on before you scare the boy half to death."

As they walked upstairs, Sera said suddenly, "I got us one room without thinking. Should I have gotten two?"

"No, I'd rather be close to you…in case anything happens."

Sera was secretly pleased. She felt safe and calm in Bhal's presence. They arrived at their room, and Sera used the key card to open the door.

She stepped into a cramped room with one large, king-size bed. Then she looked into the shoebox that was the bathroom. "Well, this isn't the Ritz."

"It's only for one night," Bhal said.

"True. Can you give me my bag and I'll charge it up?" The bag cooling panels could be charged up so they'd be ice-cold for the next journey.

Then Sera took out one of the bags of blood.

"You can feed from me, Sera," Bhal said.

How would she get out of this one? It both tantalized her and terrified her to think of drinking from Bhal again. It was too much, and Sera was frightened of either losing herself in Bhal or showing Bhal that there was something deeply wrong with her because she couldn't stomach blood.

"No, I'm okay with bagged."

Bhal's face fell. Now it looked like she was rejecting her, but she had no choice.

"I'm just going to the bathroom." She handed Bhal her phone. "Here's the folder that I made up with the information I discovered. Can you send it on to Byron while I'm in there?"

Bhal grasped her phone. "Fine."

Oh, Bhal is definitely annoyed.

Sera went in and locked the door behind her. She held the blood bag on the sink. *Come on. You can do it. Keep it down this time.*

She bit into the bag and drank it. It wasn't best served cold, but it kept it fresh. Halfway through the bag, the blood started to come up her throat.

No, please!

This was why she wanted to feed in private. If Bhal saw this, she'd probably take her straight home, and she wasn't having that. She brought up some blood and spat it out.

She couldn't stand this any more.

Sera poured the rest of the bag down the sink and cleaned up as quickly as she could. Why was this happening? Could it be due to her drug use? She would have to find out, but not until she visited the wolf packs and collected the artifacts from them.

Bhal was probably right about letting Byron know her findings. The Alphas of the packs would take Byron more seriously than her, something that annoyed her greatly.

But that was why she was doing this, to prove herself more worthy of respect and of the name Debrek.

CHAPTER FIFTEEN

Byron walked around the room holding her tablet and reading the file that Sera sent. At first she was so glad Sera was safe, then enraged that she had gone off without giving Byron the chance to think about the best way to do this, and then angry that Bhal would help her.

It was so far out of character for Bhal. Maybe Amelia was right, maybe Bhal had feelings for Sera. She didn't know how she felt about that. Bhal always put duty to the clan before anything. But love could make you do strange things. Byron knew that.

She looked up at her family and clan members in the drawing room. They all appeared uneasy, waiting to see how she would react to the news of what Sera had found and why she had run off.

"Have you all read it?"

"Yes, Principe," some said, and the others nodded as they held their phones.

It fell to Amelia to talk first. "It's brilliant. What Sera has figured out would have taken us God knows how long to discover."

Byron nodded. She was secretly proud of Sera for thinking this out so carefully, but she didn't like being forced into how they dealt with this. If she called Sera back, she'd either refuse or never forgive her, and who knew, maybe Bhal would choose to stand by Sera.

Byron needed—the *clan* needed—Bhal by her side.

"Sera is a bloody annoying little sister."

From the nervous smiles, Amelia, Torija, Daisy, Katie, and Alexis were expecting her to explode. Maybe it was time to trust Sera.

"What are you going to do?" Amelia asked.

"Let's call her. Daisy? Can you call her and put the call on the TV screen?" Byron asked.

"Yeah, no problem."

Byron thought Sera would be more likely to take Daisy's call than hers. When Sera answered, she looked shocked to see her family and friends staring back at her. It also looked like they were in a hotel.

Sera still looked pale, and her eyes were rimmed with red.

"Uh…hi," Sera said nervously, "did you get the folder we sent you?"

Byron could see Bhal. "Yes, we did. Is Bhal there? I would like to speak to her too."

Bhal came into the shot and sat on the bed. "Principe, I take full responsibility for this. I said I would bring Sera and—"

Byron held her hand up to stop her. Bhal was protecting Sera. There was no doubt in Byron's mind that this was entirely Sera's doing. Bhal really did care about her.

"Sera? You were so clever working this out. Well done."

Sera's eyes went wide. "Say what?"

"You did brilliantly working this out, but you should have come to me before leaving."

"If I had done that, then you would have sent Alexis and Torija. I needed to do this, Byron. For me, for my own self-respect. I had to be useful."

"You are an important part of this clan, Sera, and I'm sorry if didn't make you feel that way."

"Yes, we all are," Amelia added.

Byron put her arm around Amelia's waist and pulled her closer. She saw tears well up in her sister's eyes. That was all Sera had really wanted, wasn't it? Byron's approval?

"Thank you, and it wasn't Bhal's responsibility. I gave her an ultimatum—come with me, or I'm going alone."

"Now, that I can believe. Maybe I would've sent someone else, but now that you've gone, it might be the best thing. We don't know if Anka and Gilbert have worked out what they are looking for yet, but if they have spies watching us, they would be less likely to think anything of you going somewhere."

Amelia asked, "How did you work it out, Sera?"

Sera looked at Bhal beside her. "Bhal told me the story of how her people met the gods, and it stuck in my head. The artifacts sounded like the weapons the packs have."

"How did the packs get them?" Daisy asked.

"Well, Princess Scota took the Great Mother as her Goddess, promising her and her followers a society where everyone could be who they were born to be. A warrior, a nurturer, no matter their gender. Human gender norms would be the past—that kind of thing. Scota turned her back on the Egyptian pantheon, and in return the Great Mother gave Scota and her followers the ability to become wolves and live in the natural world. They left Egypt and came to the UK and gave each new pack a weapon to look after—the weapons matched Bhal's story. I'm thinking that they got them through a connection between the Tuatha De Danann and the Mother."

"Clever girl. Okay, my thoughts are these, I'll contact the packs, explain everything and hopefully they'll be willing to help, and you can pick up the weapons. Bhal, be on your guard."

"Yes, Principe."

"Wait," Torija interrupted. "What about this urn? The map to… What was it called?"

"Lochlan," Bhal said. "Our stories say it's somewhere in Scandinavia. It's a crossroads between the heavens and earth, like the one Anka opened at Stonehenge, and Daisy and Amelia were able to keep open."

Amelia asked, "I read in your email that the urn was excavated in Ireland. Maybe we should start there?"

Sera nodded. "Yeah, in Knowth."

"Excellent, I'll call Athelstan as soon as I get off the phone. Stan is usually very helpful." Athelstan was the Alpha of the English Ranwulf pack and had attended Byron and Amelia's wedding with Brona, his Mater.

"Thanks for trusting me to do this, Byron."

Byron felt guilt for not having trusted her to take charge of a mission before. Sera was obviously so happy about it. "I'll be in touch. Bhal? Keep on your toes."

"Aye, Principe."

Once the call ended, Byron said, "I think it's time to put our friends on standby. It looks like we may need them soon."

❖

Sera lay in bed while Bhal sat on the floor with her back against the side, sharpening her sword. Sera turned on her side so she could look at Bhal. Her eyes grazed Bhal's muscular shoulders, and the Celtic tattoos on each arm. Sera could see the top part of a back tattoo as well, peeking over the low collar of Bhal's sleeveless T-shirt.

She could imagine how sexy Bhal would look naked from the waist up. Sera closed her eyes for a second and could see, in her mind, Bhal walking confidently towards the bed.

"Do you do that every night?"

"Yes. You have to keep on top of it. Does the sound bother you?" Bhal asked.

"No, it's quite soothing actually." It occurred to Sera that even though she had known Bhal for a few centuries, she didn't really know her, not off-duty like this. Her experience of Bhal was simply professional. Sera knew Bhal was loyal, but under that warrior mask hid a soft, caring soul.

She reached her hand across the bed, closing the gap between them.

"I can't believe that Byron was so supportive. I thought she'd order me home and it would turn into a big fight."

"You don't give Byron enough credit. She loves you, Sera."

"I know she does. I've felt lost for a long time, but it took Byron blood bonding with Amelia to make me realize it."

"In what way?" Bhal asked.

"Well, the facts were, I was Byron's heir, not that anything would have happened to her, but it gave me a place in the clan. In fact she always told me it was my job to make Debrek heirs, since she never wanted to do the whole relationship thing."

Bhal used an oily rag to wipe down her blade. "Then she met Amelia and she became pregnant."

"Exactly. I mean, not that Byron ever thought that I would be Principe, in the event that something happened to her. She probably thought Mum and Dad would offer cousin Angelo the role of Principe."

"I know for a fact that is not true."

Sera leaned up on her elbow. "What do you mean?"

When Bhal didn't respond, Sera clambered across the bed, so she was right behind Bhal. "Bhal? Tell me?"

"Nobody knows this. Do you remember when Byron was crippled with blood sickness?"

"Of course. It was terrifying."

"I was feeding Byron because my blood was rich and I could

handle how aggressive she was being, but when it became clear that she was on the verge of slipping into madness, she made me promise something."

"What?"

"That I would take her head and her heart, the only way to kill a born vampire—and I would have done it."

"You would?"

"Yes, I would have. Alexis might be her right hand vampire, but she knew I'd be the only one who would kill her. Byron asked me to make a warrior's pledge," Bhal said.

"But I know you love Byron. Why would she know you would do it?"

"Because you wouldn't leave a warrior suffering on the battlefield. I trained Byron from a child and I love her as my family, but I would have taken her head and her heart to save her becoming what she hated."

Even though that statement spoke of violence, it was based on love. Bhal loved Byron enough to kill her. Did Bhal love her? It never seemed so, but maybe she was wrong.

"When Byron asked me to do this, she made me vow to protect you and guide you as you would be the next Principe."

"She did? Byron saw me as Principe?"

"She did, so don't think otherwise. Now that Byron and Amelia are having a child, you still have a big role to fill. It'll take the whole clan to bring up this child, just as it did when you and Byron were growing up."

Sera put her hand on Bhal's bare shoulder and felt her shiver. "Thank you for telling me that."

To Sera's surprise Bhal reached up and took her hand. "You talk about Byron believing in you, but you need to believe in yourself. I do. I mean, I believe in you."

"You do?"

"Yes."

"If I'm to be the best aunt ever, I need to conquer my demons and stop needing your help for withdrawal symptoms every couple of hours."

"You will," Bhal affirmed.

Sera's eyes fell on Bhal's neck, and her mouth watered. Imagine feeding from her neck?

Ask her to feed. Ask.

Instead she lost her bottle and pulled her hand from Bhal's. "I'm just going to feed from a bag."

She heard Bhal sigh. She was obviously taking her feeding from a bag as rejection. It was. What vampire would pass up fresh, warm blood for a cold blood bag?

An idiot that's frightened of what she is feeling, that's what.

❖

The next day, Byron, Amelia, Torija, Daisy, Alexis, and a team of six vampires arrived in Ireland.

Byron chartered a boat, just to try to fly under Anka's radar. They made their way to the ancient site at Knowth in County Meath. When they arrived at the site, it was raining, and dark clouds sat heavy in the sky above.

It was clear that the staff weren't expecting visitors on a weekday morning in the pouring rain.

Daisy looked around the site, which consisted of mounds, now covered in grass, and the perimeter of each mound had large stones. She nudged Amelia. "There's magic here."

Annoyingly the mounds were roped off, but the closest you could get was with a tour guide.

When the guide came out to meet them, she couldn't have looked more surprised at the group of unusual people wanting a tour on this wet, weekday morning.

"Hello, I'm Stephanie, and I'll be taking you around the site today. Follow me."

They arrived at the first mound, and Daisy pointed to a tunnel that went through it. Amelia whispered to Byron and she went up close to Stephanie.

Byron looked into Stephanie's eyes and used her power of compulsion on her. "We are going to look around. You stay here and never mention what we have done."

"I will never mention it. I'll stay here," Stephanie parroted back.

Daisy and Amelia stepped over the rope that kept tourists at bay and went towards the mound immediately in front of them.

"Alexis, stay here. Torija, you're with me," Byron said.

Torija pointed the stones circling the mound. "Look, there's markings on these stones."

Byron bent down at one that had concentric circles. "Could this be our planetary system?"

"Might be," Amelia said. "We're going in, Byron."

"Just be careful," Byron said.

Daisy led them, and they had to bend over to get in. Once they reached the middle, Daisy said, "Are you ready?"

Amelia nodded.

They held hands and closed their eyes. In her mind, Daisy saw ancient people carving stones and making the mounds, then saw them hold torches at night-time, while an urn was handled with care and placed in the tunnel.

Then time flashed forward to a man in more modern clothing excavating the urn, then placing it in a box.

Daisy gasped as the scene moved from this space to a lake, calm as a millpond. Her eyes shot open.

"Did you see it?" Amelia asked.

"Everything," Daisy replied. "I don't understand the lake."

"No, it was out of place."

Daisy's attention was caught by Byron talking on the phone outside the mound. They both went out.

Byron said, "Got it. Thank you, Brogan. We'll get over to Paris as soon as we can. I'll call you when we get there."

"Byron?"

"Brogan's been watching Anka. She's been to see a history professor and taken her an urn."

"We saw the memory of the urn in there," Amelia said, "and more."

"Tell us on the way," Byron said.

Byron then went back to Stephanie and said, "Thank you for a wonderful tour. You will have a great day."

Stephanie smiled. "Thank you for coming to Knowth."

On the way back to the car Torija said, "What did you see?"

"We'll tell you in the car," Daisy said.

CHAPTER SIXTEEN

Bhal and Sera weren't far from Northampton, the pack lands of the Ranwulfs. Bhal was pleased at how much faith Byron put in Sera last night. It was exactly what she needed.

Bhal looked over at Sera and had the urge to hold her hand. She so desperately wanted to be close to Sera, and she thought that they had gotten closer last night, after talking. But then Sera still wouldn't feed from her.

When she had rescued Sera from the club and she'd needed blood, Sera fed, and Bhal thought there was a connection between them. Bhal wanted to be the only one in the world to feed Sera, but obviously she didn't feel the same way.

Sera glanced around and caught her looking, so Bhal kept her gaze straight out on the road.

"What are the Ranwulfs like? I just said hello to them at Byron's wedding."

"They have beautiful pack lands, and a large stately home that backs onto the forest, where they can shift and run free," Bhal said.

"A stately home?"

"Aye. Every pack has its own way of hiding in plain sight. The Wulvers in Scotland have their whiskey distillery, the Wolfgangs in America raise cattle and have a meatpacking business, the Welsh Blaidds have huge tracts of farmland, both livestock and vegetables, the Irish Filtiarans make Irish stout and ship it all over the world."

"And the Ranwulfs?"

"The Ranwulfs own a large amount of land and are heavily involved in the dairy industry, but they realized early on that in England power lay in the class system and are the only wolf pack to be part of the aristocracy. They are the Earl and Countess of Wulford."

"Wow, proper aristocracy. How did they manage that?"

"I think they did a few favours for some of the Saxon kings."

"So they manage to fly under the radar of the humans by becoming part of the lofty class structure of England. Clever."

"Indeed. Lots of land surrounding their forest gives the pack security."

"I'm looking forward to meeting them."

They drove off the motorway and followed some country roads for about thirty minutes. The satnav didn't have the address in its database, so Bhal was directing Sera from a map.

"It should be just around the next corner."

Two large ornamental gates came into view. There were wolves and forest scenes within the ironwork of the gates.

"Wolves definitely live here," Sera said. She brought the car to a stop. "I don't see a bell or anything."

"There are wolves close—I can feel it."

Sera jumped when she looked in her driving mirror and saw two people behind them. "I think we have company."

They were both big and tall, one man and one woman. The woman approached her window.

"Just keep it calm. Vampires are not a wolf's favourite thing."

Sera nodded. They never had been natural bedfellows—vampires and wolves didn't have much in common. In fact most clans, apart from the Debreks, looked down on werewolves as merely animals, so far beneath them.

She opened the window and the female dominant wolf said, "Names."

"I'm Serenity Debrek, and this is Bhaltair, Chief of the Samhain warriors."

The female wolf looked past Sera to Bhal and said, "Welcome, Bhaltair. I'm Kendre, Second of the Ranwulf pack. Follow us up to the house."

"Well, I guess you're in charge here. They don't even want to look at me," Sera said.

"It's just a vampire-wolf thing, don't take it personally."

"Fine."

The two wolves started to march at a fast pace, and Sera followed as carefully as she could, not trying to rush the wolves and be even more in their bad books. The road took them up to the main door where Athelstan and Brona were waiting with smiles and a whole gaggle of kids and dogs.

"I thought wolves and dogs didn't mix?" Sera said.

"Only if they're not brought up together. In any case, dogs are part of the fitting in with English country life."

When they got out, Athelstan and Brona approached them. Athelstan said, "Ms. Debrek, a pleasure to see you again. I trust your family is well?"

"Please call me Sera. Yes, they are very well, thank you."

Sera was surprised at their welcome. Not only did they play the part of the country lord and lady perfectly, but they were so warm.

Stan went to shake Bhal's hand. "Welcome, Warrior. Come inside and we can talk."

Brona, a beautiful auburn-haired woman, who could be described as an English rose, approached her and shook her hand.

"I'm so pleased to meet you, Sera. How was your journey?"

"It was okay, thanks."

Sera had a flashback of sitting in the car on the motorway lay-by. Her fingers were scrunched into her hair as Bhal prepared her very own methadone substitute. She hated the way it made her feel, and she doubted that she could stay away from Malum without Bhal's help.

"Excellent," Brona said. She slipped her arm through Sera's. "I hear your Principessa is having a baby?"

"Yes, she's seven months along. We're all very excited."

"Cubs are such a blessing."

Sera watched three young wolves follow Stan and Bhal into the entrance hall.

"Is it three cubs you have?" Sera asked.

"No, five cubs in all. My oldest daughter Avery and my son Eldred are working in the forest. We feel it's important for them to work the land and understand our lands from the bottom up."

Brona led them into the hall, and Sera gazed at all the tapestries covering the walls. Most had wolves, forest scenes, and battles.

"Those are beautiful."

Brona looked up. "Yes, they are extremely old, some of them. It's important to preserve your past."

Sera saw weres walking through the hallway and giving them suspicious looks. Well, mostly her, probably.

Stan turned around and said, "We thought we could have lunch and speak about the weapons that you are trying to collect."

"That would be lovely. Thank you."

❖

"This is beautiful," Sera said.

Bhal smiled at Sera thoroughly enjoying her lunch. Vampires didn't need to eat but could simply eat for pleasure, and Sera was certainly feeling pleasure.

After settling in, Bhal and Sera were taken into what Brona had called the breakfast room, a more intimate setting for lunch, rather than a dining room, Bhal assumed.

Sera was enjoying the biscuits and cheese after the meal. "This is so delicious."

"I'll have some Ranwulf cheese sent to your home in London. We love it when people enjoy our produce, don't we, dear?"

"Indeed we do."

Bhal was sure that no one would ever guess that two delightful, polite English people were werewolves. Bhal supposed that was the point. They had made their pack synonymous with the English elite. There would be few questions asked by those who lived around their land. You don't question the lord and lady of the manor.

"Lord Stan, did my Principe explain over the phone what was going on?" Bhal said.

"Yes, it's troubling. This witch Anka becoming powerful and bringing back Balor to this world suits no one in the paranormal community."

Brona shook her head. "The deaths of the humans are piling up every day. It's shocking. Your Principe said that a drug in the community is making some of us turn to some of our baser instincts."

Sera looked across at her nervously, but answered truthfully, "Yes, it's a drug that makes you think of only yourself and the oblivion the drug offers. I understand it makes those of us who would never normally be involved in violence against humans lose all control. Bhal?"

"Aye, on Samhain night I saw paranormals who were dead behind the eyes and acting only on their impulses."

Stan clasped his hands under his chin. "And you need the werewolf packs' weapons so that this witch Anka cannot open the doorway that will let Balor in?"

"Yes. I know it's a big ask to trust us and relinquish your shield, but Balor would kill and enslave millions of humans and paranormals."

"My Second, Kendre, is against it, so too many others of my elite wolves. As much respect I have for Byron and the Debreks' way of life, it is difficult to give away what Princess Scota gave us. It's part of who we are as wolves."

Sera looked to her for help. Bhal needed to make a good case for this. "Alpha, I have seen the devastation that Balor can cause, and that was in a time before weapons and modern technology. We need to stop him coming back."

Stan looked at his mate. "What do you think, Mater?"

"Come running with us tonight. Then we can make a decision in the morning."

"Thank you, Mater."

An invitation to go running with the pack was as good an offer as they were going to get. It was a test, and Bhal was sure she and Sera would pass it.

❖

At seven in the evening, Sera was feeding before going out for a run with the pack. Why she was doing this, she had no idea. What did this have to do with trusting them?

Sera was still forcing down the blood bags. Forcing was the right word for it. She couldn't describe the feeling other than force. Blood usually tasted good hot or cold. She preferred hot, but even cold, it still sated her hunger. Now it tasted wrong, bitter, vile, but her body needed it so badly. Bhal's gift was helping with the drug withdrawal, so why wasn't it helping with this symptom?

Sera finished the bag and threw it to the side. Almost immediately a wave of sickness came over her. She hurried to the bathroom and vomited up the blood she had drunk. Her body was retching violently, as if trying to get rid of every drop. Once it was over, Sera sat slumped by the toilet, shaking.

Her whole body was crying out for blood but at the same time making her sick. What was going on?

So cold, Sera thought.

She heard a knock at her bedroom door. "Sera? Are you ready?"

"Shit."

She couldn't let Bhal know what was going on because she would take her back home to work out what was wrong with her. Sera had to do this mission. She had to feel like she had a purpose to live from now on.

She forced herself up on to shaky legs. She shut the bathroom door and shouted, "Come in, I'm just in the bathroom."

"Good enough."

Sera looked at her bloody mouth, lips, and neck in the mirror, then grabbed a towel. She soaked it and rubbed soap into it, before trying to clean her face.

Sorry for ruining your towels, Mater.

Once she was presentable, she hid the towel in a cupboard and stepped out into the room. Bhal was sitting in a chair with her sword in her scabbard resting between her thighs.

"You don't look well," Bhal said.

"Thanks a lot."

"You know what I mean."

It was then Sera spotted the discarded blood bag on the floor. "Shit, I forgot to pick that up. Let me get it." Sera got it and one of the bags the clan used for disposing of them and put it in her rucksack. You didn't want to leave blood products around.

"You need some water before we go out."

Without arguing or any snipey comments Sera said, "Yes, I do."

Before Sera knew it, she was kneeling before Bhal and looking up at her. They hadn't done it in this position before and Sera felt it—the moment was now charged with something else. Sexuality.

Bhal's lips parted, and Sera was sure she could see hunger in her eyes, and it lit Sera up inside.

Sera's heart was beating hard, and she couldn't stop herself from putting her hand on the handle of Bhal's sword. Bhal shifted uncomfortably in her seat but didn't take her eyes off Sera.

"May I have some water, please?"

"Yes, but Debreks don't kneel, especially to a warrior who has pledged their sword to your clan."

Sera still hadn't taken her hand off the sword handle. "I can kneel before anyone I choose, Warrior."

Instinctively Bhal covered her hand with hers. "I need to move this to give you what you need."

God. Sera felt like her head was scrambled. She was sick, she was hungry, she was weak, she needed sex, she needed Bhal—all at once.

A spasm of pain in her limbs reminded her that she needed Bhal's healing powers most at the moment. She took her hand off and sat back.

"Sorry."

Sera noticed Bhal had a tremor in her hands as she put her sword to the side and fought with the water bottle. Was Bhal as turned on as she was? She hoped so.

Bhal offered the water in her hands. Sera cradled them and sipped at the life-giving water.

As the calm and energy returned to her body, all Sera could think was *I want her. I need her. Bite her, bite.*

Sera shook, finished the drink, stood up quickly, and turned away.

Bhal dried her hands on her utility trousers and tried to calm her body. What had just happened? The image of Sera kneeling before her was wrong but had caught her with such surprise that she couldn't temper her body's reaction. Heat and hunger had rushed through every cell in her body. Then when Sera touched her sword, it was as if she was caressing her body. She was sure Sera knew exactly what she was doing because her eyes were red for Bhal.

A vampire's eyes were red for either arousal or hunger, and Sera had just fed. That was why Sera turned away from her, to try to hide.

Bhal was sure she had loved Sera for a long time, but her wake-up call had been slow. How was she going to deal with this?

Just get her through this mission and her addiction. Then she could worry about love when they defeated Bhal and Anka.

She stood up and strapped her sword to her back again. "Are you ready?" Bhal asked.

When Sera turned back around, her eyes were normal again. Bhal was glad. She didn't have to face what it meant.

"What exactly are we doing, going running with wolves?"

"It's part of their culture. They let their wolves size you up. A wolf bonds or doesn't in a physical way. Sharing this with us is an honour and our chance to prove we are trustworthy."

"You sound like you have a lot of admiration for wolves."

"I do. Their culture has similarities to my own."

Sera wished she knew more about Bhal's past, especially after what Morrigan had hinted at. But she always got the impression Bhal didn't like talking about her past.

"Are you just wearing your T-shirt and the sword?"

"Aye, we're running with wolves, and I never go anywhere without my sword."

Sera nodded. "I'll just change."

Sera slipped out of her thin jumper, leaving her in a figure-hugging top with thin straps on her shoulders.

Bhal scanned Sera's bare shoulders and her cleavage that was barely showing. She was absolutely beautiful.

They went downstairs and found some wolves in pelt, waiting for them. Brona was still in her human skin. Some growled low as they looked at Bhal. But the wolf by the Mater's side bared his teeth, and they stopped.

"I thought I'd stay in skin so we could talk. The Alpha will lead the run with you, Bhal."

So the wolf at Brona's side was the Alpha.

"Okay, that would be nice."

The Alpha howled, and he and Bhal started to run. It was lucky that Bhal was a fit immortal warrior.

"Don't worry, Sera. Stan will make the wolves keep pace with Bhaltair."

She looped her arm through Sera's. "So, tell me about yourself, Sera. How long have you and Bhal been together?"

Sera's eyes went wide. "We're not together. Why did you think that?"

"All the little things that wolves notice. Looks, touches. You look at each other like you've been in love for a long time."

Other people were noticing it now? It was getting harder to deny her feelings. She looked up ahead at Bhal running with the wolves, and her stomach tightened. She looked so sexy. Those shoulder muscles, arms, and tattoos excited her.

"I like her, I really do, but it's difficult."

"All love is—that's why it's worth fighting for."

They carried on walking, Sera telling Brona all about her life, but with each step she was feeling worse and worse, until dizziness overcame her and she fell to her knees, then to the ground.

❖

When they got to the stairs Bhal lifted Sera into her arms.

"I can walk myself." Sera struggled.

"Why walk when you have a warrior at your service?"

"I don't have the energy to argue," Sera said.

Bhal hated seeing Sera like this. She longed for the day Sera was back on her feet and arguing with her. When they got back to Sera's room, Bhal pulled the quilt back with one hand and then placed her carefully on the bed.

"There. Are you more comfortable?"

Sera nodded.

Bhal touched her cheek and forehead. "You feel clammy. Maybe Magda was wrong about the drugs. Maybe they've done more damage than we realized. I think I should get the Ranwulf healer."

Sera's eyes sprung open. "No, I don't want to see a doctor or a healer."

"What harm would it do? I'm worried about you," Bhal said.

"I said no, and I don't want you asking for the healer when you leave this room. Promise me?"

Bhal scrubbed her face with her hands. "I don't know."

"Please, Bhal. I want to trust you, and I don't want to see a doctor or a healer."

"Fine, but only if you promise to see the Wulver healer if you don't feel any better," Bhal said.

"Okay, okay—deal. Do you promise?" Sera asked.

"Aye, I promise. I'll be back in a second."

Bhal went to the bathroom to fetch a wet towel to cool Sera's face. There wasn't a towel hanging on the rack, strangely. "There must be some towels in here somewhere." Bhal rummaged through drawers and cupboards to find them. She opened a cupboard under the sink and found a pile of towels waiting. Bhal grabbed one, but as she did, she noticed one stuffed at the back.

She pulled it out and found it covered in blood.

Bhal didn't think Brona would leave something like this in a guest room. She was very proud of her home. Bhal wanted to run and get the healer, then return to London with Sera. But she had given her word. They would be leaving for Scotland in the morning, and Sera had promised to see a healer there if she was no better.

Bhal saturated a towel with cold water and wrung it out. She went to Sera and placed the towel on her head.

"That's nice and cool. Thanks," Sera said.

"You're welcome."

Sera grasped her hand and said, "Don't go. Stay with me?"

Bhal smiled. "I wasn't going anywhere. I was just going to sit on the armchair."

Sera patted the other side of the bed. "Lie here with me. Then I won't feel alone."

Bhal was surprised at Sera's request. She'd thought Sera would want to get rid of her. She walked around the bed and took her boots off. When she lay on the bed, she felt awkward. Bhal didn't want to get too close and make Sera feel uncomfortable.

But then Sera's hand searched for hers and held on to it. Bhal squeezed her hand. "You doing all right?"

"Yeah, I'm okay. I feel hot and cold at the same time. I suppose, being an immortal warrior, you probably haven't felt ill."

"I have. I haven't always been immortal, remember. In fact I nearly died when I was six."

Sera turned around as quickly as she could. As bad as she felt, Sera wanted to know everything about Bhal.

"Really? Will you tell me about it?"

"If you want. I was only six, but I do remember a lot. My brother Donel and I were sick at the same time."

"You had a brother? Was he older or younger?" Sera asked.

"We were twins."

Sera's eyes went wide. "Twins? You must have been close."

Bhal smiled softly. "We were never apart. Did everything together, even got sick together."

Sera scooted closer to Bhal. "What was it, the sickness?"

"Hmm. I suppose you might call it something like COVID or flu. We coughed and had difficulty breathing."

"Sounds horrible. Were your parents all right?"

"My mathair was fine, but my athair was already dead. He died in battle, trying to defend our village from raiders."

"*Athair* is father?" Bhal nodded. "That must have been so hard for her, for you all."

"That's the wonderful part of being in a village or tribe—they were our family," Bhal said.

"So what happened?"

"We were both struggling to get any air into our lungs. Our tribe's healer didn't know how to help. Donel slipped away one night, two weeks into it."

Sera squeezed Bhal's hand. "I'm so sorry, Bhal."

"Even though it's such a long, long time, I still miss him."

Sera pulled Bhal's hand to her lips and kissed it. There was so much more to Bhal than the tough warrior, and she loved it.

"You were twins. It's no wonder you always miss him. What happened to you?"

"When I was almost at my last breath, a Druid priest came to our village and asked to see me. The priests were almost godlike to us, they were so wise and so respected."

"What did he do?" Sera asked.

"He came to see my mother and said he'd had a vision. The Goddess Danu wanted me to be a warrior in her name. I was chosen to be a Samhain warrior."

"Wow. Is Danu part of Tuatha De Danann?"

Bhal shook her head. "No, they actually worship her. Danu is a Mother Earth type of Goddess."

"Like the werewolves' Great Mother?"

"Aye, they are similar. I've often wondered if they are one and the same."

"What did he do?" Sera asked.

"Gave me some water from a wooden bowl, and within minutes I was taking big clear breaths."

Sera took the towel off her bed and leaned up on her elbow. "Just like you can do? Is that when you became immortal?"

"No, I didn't become immortal till I was eighteen."

"Why didn't he come and help Donel too?" Sera said.

"I always asked that. I felt guilty. If only he had lasted longer, he could have been saved too. It was later in life I found out the truth."

"Which was?" Sera could see the strain that looking back was taking on Bhal.

"The priest, Mogh, became my mentor throughout all my years of training as a warrior. He told me that he had only been given the vision of saving me the day before. He said he saw me as chief of the Samhain, and I was to be protected until then. *Twins born carry on as one.* Mogh said Donel's fate was already sealed. It doesn't seem fair. I would give anything to let Donel have a life here on earth."

"That's why you are special and the perfect warrior. You would lay down your life for the greater good, or the ones you love."

Sera said the word *love* on purpose. She wanted to make Bhal feel what she was feeling. She was falling in love with Bhal even more after hearing that story.

Bhal turned her head and looked deeply into Sera's eyes. "I would do anything for those I love."

Sera laid her head on Bhal's shoulder. She just wanted to be connected to her.

"How are you feeling?" Bhal asked.

"Much calmer."

"Remember, you promised to go to the healer if you're no better."

"I remember." Sera wanted to change the subject. "Do you think the Ranwulfs will give us the shield?"

"Aye, Stan was talking to me and said he would. We bonded on the run."

"His Second, Kendre, was against it. She may talk him out of it," Sera said.

"Seconds are supposed to challenge and be overprotective of their pack. It will all be fine."

"I wonder where it is. They haven't shown it to us yet."

"They wanted to size us up first. And the Wulvers should be willing. The clan has a good relationship with them," Bhal said.

"Let's hope so."

They lay in silence for a while. Sera was enjoying the comfort of resting her head on Bhal's shoulder. She wished she could put her arm around Bhal's middle. She wanted to be closer than close.

If her younger self could see her cuddling with Bhal, she wouldn't believe it. When she was very young, before she hit puberty, she'd had a crush on Bhal. She was this big, tough warrior. She'd listened and trained with weapons, just as Bhal instructed, but in her teenage years everything changed, and things got worse as she got older.

They argued every time they had weapon training. Bhal was always concerned about her commitment, but Sera resented spending all this time learning to fight.

Once she undertook her ascension ceremony and became an immortal born vampire, she felt she didn't need to practise any more. Sera was stronger and faster than any human or turned vampire. Why did she need to work on combat skills?

Byron did. Even to this day, Byron and Bhal sparred most days. Sera just wanted to party and have fun, and she had for a few hundred years. Now, looking back, she could see why training was important, but she wasn't going to admit that to Bhal though—not yet.

She felt her body start to shake. She was cold. Why was she so cold?"

"Are you all right?"

"I'm cold. I don't know why, and the lamplight is bothering my eyes."

Bhal reached for the switch and the light went out. The room was now in darkness. "Do you mind if I get close to warm you up?"

"No," Sera croaked. There was nothing she'd like better.

Bhal spooned her and put her arm around her. "Is that better?"

"Yes, it's nice."

There was a tense silence in the air.

Sera felt so secure, so much warmer, and like Bhal was meant to fit with her. Her voice filled the silence. "I was just thinking earlier, imagine what our younger selves would make of us being close like this. You caring for me."

"We did butt heads. You don't take instruction well."

Sera laughed softly. "No, I'm kind of stubborn. A bit like a warrior I know."

"I've always been used to people obeying orders. Even Byron, although she has a strong alpha personality, took my instruction," Bhal said.

"There was always a tension between us. Don't you know what I mean?" Sera asked.

Bhal shuffled even closer so that her lips were next to Sera's ear. "There was fire between us."

Sera shivered, not from the cold but from the feel of Bhal's breath on her ear. The shiver travelled through her body and made her nipples burn and her sex throb. If she was feeling any better, she would have turned around and kissed Bhal. Then where would they be?

She closed her eyes, and images of them fighting and squabbling floated across her mind. There was fire, always fire. Why had it taken this long to see it?

She remembered the last time it happened, on Samhain night. They'd almost kissed, but this was her memory, and this time in her imagination, Bhal had kissed her deeply. She then wrapped her arms around Bhal and sank her teeth into her neck.

Her eyes sprang open.

Out of the blue Bhal said, "I've always cared for you, Sera, always. When Anka kidnapped you, I thought...I felt true fear."

"Why are you telling me this now?"

"Sometimes it's easier to say things in the dark."

Sera lifted Bhal's hand and brought her wrist to her lips. She could hear the strong blood pumping through her veins.

Her teeth punctured her gums. *Bite, bite, feed. Bhal would be willing.*

She might be, but Sera didn't want her to consent through obligation, and as much as Sera thought Bhal was trying to show her feelings, Sera wasn't in the right mindset to judge that.

It took most of her strength, but she let Bhal's wrist drop. "Tell me more about your life, after your illness."

"If you want. I stayed with my mathair for another year before joining training for the Samhain warriors."

"It must have been hard leaving your mum," Sera said.

"It was at first, but she kept telling me that it was my destiny. I didn't want to let her down."

"Where did you go?"

"The warriors had a training village about ten miles from my home…"

Sera drifted off to sleep.

❖

"Bring me back the Blaidds' spear," Anka said.

She was lounging in Gilbert's bedroom in the Dred castle. Two bodies were lying beside the bed, having been used and dispensed with the night before.

Gilbert pulled on his trousers and buckled his belt. "I promise I will. I can't tell you how good it will be to get back to what I'm good at. Raining terror on our enemies."

"You are so good at it."

The door opened and some vampires came in to take the bodies away. Once they were gone, Gilbert said, "What about the Debreks? Have they found out about the weapons yet?"

"I don't know for certain, but they haven't approached the wolf packs. My spies tell me Byron and your daughter went with their women to Knowth. They are well behind."

"Excellent."

Gilbert put on his boots and Anka said, "It's astonishing Victorija is your daughter. Where on earth did you get her?"

"She is my wife. I thought I could mould her into a true born vampire, but she was weak. Weak and pathetic. I cannot wait to kill her and her woman."

"You will get the chance."

"Then…?"

"Then we rule the world—at Balor's side."

Gilbert had been thinking a lot more about after. Balor was a terrifying creature. He would rather help subdue the population far away from Balor. "Maybe Balor could carve the world up between us?"

Anka was silent for a few seconds. "It's certainly something to think about."

"Maybe you can mention it to Balor the next time he pops into my body."

Anka pursed her lips and nodded. "I will, I will. Now go and get me that spear. The first of many."

"It will be easy," Gilbert said.

CHAPTER SEVENTEEN

"S tan won't be long," Brona said. The Mater had come to find Bhal a little while earlier to say Stan and his higher ranking wolves would bring the shield to them shortly.

Bhal was waiting in the entrance hall with Brona while Sera got ready to leave.

When Bhal had woken up this morning, she left the bed and Sera's warm body. She had tried her best to explain how she felt, but Sera hadn't said anything similar and again refused her blood.

She was sure her blood would help Sera, but for some reason she wouldn't take it. Bhal thought they were getting closer, but were they? A few months ago, Bhal could quite imagine Sera refusing her blood out of stubbornness, but after everything, why wouldn't she take it now? After all, her blood had gotten Byron through the worst parts of the blood sickness until Amelia came back to her.

Footsteps on the stairs made her look up. Sera looked terribly ill, deathly white with dark red rings around her eyes.

"Is your friend all right?" Brona asked.

Then a thought hit her like a sword to the guts. The bloody towel, blood bags that were leaving her still hungry for blood, and refusing Bhal's own multiple offers to feed. That's exactly how Byron looked when she had the blood sickness, when her body was crying out for Amelia.

Bhal's whole body and mind went into a blind panic. "Excuse me, Mater. I'll just be a moment."

She ran out the front door and right around to the side of the large stately home to get some privacy.

Bhal fell to her knees on the hard stones and grasped her head in her hands. "I've lost her, I've lost her." Tears fell from her eyes and the sword she felt puncturing her guts twisted inside. It wasn't just the withdrawal from the drugs. Sera was blood bonded with someone.

Bhal scrambled to her feet and leaned against the side of the building. She thought about the way she had found Sera at the No Such Place club, a vampire assaulting her while Sera was unconscious. Someone had either forced a bond with her, or Sera had done it while high. "Why?"

Bhal thumped her fist against the wall. Why had some no-hoper from that place been compatible with such a beautiful soul?

"Are you all right, mate?"

She hadn't even heard one of the were gardeners walk up the stone path.

"Aye, I'm fine."

Get yourself under control, Bhal told herself. She used her jacket sleeve to wipe away the tears. She couldn't remember the last time she'd cried. The stoic mask that had been slipping away over the time since Sera's kidnapping would need to be put firmly back on.

"Okay, think."

She had to get the shield, then drive to Scotland and the Wulver pack lands, get Sera to a healer, and then Byron would need to find the person her sister had bonded with, or Sera would lose herself to madness, then death.

A blood bond was supposed to be a loving thing. Not this, a drug-fuelled mistake.

Act like a warrior, you fool.

Bhal closed her eyes and rolled her head from side to side. When she opened them, an iron core was running through her.

She walked back into the house. Stan and Brona were standing with their wolves and an old wooden case. Sera came walking towards her.

"Where did you get to?"

"I just needed some air." She walked past Sera coldly.

"Bhal, Sera?" Stan said. "Here is our shield. Open it, Kendre."

Kendre laid it down on the floor and pressed open the catches. When the lid was opened, Sera walked forward to see it more clearly.

"It's beautiful."

It was. It was a round, hammered gold shield, and in the middle was a clear crystal. It truly was a special weapon. The stone on the middle must be one of the stones needed to open the portal.

"Shut it up, Second," Stan said. "We are giving you this weapon on your word of honour that you will take care of it."

"Or I will hunt you down and rip your throat out," Kendre added.

"Manners, Second," Brona said.

Bhal placed her hand on her heart. "I give you my word of honour that we will look after it."

"I give you my word too," Sera said.

Stan took the case and handed it over to Bhal. "Forgive us, Bhal, this shield is such a great part of our identity. It's so hard to let it go."

"No apology needed."

Bhal picked up the case, and Sera said, "Thank you for your hospitality, Stan and Brona."

Bhal beat her chest with her fist in the traditional werewolf way, out of respect. She then turned and walked out of the house, leaving Sera to catch up.

Bhal put the case in the back seat of the car, then opened the passenger door for Sera. "Give me the key fob. I'll drive—you're not well enough."

"What's wrong with you?"

"Nothing. Get in and we can get going," Bhal said flatly.

Sera looked back and obviously saw they were being watched. So she handed Bhal the key, got in, and slammed the door.

Bhal felt a twinge of guilt, but the devastation at losing Sera to some unworthy vampire or shifter twisted that sword that was stuck in her gut.

Keep your eyes and mind on the mission.

❖

Alexis leaned over the front passenger seat and said, "We're just arriving at Brogan's now."

The car pulled in and one of the guards opened both side doors.

"This looks like an old warehouse," Amelia said.

"It is. It's Brogan's office for her artwork and her private eye tracking business. Let's go."

Leaving the guards at the two vehicles outside, only Alexis went up with them. Brogan met them at the door of the lift and welcomed them into her loft space.

"Hi, nice to see you. I haven't met you before, Principessa."

Byron said, "Yes, this is my wife, Amelia."

"It's an honour."

Amelia loved her Irish brogue. "Thanks, this is my friend Daisy, who I understand you helped track for Byron, and her blood bond, Torija."

Brogan made a show of kissing Daisy's hand. "Welcome, Daisy, and your—vampire."

Torija gave her a dirty look. "Still scratching a living as an artist, Brogan?"

"I'm doing well, thanks for asking, Victorija."

"It's Torija, Brogan," Daisy said defensively.

"Sorry, Daisy. Come in, and I'll make coffee."

Amelia and Daisy looked at Brogan's canvases while she made the coffee. Torija and Byron sat on the couch while Alexis stood at the window, scanning outside.

"These are beautiful," Daisy said.

Brogan walked through with a tray of coffee. "Thank you. I like to concentrate on the natural world."

Brogan handed out the cups, and Daisy and Amelia sat by their partners.

"What have you found?" Byron asked.

"Anka and Gilbert." Brogan handed over a tablet, and Byron flicked through the pictures. "The first at a Dr. Marie Beaufort's house. They visit, then leave and go to an antiquities collector."

"I can see they've caused quite a scene." Byron handed the tablet to Amelia.

"They killed him?" Amelia asked.

"And all the staff. Whatever they took from him, they then went back to Marie Beaufort's house. If I tell you that she is a professor of ancient history, I think you'll get a clue as to why they went back to her."

"What did you make of Professor Beaufort?" Daisy asked.

Brogan tapped her fingers on the coffee table. "I could feel her fear. I kept a close watch on them from her back garden in case I had to break my cover and help her."

Daisy turned to Amelia and said, "I think she will talk if we can help her feel less alone in this. She must be terrified."

"Yes," Amelia agreed, "let's do that."

"I'll come with you," Brogan said.

❖

An hour into their drive and Bhal hadn't said one word to Sera. It was driving her insane, which was made harder by how terrible she felt. When her eyes had opened this morning, it was almost painful.

She was so hungry. Why wasn't the blood doing its job? She was determined not to show how ill she was, but it was so hard.

"Ugh," Sera moaned.

"Do you need me to stop?" Bhal said.

"Oh, now you speak? I don't need anything from you," Sera said angrily.

"Clearly."

Sera could not stay silent any longer. "What is your problem? What happened to the kind and understanding Bhal?"

"We have a mission to do. I'm protecting the Principe's sister. Let's get back to it."

"We spent last night cuddling, going to sleep. What has changed?" Sera said.

"Nothing has changed. We weren't *cuddling*, I was keeping you warm."

That hurt Sera. Bhal was so tender, so caring. It was real, wasn't it?

"Do you know what? Fuck you. Now I remember why we don't like each other. I wish I'd come on my own."

Sera turned to her side so she wouldn't have to look at Bhal. She closed her eyes and tried to fall asleep.

Another two hours into the journey, and every cell in Sera's body was shaking, and whatever liquid there was in Sera's stomach was sloshing around in a sickening way. Bhal had asked her a few times if she needed water, but she ignored her.

Not only was her body breaking down, but her heart was crumbling.

Why did it have to be her? Of all the people in the world she could have fallen for, she'd fallen for her unemotional arch nemesis.

The sloshing in her stomach got worse and made her heave. "Stop the car, stop."

"What is it?" Bhal asked.

"Going…be…sick."

Bhal pulled over to the side of the country road, and Sera got out just in time to be violently sick. There was blood everywhere, and Bhal was going to see exactly what had been happening to her.

Sera felt a hand on her shoulder. "Are you all right?"

She shrugged the hand away. "Obviously not."

"You are going to see the Wulver healer. Even if I need to carry you there." Sera said nothing, then heard Bhal say under her breath, "When I find out who's responsible for this, I will kill them."

Sera had no idea what she was talking about. The retching became worse, and her vison started to narrow as she was hit by a wave of dizziness.

Bhal saw Sera swaying and grabbed her while she was falling. She cradled her by the side of the road and got some water out to help her, but it wasn't helping this time.

Of course Bhal's magical powers could help with withdrawal symptoms, but not blood sickness. She lifted her into the passenger seat and hurried round to the driver's side.

She had to get her to the Wulvers' healer as quickly as possible. Another hour and a half and they should be there, deep in the Highlands of Scotland.

CHAPTER EIGHTEEN

B hal drove along the side of Wulver loch. She looked over at Sera. She was sweating and murmuring in her unconscious state. Bhal wasn't much better. Her mind was whirling with questions, and her heart was broken.

She was so much in love with Sera, and before she'd a chance to express it, Sera was already bonded to someone else. Bhal didn't know how she could live with it, be around someone who she loved while they were blood bonded to someone else.

Bhal would have to leave the clan. Perhaps Byron would want her to when she found out that Bhal hadn't told her about Sera's drug addiction and how she found her at the club. Only the gods knew how Byron would get the blood Sera needed from whoever the bastard was who shared her blood.

Money, probably.

On the road ahead was a crossroad. One carried on following the loch down past the whiskey distillery and gift shops and tea rooms that the humans used. It was essentially the human face of the clan.

But the road she took was the one that led into the inner sanctum of the Wulver pack, the Wulver forest. The Wulvers made their lives in the trees. Their homes sat like tree houses up in the tree canopy.

She came to a security gate, aimed at stopping humans. She was flagged over by two male wolves in security uniforms.

"Hello, I'm Bhaltair of the Debrek clan. Your Alpha is expecting us."

"Yes, welcome."

The wolf looked at Sera in the passenger seat.

"I need to see the healer quickly. Ms. Debrek is sick."

"Come through and park there. I'm Jansen. I'll take you right to her."

Bhal parked and carefully lifted Sera from her seat. She was murmuring incoherently.

"Can I help you with her?" Jansen said.

"No. I'm fine." She's my responsibility. "But can someone guard the car? We have a precious artifact in the back seat."

"Aye, of course."

Jansen shouted over to another wolf to stay by the car. Then they made their way into Wulver lands.

They arrived at huge grey security gates. Jansen lifted his hand to the gate, and it beeped and started to open. When it did, a whole other world opened up. Ahead of them was a modern marketplace with shops that were busy with Wulvers going about their daily business. Behind that was ancient forest.

"If we go through the trees we can avoid the shopping area," Jansen said.

"Aye."

Bhal jogged with Sera in her arms, and Jansen alongside.

Jansen made a call through her earpiece. "Can you get the Alpha to meet me at the healer's? Bhaltair from the Debreks is bringing a casualty."

Bhal's heart was pounding, not from the exertion but from the worry of what was happening to Sera. She had to put her heartache to one side, and if she had to go through every patron of that club to find Sera's blood bond and drag them back here, she would.

Then it hit her. What if the blood bond was the one she'd found with Sera? Bhal had killed her. She felt sick and began to run faster.

The forest opened up into a clearing with huge, ancient looking tree trunks that passed the balcony of a large wood-framed house up in the canopy. Bhal had heard that the Wulvers lived up in the trees, but she could never have imagined it looked like a forest from a storybook.

"Not long now," Jansen said.

They passed another few wooden houses in the trees before they reached what looked like the centre of the tree village.

"This is the healer's hut." Jansen pointed to a wooden structure that was on the forest floor but had stairs all around the trunk of a thick tree, leading to higher levels.

A female wolf was waiting at the door for them. "Bhaltair?"

"Yes."

"Come in." She led Bhal into a consulting room. "Put her there."

Bhal put Sera onto the treatment table.

"My name's Dr. Olivia. Who is the patient?"

Bhal bent over, resting her hands on her thighs trying to get her breath back. "Serenity Debrek."

"Byron Debrek's sister?"

Bhal nodded. "Aye, she's been suffering with withdrawal from a drug called Malum. I was helping her with the cravings. I'm able to heal by offering water from my hands."

Olivia smiled. "I have heard of you and your gifts, Warrior."

"She can't feed, and she's been bringing up blood. Really pale, hot and cold—I don't think it's the drug."

Olivia placed her hand on Sera's forehead. "She feels hot now." Olivia got the thermometer.

Another woman walked in. "Olivia, can I help?"

"This is one of my nurses, Keres," Olivia said. "The patient has a very high temperature. We need to get this down."

Bhal's guts twisted inside, as she watched Sera murmur and move, and shiver. "A vampire shouldn't have a high temperature."

"No, and she shouldn't be rejecting blood. Is there anything else you can tell me about her?"

Keres brought over some cold packs to put on Sera.

"I think it might be blood sickness. I saw it when my Principe went through it."

Olivia looked surprised. "Does she have a mate, partner? Girlfriend? Boyfriend?"

Bhal wanted to scream *Me!* but she shook her head. "It may be someone she met casually."

"I see."

Sera shouted, "No, no," and thrashed around.

Bhal ran to her, but Olivia and Keres held her. "Go outside, Warrior, and let us do our work."

"But you don't—"

"Look, I studied as a human doctor and in paranormal medicine. We'll start and try to lower her temperature, then I'll test her blood. It will tell us if she has blood sickness. Now go."

It took everything in Bhal to walk out the door. Once outside she heard her name being called. A tall, well-built, dominant wolf came striding up to her. She was sure this was the Alpha. She had a dark mane of hair, dreadlocked and held in a leather strap at the back with undercut sides, and the Celtic sign of the wolf shaved on one side.

"Bhaltair? I'm Kenrick."

Bhal managed to pull herself together enough to thump her fist to her chest in respect. "Alpha, thank you for having us."

"It's an honour. This is our Mater, Zaria."

"Mater." Bhal bowed her head.

Kenrick slipped her hand around her mate's waist. "How is Ms. Debrek?"

"Not well. I'm worried about her, to be honest."

"Olivia will look after her," Kenrick said. "You won't find any better. Whatever you need, it's yours."

"I can't thank you enough."

"The Wulver pack will stand shoulder to shoulder with the Debreks. My cousin, Dante Wolfgang from the American pack, is arriving with her Second tonight to join the fight."

Bhal didn't think she could feel any more emotional, but she had never seen the community come together like this before. "Thank you, from our hearts."

"We've prepared a house for you if you'd like to take your things to it and settle in?" Zaria said.

"No, I'd like to get a bit of air," Bhal said.

"Aye, no problem. I'll have someone find you if there's any news," Kenrick said.

As soon as Bhal got out of sight, she broke into a run. When she was far enough from the wolves milling about, she leaned against a big tree truck and couldn't stop the tears from rolling down her cheeks.

I've lost her.

Sera woke on the muddy ground of a woodland area. Everything looked hazy, as if there was smoke permeating the air. She pushed herself up onto her feet. Were they in the Wulver pack lands? Where was Bhal? No matter how angry Bhal was with her, she would never desert her.

The smoke began to clear slightly, and as she took a few steps forward, Sera heard the rhythmic beating of drums.

"What is going on?"

Sera followed the sound of drums into the woods. She caught sight of a young boy with dark hair and ragged brown trousers and tunic. He froze when he saw her.

"Can you tell me where I am?"

But instead of answering, he ran. Sera broke into a run to follow him. The beating of the drum got louder and louder, until she heard the shouts of men up ahead. She slowed and took quiet, careful steps to the edge of a clearing.

The area was packed with warriors bedecked with swords, shields, and spears. Up ahead there was a large bonfire billowing smoke into the air, and a big dais. She caught sight of the boy to her side, and he pointed ahead.

The crowd parted, and a warrior walked out into the circle of warriors. *It's Bhal.*

Her clothing was different, but Sera would spot her warrior anywhere. Her warrior? She wasn't that at the moment, but in her heart, Bhal was hers.

Sera looked to the side, and the boy had disappeared. What was happening?

Bhal was wearing only a green tunic and trousers, not her traditional sword that she took everywhere. She looked powerful, strong, and confident.

She began her walk towards the dais. Sera could feel the beat from the men, deep in her bones. Smoke filled the air, and wood crackled from the many ceremonial fires around the camp. This felt like an important day in Bhal's life, and Sera could feel the expectation in the air around her.

On the raised platform in the middle of the camp was a stocky man with a full head of curly red hair. Next to him, an elderly man stood in long robes, tall and thin, with long salt-and-pepper hair and a beard to match. The warriors stood before him, banging their swords on their shields and chanting, "Bhaltair, Bhaltair."

As Bhal approached the dais, she saw the younger warriors had formed a guard of honour, with spears standing proud, around the platform.

Bhal took the first step up onto the platform and kneeled before the large man. The warriors quieted down and Bhal said, "Chief, I have killed many for you in battle, given you countless victories, and protected the people of our land. I now come before you to claim my right of leadership as your heir."

"Wow," Sera whispered.

This must have been when she was made Chief of the Samhain warriors.

The warriors cheered their approval.

"Warriors of Samhain. You have all proved yourself worthy to me, from the first day you marched into this camp, but one warrior has shone above all. She is the fiercest and most noble warrior I have ever trained, and I know that you are proud to serve with her. Will you accept Warrior Bhaltair as your Chief?"

Even though this was so long ago, Sera felt pride in Bhal, and the love in her heart only grew.

The men shouted, "Aye!" in unison and banged their shields.

"Very well." The stocky man looked to his side and ushered the tall man in robes to step forward.

"Mogh, Warrior Finnian has consented."

Mogh? That was the priest that Bhal said came to save her from her illness as a six-year-old.

He stood now in his long green robe, his silver hair buffeting in the breeze. He must be unusually old in the time period Bhal was going through this. He reminded Sera of Merlin from the King Arthur myth. There had to be magic involved in this.

"Warrior Bhaltair. At your birth, I had a vision that your life would be an extraordinary one. A life filled with honour and fighting the evil that surrounds us. It is my honour to perform this ceremony for you."

Mogh asked his assistant for the bunch of burning twigs he was holding and began to wave the smoke around Bhal. "May the Goddess Danu make you strong and give you many victories in battle."

Mogh then dipped his finger in ashes and used them to draw the mark of Samhain on Bhal's forehead.

As he finished, everything around her appeared to slow down gradually, until everyone was frozen except Bhal and Mogh. The air around Sera grew cold.

This is incredible.

A ball of light appeared from Mogh's hand and hovered above, and Mogh smiled warmly at Bhaltair.

Wow. Bhal really is magical.

"Do not fear, Bhaltair, you are so important to us. We have planned for this day since you were first conceived in your mother's womb, and here you are, as brave and as strong as we ever planned."

He cupped her face. "Your path is a hard one, a lonely one, but you are the only one who can make a stand against evil. Never lose hope because the end will come. You will not face the end alone. Look not with your eyes but with your heart."

There was a flash, and they were immediately thrown back into the reality with all the men shouting and stomping.

Bhal looked around herself. She wasn't expecting that magic, clearly.

"Stand, Warrior." She looked all around herself in confusion.

"Warrior Bhaltair, Stand!" Mogh repeated. Bhal shook her head and stood. Mogh clasped his hands on her shoulders and whispered, "Take deep breaths—we must continue."

The chief handed Mogh a leather belt that was adorned with a phallus, and he placed it around Bhal's waist. "This phallus represents your power over this clan, and the power over the spirits that we fight against."

Sera's eyes went wide. *I didn't see that coming.*

Bhal then was handed the Chief's fur cloak with a bear's head hood, and this was fixed across her shoulders. "The bear cloak represents your power over nature and the forests."

The last item was the outgoing Chief's sword. It was a large silver sword adorned with a green stone on the hilt.

That's it. That's Bhal's sword. She'd recognize it anywhere. It had to be magical too because it hadn't changed one bit over all the long, long time it been in Bhal's possession.

"I give you my sword willingly. Use it honourably, and may it bring the Samhain warriors many victories."

Bhal took the sword in her hand, and then she was presented to the crowd. "Warriors, hail Chief Bhaltair, your new leader!"

Sera watched Bhal hold her new sword aloft, and she looked powerful as her warriors chanted her name. She was so sexy. Bhal held such power in her body, and yet this was the same person who held her so tenderly in bed. Power and gentleness in the one wonderful package.

To Sera's surprise she was knocked off her feet and slammed into the floor as the scene turned upside down.

"What now?"

Sera jumped to her feet and brushed herself down. But she stopped and paid attention when she didn't her the thump of drums any more. What she heard was screaming. Blood-curdling screams.

She ran through the trees, hearing the clash of swords as well as screams. Sera found herself running out into a scene of absolute carnage.

The village huts were burning, and Sera could taste the acrid smoke on her tongue. The butchered bodies of humans were everywhere. Some humans were fighting, but something more frightening—void patches of space were extracting the souls of the nearly dead.

Balor's Sluagh Horde. The entities that Bhal's warriors were created to fight. Sera ran towards one human and placed herself in between the Sluagh and a human male on the ground.

It just went through her—but then she was not really here. She was just an observer.

Sera heard a familiar voice and looked to her left. Bhal was there, cradling an older woman. She hurried over and kneeled across from her.

"I'm sorry I wasn't here on time, Mathair."

That's her mother? This must be Balor's doing. He destroyed Bhal's home village.

Bhal's tears ran down her cheeks, and Sera's heart broke for her.

"Warrior?" The older man called Mogh stumbled towards them with a bad looking stab wound on his side. He was holding a stone urn. "Bhaltair, come quickly."

Bhal laid her mother's head down carefully and moved over to Mogh's side. "What happened, Mogh?"

"No time for that. Drink out of this bowl quickly."

Sera saw that the urn had markings all around.

"What is it?" Bhal asked.

"You and your warrior's task is to beat Balor," Mogh said.

"I will find him and destroy him," Bhal said fiercely.

"It will be hard, and the chance to stop him forever will not come for a long time. Drink this water and do the same with your warriors. It will make you immortal," Mogh said.

"Immortal? That's not possible."

"I was given this by the Tuatha De Danann. Believe in my words, in me, and it will work."

Bhal took a big gulp from the urn, and a golden light started to run through her body, from her head to her feet.

"How do you feel?" Mogh asked.

"Stronger and more powerful than I ever have been," Bhal said.

"Good. From now on you will not only be immortal, but if you give people water from your hands, they will heal, even on the brink of death, just as this urn has given you life."

"How do I beat Balor?"

"Trust in yourself, your friends, and your heart. In the meantime, protect the people from the Sluagh, every Samhain."

"Then let me heal you, Mogh," Bhal said.

"No, I have completed my task in this realm. Promise me you and your warriors will protect those innocent lives?"

"I pledge to you with all my heart."

As Mogh breathed his last Bhal said, "I have no one now."

Sera tried to put her hand on Bhal's shoulder, but it went right through her. "You have me, Bhal. Wait for me?"

Bhal looked at her for a second as if she felt Sera's energy beside her, but then two little girls were dragged out of their hut screaming by an assailant with dead, empty eyes.

Bhal ran to them with sword out, and Sera followed her, screaming, as the assailant tried to slash at the children.

"No," Sera screamed.

❖

Bhal sat against the tree trunk, slumped with her head in her arms. Her guts were twisted, and pain stabbed at her heart.

"Get a grip of yourself, Warrior."

Bhal wiped her tears on her sleeve. If it was blood sickness that Sera had, then it wasn't her, and if they couldn't find who it was, Sera would slip into madness and death. It was happening already.

"Long time no see, Warrior."

Bhal looked up and saw a woman with ringlets of copper hair cascading down to her shoulders dressed in a long green robe embroidered with gold and a gold tassel tied around her waist. It was Hilda, the leader of the BaoBhan Sith. "Hilda? What are you doing here?"

Bhal jumped up and bowed her head.

"I come down from the castle every week. The Wulver Second takes care of her niece, Milo, who's part witch. I come to teach her the skills she will need as a witch. Come over here and we can talk."

There was a bench not too far away from them and they sat down. The BaoBhan Sith were a clan of vampires with a deep connection to nature and magic. They were part vampire and part fae, and they didn't drink the blood of humans, only of humanely caught animals.

The BaoBhan Sith lived further up north at the tip of Scotland in the Debrek castle there. The Debrek clan were very close to them and allowed them to live in the castle.

"I went in and visited with Sera," Hilda said. "You've known her for a long time, Bhal. Why didn't you ever tell her you were in love with her?"

"How did you…?" Bhal asked with surprise.

"Bhal, I've known you both for many years. People don't argue like you two did with no passion in their hearts."

Bhal shook her head with resignation. "I didn't understand my feelings until recently, and Sera was young, in vampire terms."

Hilda clasped her hands. "When Zaria told me that Sera was in the healer's hut, I went in to see her, I hope you don't mind."

"Of course not. How was she?" Bhal asked.

"Thrashing about in delirium, but the doctor knows why. She tested Sera's blood and it is blood sickness."

No matter how much she thought it was true, it was still like being doused with a bucket of cold water to have it confirmed. Bhal put her head in her hands.

"I knew it. I knew it. I've lost her."

"Tell me—what's been happening with Sera recently?" Hilda asked.

Bhal sighed. "Byron doesn't know this, but Sera has felt a bit lost for a while. She got involved with this new club where they were peddling drugs to the paranormals. The witch Anka and Gilbert have been swamping our world with them."

"Has she stopped?"

"Ever since I found her unconscious at the club, I've been helping with the withdrawal symptoms. Giving her my healing water. It helped for a while, but she's been getting progressively worse. Rejecting the blood she brought in blood bags."

"Did you feed her?"

"Once or twice, but after that, I offered but she didn't want to," Bhal said sadly.

Hilda rubbed her back. "We need to find her blood bond."

"Hilda, it could be anyone. I don't know how I'll find them. This club Sera was involved in, back in London…she was so drugged up she didn't know who she was."

"Bhal," Hilda said, "will you come with me? I want to try something."

CHAPTER NINETEEN

When Hilda and Bhal entered the healer's hut, the doctor, the nurse, and Zaria were trying to hold Sera down as she thrashed about.

"Bhal, feed Sera quickly," Hilda said.

"What?" Bhal was confused. "How will that help?"

"Just do it now, before we lose the ability to control Sera. She's a born vampire. If she wakens, confused, she could destroy this place."

Bhal moved over quickly to Sera and took out a knife that was strapped to her leg, while everyone struggled to hold Sera. She cut into her wrist and held it over Sera's lips.

The blood dripped into her parted lips and pooled on her tongue. Bhal squeezed her wrist to make it flow faster. She saw Sera's teeth spring out of her gums, and on instinct held her wrist against her mouth.

Sera's teeth latched on and greedily sucked on her wrist.

"She's calming," Olivia said.

And she was. They were all able to ease their grip. Bhal was astonished to see the colour return to Sera's cheeks. After a minute Sera's hands reached up and cradled Bhal's wrist. Then all of a sudden her eyes popped opened.

They were deep red.

"*You*," Sera gasped, then fell back into sleep.

"What the hell happened there?" Bhal said.

Nurse Keres brought over a bandage for Bhal and held a gauze over the wound.

"I think she needs to rest now," Olivia said.

"You are her blood bond," Hilda said.

"What? We didn't share blood. I can't be." There was no way that was true.

Just at that moment Kenrick ran into the room. She must have felt her Mater's tension. "Zaria?" Kenrick wrapped her arms protectively around her mate.

"It's okay, Ricky. Everything's calm now."

"Doctor, can you test Bhal's blood on Sera's, please?" Hilda said.

"Bhal, come over here."

Olivia drew some blood from Bhal and placed it in a petri dish with Sera's. Bhal's mind was reeling while Olivia checked it under the microscope.

"Yes. Ms. Debrek's cells are not breaking down any more and are returning to normal now."

"How can this be?" Bhal asked Hilda.

Hilda took Bhal's hands and turned them over to her palms. "Your hands have the ability to send your DNA into another person and to draw theirs to you, to help them heal. A blood bond, under normal circumstances, is sharing DNA through blood. Then if you are compatible, a bond takes place. You have done that, in an unconventional way, but it has the same outcome. Look at Sera. When was the last time she looked as healthy as this?"

Bhal stepped back over to her and was shocked at how well she looked. Her skin was pink with a healthy glow. Sera hadn't been like this since after she was kidnapped. She couldn't take this in.

"Why is she still unconscious?"

"She's sleeping," Olivia said. "From what you said, Ms. Debrek's not been well for a long, long, time."

Bhal had to think.

"I'll be back soon." Bhal hurried out of there and had the intention of walking deep into the woods.

"This is the place," Brogan said.

After touching down in Paris, Byron, Amelia, Alexis, and Torija picked up Brogan, and she led them to Professor Beaufort's house.

"It's the red door on the right."

"Okay, Torija, Brogan, you're with me and Alexis. Amelia and Daisy, you stay here with the guards."

"Oh, not a chance," Amelia said.

Quickly followed up by Daisy. "I'm going."

"No, Daisy. I agree with Byron," Torija said.

"Of course you do because you think I'm this little woman who you can wrap up in a box. That isn't happening." Daisy pointed at Torija.

There was an awkward silence for a few seconds, and then Brogan cleared her throat. "As much as I hate to get involved in this old married couple fight, I think it's a good idea to take the Principessa and Daisy. I've watched this woman be terrified by Anka and Gilbert. She knows what happened to the owner of the urn she decoded. I think she might be less intimidated by Amelia and Daisy."

"Fine," Byron said.

Torija sighed and said to Daisy, "Stay close, cherie."

Byron helped Amelia and Daisy out. "Alexis, stay here for the moment."

They arrived at the door. "I'll take the lead, Byron," Amelia said. She rang the bell, but no one answered.

"She's in there. I hear voices," Byron said.

Amelia knocked and knocked again, but nothing.

Torija had enough. "Let me burst in the door and compel her to tell what we need to know."

"Don't you dare. No compulsion," Daisy said. "Let me try."

She kneeled down and opened up the letterbox. "Hey, listen—we just want to talk, I swear to you. We're the good guys."

Still nothing, but Daisy had an idea. "My name's Daisy MacDougall, and I fight against people like Anka and Gilbert. Look up Monster Hunters on YouTube, and you'll see that you can trust me and my friends."

"She won't do it," Torija said.

Daisy stood up and shrugged. "If she doesn't, she doesn't. We are not busting our way in your way."

They waited and waited. Byron looked at her watch. "How long do we leave it?"

Just then they heard a click on one lock, then the other. The door opened, and they saw a woman as white as a sheet and trembling. She had her phone in her hand.

"Are you Daisy?" Professor Beaufort asked.

"I am. Can we talk to you, Dr. Beaufort?"

Daisy watched Professor Beaufort look around at everyone behind her and shrink back inside the door.

Daisy took Amelia's hand. "This is my friend Amelia, and don't worry about those two scary looking people behind me."

"Please believe we mean you no harm," Amelia said. "We just want to talk."

"Just you two," Professor Beaufort said.

"Yes, no problem," Daisy said.

Amelia shushed Byron and Torija before they ruined this. "You will be able to hear if there are any issues."

As Daisy and Amelia walked in, Daisy heard Torija say, "I can't believe you allowed that."

"I didn't see you jumping in and overruling your blood bond either."

Daisy had to chuckle to herself. Both Byron and Torija picked the wrong women if they thought they could be overruled.

Professor Beaufort led them to the kitchen. "Sit down."

"Thank you for talking to us, Doctor," Amelia said.

"Marie, call me Marie."

Daisy looked at Amelia, and she nodded for her to take the lead. From her time with Monster Hunters, Daisy did have a skill at getting people to feel comfortable, and to talk.

"Marie, you saw on YouTube what I used to do? Yeah, then I found out, like you, that this paranormal world did truly exist, and what Madam Anka and her people wanted to do with it. I met Amelia, who is married to the sophisticated one in the suit outside, and then I met and fell in love with the blond-haired one."

"What are they?"

Again she and Amelia shared a glance. She had to tell the truth to gain Marie's trust. "They are vampires."

Marie gasped and her hands started to shake.

"No, please don't be scared. They are not like the vampires that Anka brought with her," Daisy said.

Amelia jumped in and added, "You saw how easily we got them to stay at the front door. If they had any ill intent, they'd already be in here. Not everyone is malevolent in the paranormal community."

"Exactly," Daisy said. "We are from a group that is fighting against Anka and trying to protect humans."

"Are Anka and people like her behind the deaths that've been happening all over the world?" Marie asked.

"Yeah, she is letting her bad crowd run riot. That's what we are trying to stop, but if we don't find out the information that you decoded on the urn, we won't be able to."

"If I tell you, she'll kill me and my whole family."

"If you don't, your family and everyone else's will be killed or enslaved. There's no other outcome," Daisy said.

"In the meantime, she could send someone to kill me and my family at any time. I live with my elderly father. She's used me twice to help her with artifacts and information. I'm sure she'll hear if I tell you anything," Marie said.

"Could I suggest this?" Amelia said. "What if we left two guards to protect you? This is going to come to a head soon. They can protect you till this is over."

"Let me meet them first?" Marie said.

"Give me two seconds." Amelia left the kitchen.

"Your friend is pregnant," Marie said.

"Yeah, she is." Daisy smiled.

"But you said she's with one of the vampires at the front door. How is that possible?" Marie asked.

Daisy chuckled. "It's complicated."

"It must be. I saw on your YouTube channel that you tried to expose the paranormal. Why did things change?"

"Honestly? I found out about my friend and that she fell in love with the leader of a vampire clan. I got to know the clan, and how it was not harmful to humans."

"How can that be? Vampires need blood," Marie said.

"This clan only takes blood by consent. They have human families that have worked for them for generations. They are very well taken care of. But the vampires in Anka's group, they see humans as food, nothing more," Daisy said.

Amelia came back with two vampires. "These two vampires will protect you. This is Owen and Trista."

Amelia nodded to them, and Trista said, "At your service, ma'am."

"Okay, I'll tell you. I pray I'm doing the right thing," Marie said.

"You are," Daisy said.

"The urn gave the location of a crossroads of worlds, of realities, that the ancient Celtic people believed in."

"How did they get this urn?" Amelia asked.

"From a race of people called the Tuatha De Danann. They came to Ireland with great technology or supernatural powers, depending on which way you see the story."

"Can you tell us the coordinates?" Daisy asked.

Marie got up. "I'll write it down for you."

Minutes later, Daisy and Amelia walked to the front door, and Daisy waved a piece of paper at Byron and Torija. "Told you our way was better."

"Well done, Daisy," Byron said.

Torija shook her head. "Hmm..."

Marie followed them to the door.

"Thank you, Professor Beaufort. Your two guards will stay with you until this is over. Owen, Trista, protect the professor and do as she says," Byron said.

"Yes, Principe."

"Don't be frightened to have them do any heavy lifting you need done," Daisy said. "Vampires are strong and handy to have around."

"Thank you, and good luck," Marie said.

They walked back to the car and got back in.

"Time to regroup," Byron said.

Bhal had wandered for an hour or so while she tried to make sense of her jumbled mind. She was the blood bond of the woman she loved. It was what she would have given anything for a short time ago.

The thought of her beautiful Sera being shackled by blood to one of those people at that club had been horrifying, but getting what she wanted was overwhelming too.

What if Sera hated her for it? There was nothing else in the world Bhal wanted than to go back to Sera's side, but she was frightened.

"Bhal?"

Ricky caught up with her. "Bhal, Sera's wakened up, and we've taken her to the house we set aside for you."

"She's on her own? Is she safe?"

"Perfectly safe and well. Follow me, I'll take you to her," Ricky said.

Bhal followed Ricky until they arrived at one of the large houses, supported by trees.

"Just take the stairs up the side, and you'll reach the top in no time."

"Thank you, Ricky."

"Let us know if you need anything, and we can talk about the sword when you're ready."

Bhal had almost forgotten about their mission here and the imminent threat to humanity. Nothing ever disturbed her from mission goals, but that was all different now.

She walked over to the stairs and put her foot on the first step. Taking the second one and the third would be the difficult thing.

Don't be a coward.

She took another step and another and was soon running upstairs to the front door of the wooden house. Bhal opened the door and stepped into the modern home. In front of her was an open plan kitchen, with a dining table. At the other end of the room was a huge bed. Behind it instead of a wall was glass. You could see the tall trees as they were now above the canopy.

What a view.

To the left hand side of the kitchen was a corridor and another door. Maybe another bedroom, Bhal thought.

She didn't see Sera. Maybe she was in the bedroom down the corridor. Bhal walked up to the kitchen just as Sera walked out of what must be the bathroom in a white dressing gown, a white towel twisted around her hair, just out of a shower.

Sera stopped dead when she saw Bhal. They stood in silence for what seemed like an eternity.

"Hi," Sera said.

"Hello, you're looking much brighter," Bhal said nervously.

"I feel so much brighter. I've got energy that I haven't had in such a long time."

It was time for Bhal to do the right thing and take the lead in this situation. She walked over to Sera, dropped to one knee, and held up her wrist to her. "Serenity Debrek, I offer my blood, and I offer my life to you."

Sera took her hand. "Get up, Bhal." When she did, Sera asked, "Are you saying this out of obligation, Bhaltair? Tell me honestly."

Bhal took Sera's hand and put it on her heart. "You might know me to be many things, but never insincere. When I realized you were blood bonded, and I assumed to someone else, I was destroyed." She took a step to Sera, and they were only inches apart. Bhal rested her forehead on Sera's and closed her eyes. "I will serve you loyally for eternity, because I lost my heart to you long ago. I just never allowed myself to recognize it, but—"

"But what?"

"But if you don't feel that or never will, it's all right. Just know I will serve you with love."

Bhal kept her eyes closed. She was frightened to open them and look Sera in the eyes if she was rejecting her love.

She felt Sera's lips press against hers and give her the softest of kisses. Bhal kissed her back.

Was this really happening?

She opened her eyes and looked in Sera's.

"I've fallen in love with you, Bhal."

Bhal could hardly take in what was happening. "I give you my life, Sera."

She watched Sera's eyes scan over her face and down to her neck. Bhal clutched her chest and lurched forward.

"What is it?"

The pull in her chest she could only describe one way. "You're hungry."

"Yes, but you don't have to…"

Sera's words faltered when Bhal took off her sword and set it on the kitchen counter. Sera's heart had never thudded so much since she realized she was having feelings for Bhal, and now it beat like a drum as she watched her blood bond pull off her T-shirt and throw it to the side.

She had dreamed of seeing Bhal like this. Her tattoos had teased what lay beneath her T-shirts, and now here was Bhal walking towards her, about to offer her blood.

Intricate black Celtic designs and geometric patterns covered Bhal's arms and her chest. On her stomach was some kind of ancient writing, she guessed. She loved the stomach muscles underneath the words. When Bhal got close, she lightly placed her fingertips on them.

Bhal's stomach contracted at her touch, and she had an intake of breath. Sera took off her head towel and threw it to the side. Her wet hair hung loosely around her shoulders.

She saw Bhal smile at that, then reach up to touch her hair, but before anything else happened, Sera wanted to see the muscular, tattooed back that had invaded her thoughts for so long.

She walked around Bhal, trailing her fingers as she went. Sera heard Bhal's breathing become heavier. Then she saw what she'd been dreaming of.

Bhal's tattoo hung like a thick chain around her neck and was connected to a design that went down to the base of her spine and spread wide over the rest of her back. She didn't understand the design or what it meant, but Sera knew that it was beautiful and sexy on her strong back.

Sera walked back around and noticed that her teeth had erupted. She wanted Bhal so much.

"You're hungry," Bhal said.

"I'm hungry for you, all of you."

Sera untied her dressing gown and slowly let it drop. Bhal's eyes widened, and her lips parted.

Bhal went to touch between her breasts but stopped as if wanting permission. Sera took her hand pushed it onto her.

Bhal's fingers trailed between her breasts and grazed her breast and nipple. Her hands were rough and calloused like a warrior's should be, and they made Sera instantly wet.

"I hunger for you too. I would give up my life for just one kiss," Bhal said.

"You don't need to do that. Kiss me and let's live for each other."

Bhal's lips found hers, and Bhal's hands found her hips. Their kiss was soft, and then Bhal's tongue slipped into her mouth, and it felt overwhelming.

Sera had enjoyed casual sex in her life, but nothing had felt like this, and they'd only kissed so far.

She wrapped her arms around Bhal's neck and said, "Take me to bed, Warrior."

❖

Bhal carried Sera over to the bed on the other side of the room, like the most precious cargo. Sera's kiss and the feel of her body were driving her wild. This was what she had been looking for her whole life.

She placed her down on the bed carefully and took off her boots and trousers. She hesitated and took a moment to appreciate Sera's beauty waiting for her to love. Sera's eyes were a deep red. To know that was for her made Bhal feel fire.

"Come," Sera said.

Bhal laid herself on top of her blood bond, stroked a strand of wet hair from Sera's cheek. "I've waited for millennia to worship you."

"God, the things you say destroy me," Sera said.

Bhal kissed her and heard her moan. "You really do want me, don't you?"

"Bhal?" Sera cupped her face and said, "Yes, you are the one. You are my heart. I don't ever want to sleep apart from you again."

Bhal couldn't hold herself back any longer. She kissed Sera's chest and was soon kissing one ample breast while squeezing the other. Sera moaned and ran her hands over Bhal's shoulders and arms.

She licked all around Sera's nipple, teasing her, while her hand found Sera's wet centre.

"Oh yeah," Sera moaned.

Bhal sucked Sera's nipple then lapped at it while gently squeezing Sera's sex with her hand.

She then made sure to give the same treatment to Sera's other breast. As she did, Sera pushed Bhal's hand into her sex.

"Inside," Sera begged.

Bhal stroked her clit first, making Sera all the more desperate. Bhal teased at her opening as a promise to what would be coming and looked deeply into Sera's hungry red eyes.

"I offer you my neck and my undying love and worship for as long as our lives will last."

"Yes," Sera said simply.

It was then that Bhal pressed two fingers inside her lover. Sera gasped but they didn't stop looking in each other's eyes.

Bhal pushed her fingers in and out of Sera's wetness, going deeper with each thrust. "I love you."

She lowered her neck to Sera's mouth. Bhal could feel Sera's teeth scratch her neck, which made Bhal shiver. In moments, though, that feeling was nothing to the experience of Sera's teeth piercing her neck.

The feeling was exquisite and went straight to her sex. Now she was inside Sera, and Sera was inside her. There was nothing more intimate than what they were giving each other.

Every time Sera sucked on her neck, it was like her clit was also being sucked. This was nothing like she'd ever experienced. As Bhal thrust inside Sera faster, so Sera sucked faster. They built up and up until Sera dug her fingers into Bhal's shoulders, and Sera's walls fluttered against Bhal's fingers.

Bhal's orgasm exploded from her sex, and she thrust her hips frustratingly into nothing. Sera pulled her teeth from Bhal's neck, gasping for breath.

"Oh my God, oh God that was—"

Bhal looked down at Sera, with her own blood around her mouth. "I need more."

She went between Sera's legs and pressed both their sexes together.

"Yes," Sera said, wrapping her legs around Bhal's thighs, bringing them closer together.

After coming with just Sera's bite, Bhal had the urge, the desperate need to thrust into her lover. They moved together naturally and easily as they were both so wet. Sera grasped Bhal's hair and hung on tightly as they moved together.

"Kiss me."

Bhal met Sera's lips and kissed her, thrusting faster and faster.

"Faster, baby. I'm going to come," Sera pleaded.

Bhal's body exploded, and deep pleasure and heat rushed from her sex all over her body and was heightened when she heard Sera scream out her orgasm.

She collapsed down onto Sera, both of them sweaty and breathing heavily.

"You are my Goddess," Bhal breathed.

❖

Anka sat by the fire in her rooms at Dred castle, enjoying a glass of wine. She looked at the clock on the fireplace and imagined her vans full of her troops moving across Wales, ready to strike tonight.

"Balor, we are getting near the endgame. Your feet will soon walk this earth."

There was a knock at the door, and Asha walked in. "Madam, I've heard from your spies."

"Sit down with me, Asha, and tell me."

Asha smiled. He had been neglected as of late because of Gilbert's presence. Asha had been loyal to her for a very long time, and she had a care for his existence, as much as she ever had a care for anybody's.

But Gilbert was strong and brought her closer to Balor. That was their connection, why she wanted to fuck him, why her body became alive for him. When Balor returned, who knew if that would still be the case.

"The Debreks were last seen visiting the site at Knowth in Ireland. They left there but we don't know where they are now."

"Find out, Asha. At least they are a few steps behind us," Anka said.

Asha looked down sheepishly then back up. "There's something else."

Anka sat forward. "What is it?"

"Serenity Debrek and Bhaltair are on the trail of the keys. They have the English shield and are in the Wulver pack lands now."

Asha looked surprised when Anka burst out laughing. "Byron sent Serenity on a mission to find the keys? What a fool. Serenity is a failure of a vampire, a party girl hooked on our drugs. This will be simple."

"They will have two keys, Madam."

Anka sat back and crossed her legs. "Tonight we will have the Welsh spear, then go and take the Irish axe. Believe me, if Serenity is involved, then they are simply keeping them safe for us. Besides, the Debreks have no idea where to take them."

"Shall I have our spies follow them in Scotland?"

"Yes. Next they'll cross the water to Ireland, and that's where we'll take them from them. We need to know when they leave for Ireland."

"Yes, Madam."

Anka took a sip of her wine, then said, "Good work, Asha."

Asha's whole demeanour lifted. "Thank you, Madam."

❖

"This is a nice place," Amelia said.

Torija led their group into the drawing room of her Paris home. "It once belonged to Daisy's ancestors," Torija said.

Daisy smiled at her. "We stayed here when Torija and I ran from the Dreds. Sit down."

Byron and Amelia sat with Daisy on the other couch, while Torija went to the drinks table, but Alexis remained standing. She looked jumpy.

Byron looked up and must have sensed her discomfort. "Alexis, tell our vampires to feed and go and check in with Katie."

"Thank you, Principe," Alexis said before nearly running out of the room.

"It must be difficult for Alexis, leaving Katie at home. Especially after..." Torija's voice drifted off as the guilt enveloped her.

"Tor, don't," Daisy said.

Byron sat forward. "Torija, we all agreed to move on from the past. Now get us a drink."

Torija cut the tension by bowing. "Yes, Principe. What would you like?"

"Brandy, please. Darling?" Byron said to Amelia.

"I don't want to drink alcohol. Just in case." Amelia rubbed her stomach.

Daisy jumped up. "I've got us covered. There's a nice white wine in the fridge for me, and sparkling water with lime?"

"Perfect," Amelia said.

"Just be a second."

Byron took out her cigar case and offered one to Torija when she brought her glass.

"Byron? No cigars," Amelia said.

Torija handed over the brandy and went back to get her own. She couldn't help but smirk at Amelia and Byron's conversation.

"Why? You usually say you like the aroma. We're all immortal here. What harm is there?"

"I do like the smell, as long as a window's open, but not around the baby. They are not immortal till they decide at eighteen whether they want to turn. I've given up caffeine. I don't think giving up the odd cigar is too much to ask."

Byron nodded. "You're quite right. I didn't think of it that way."

Torija poured a whiskey for herself. It was eye-opening to think of something else apart from your blood bond in that way. She wondered if Daisy had ever thought about children. Maybe it was something they should do, now that it was possible for them, and especially as it was something that caught Byron and Amelia unawares.

"What are you thinking so hard about, Vamp?" Daisy said.

"Nothing. We can talk later."

Daisy gave her a strange look and took the bottle of wine and two glasses over to Amelia.

"Here we go. Nice chilled white wine."

Daisy handed Amelia her sparkling water, then poured out a glass of wine, then fell back onto the couch. Torija put her arm around her as she cuddled up to her. She could never take this for granted. She was the luckiest vampire alive.

"So what now?" Daisy asked.

"We need to contact Sera and Bhal," Byron said. "I tried to call both their phones on my way back, but neither are answering."

Amelia lifted her glass to her lips, then laughed. "They're probably killing each other as we speak."

They all laughed.

"Let's hope not," Byron said. "They have to collect the weapons. Hopefully they have the Ranwulfs' shield at least."

"And are in Scotland with the Wulvers," Amelia added. "We know where Lochlan is now, but what's our next move?"

Byron took Amelia's hand. "Get our heads down tonight. Then tomorrow get in contact with my sister, and meet them in the Irish pack lands, hopefully with the shield and sword."

"You realize they have weapons to kill each other?" Torija joked.

"Here's hoping it's just a mild skirmish," Byron said.

❖

Sera rolled over and held Bhal's arms above her head.

"I surrender," Bhal said breathily.

Sera smiled and then laid her head on Bhal's chest. They were both trying to get their breath back. They hadn't stopped exploring their bodies since Bhal had come to her earlier in the afternoon.

Bhal stroked her head. "How are you feeling?"

"Never more alive. Thank you. It seems such a long time since I've felt like myself, experienced so much energy."

"I would have fed you from the start, but you kept refusing me, so I thought you were rejecting me," Bhal said.

"I was never rejecting you. The first few times I fed from you, I got scared," Sera said.

"Why?"

Sera lifted her head and looked into Bhal's eyes. "Because I'd never felt anything so overwhelming in my life. I knew that if I kept feeding from you, I would have to face my feelings. I wasn't ready for that."

"Aye, neither was I."

"It was hard coming to terms that you cared for the person who annoyed you more than anyone in this whole world."

"Something like that," Bhal said. She caressed Sera's cheek. "I'm sorry I was harsh to you on our way to Scotland. I suspected you had blood sickness and thought I had lost you to someone at the club."

"Why would my blood bond be someone I didn't know and didn't care about?" Sera asked.

"Look at Daisy. She was bonded to the then-most-evil vampire we knew of."

Sera lay back down, and Bhal cuddled her in under her arms.

"But they were destined to be together. Just like us," Sera said.

"How did you take the news when the doctor told you it was me?"

"I knew before I opened my eyes."

"How did you know?" Bhal asked.

"I experienced a vision while I was unconscious, of you," Sera said.

"What kind of vision?"

"I woke up in this forested area, saw this little boy with dark hair. He got me to follow him, and he led me to your Samhain warrior village. I watched your ceremony to become chief of the Samhain warriors. Somehow I knew this was because you were in my blood."

"You saw that? Really?"

"Yeah, and even though it happened such a long time ago, I was so proud of you," Sera said.

"I was the first female to ever be chief," Bhal said.

Sera laughed softly. "I gathered that since they put the big strap-on thing around you."

"Aye." Bhal laughed. "It was a big masculine society. Luckily, I've always been in touch with my masculine side. The phallus was seen as a symbol of power."

Sera stroked her fingers along Bhal's stomach, making her muscles contract. "Don't worry, you have power, Warrior."

Bhal took her hand and kissed it. "You are my Goddess, and I will worship at your feet for all time."

Sera rolled on top of Bhal. "You say things like that, and my heart turns to mush."

"I don't say things I don't mean," Bhal said.

"I know." Sera ran her finger over Bhal's lips. "That's why I've fallen in love with you."

Bhal caught Sera's finger and sucked it into her mouth. Sera loved this. The intimacy they were sharing was natural and perfect. She hadn't ever had intimacy with anyone else she'd slept with.

But then she'd never made love with any of them. They were purely about sex. This was a whole other world.

"Did you see anything else in your vision?" Bhal asked.

Sera didn't want to upset Bhal, but she had to tell her the truth.

"Yeah. The little boy I mentioned took me to quite a different place and time."

"I wonder if he was my brother."

Sera nodded. "I felt like he might be."

She saw Bhal gulp hard. "Tell me what you saw."

"Balor's Sluagh entities were stealing the souls of your people, after they'd been slaughtered."

"When Balor attacked my home village? My mathair died in that attack," Bhal said.

"I know. I saw you crying over her body, and it broke my heart."

Bhal's eyes were filling up with tears. "After she died, I was truly alone. I had my warriors, but you can't show that emotion to them. You have to keep a stoic mask on."

"That's probably why we didn't get each other. You have a stoic mask, and I show every emotion known."

"True. I have to tell you something. That's when Morrigan came to me, and it only happened once, but I was so alone, so needing to feel something, that I gave in to her."

"You slept with her?"

Bhal nodded. "Only the once, but she's tormented me about it ever since."

Sera stroked her head. "Everyone has a past, and I can understand why you needed to feel something."

"But I felt nothing with her. But I can't be like that—I mean, I can't have that stoic mask—with you. I can't control my feelings any more. I love you, Serenity."

Sera's heart tightened. "I want you to show me everything, and you'll never be alone again."

Bhal flipped them over so that she was on top. "I know we are blood bonded. We got there in a different way, but I'd like to share blood in the normal way to bond."

"Yes." Sera's eyes flashed red and she bit her own lip to let her blood flow. "Kiss me."

Bhal placed her lips to Sera's and sucked in her blood. Bhal jumped slightly when Sera's vampire tooth bit Bhal's, allowing her blood to flow.

Their kissed deepened, and Bhal savoured the sensation of sharing blood. They were truly bonded in every way now.

CHAPTER TWENTY

Sera had her second shower of the day. She and Bhal took a shower together, but Sera had gotten out so they didn't get even more caught up in each other again. She was standing outside the shower brushing her long, wet hair, but her eyes and concentration were fixed inside the big open shower.

She was intensely interested in the way the water ran over Bhal's muscles and tattoos, and trickled down her body. Sera had never been as attracted to someone as this before, and to be bonded just made it all the more intense.

"Are you sure you don't want to get back in?" Bhal said.

"I'd love to, but we can't. We have just abandoned our hosts for hours and hours."

"They're wolves, they understand bonding."

"If you remember, we have to save the world. We need to talk to Kenrick about the sword," Sera said.

"True." Bhal sighed. "When this is over, I'd like to go away, just us—no clan, no world in danger—and be together. What do you think?"

Sera smiled. "It sounds perfect." She heard footsteps walking up to their tree house. "There's someone coming."

Sera quickly tied the towel around her head. She heard a knock at the door and then, "Hi, it's Zaria."

"It's the Mater. I'll go out. Get dressed quickly," Sera said in panic.

"Calm down, it's all right. I won't be long."

"She'll know what we've been doing if we both come out of the shower room."

"Like I said—they're wolves. They understand. I don't remember you being such a prude."

Sera sighed. "Just hurry up." She skipped through the house and opened up the door. There were two dominant wolves following Zaria with Bhal's and Sera's bags. "Mater, come in."

Seeing that Sera wasn't dressed properly, she turned to the wolves and said, "About turn, guys, and leave the bags there. I'm sure Bhal will get them for us."

Carrying bags didn't worry Sera, but she supposed wolves saw things differently. Zaria probably thought Bhal's feathers would be ruffled.

"Would you like a drink, Mater?"

"*Zaria*, please. No, I'm okay. I just wanted a quick chat. I haven't disturbed you both, have I?"

"No, just a quick shower before coming over to talk to you and the Alpha."

Scra led her over to the island in the kitchen.

"We're having a barbecue and bonfire night for your arrival. It's getting going now, but whenever you're ready, if you'll be up to it."

"Absolutely. I feel better than I ever have, now that I have Bhal."

Zaria smiled. "It's working out for you both, then?"

Sera could feel her cheeks heat up. No doubt, she was blushing. "Yes, it's perfect."

"I'm glad. Bhal was so distraught while you were unconscious," Zaria said.

"She was?"

"Oh yeah. Seriously. I knew she must be very much in love with you."

Sera didn't want Bhal to be upset, but it was nice to know how much she really cared.

At that moment Bhal walked out and bowed her head to Zaria. "Mater."

"Zaria and her wolves brought our bags." Sera pointed to the door.

"Thank you." Bhal went and brought them into the house.

"The pack are having a barbecue and bonfire night for us. I said that it was wonderful of them."

Bhal stepped beside her and put her arm around her waist. "That's very kind."

"We can talk about the sword and the details of the battle ahead. The Wolfgangs have just arrived too," Zaria said.

"We'll be there in half an hour."

After Zaria left, Sera went to dry her hair. Bhal lay on the bed, unwilling to be far away from her blood bond. Sera watched Bhal take her phone out of her bag and saw a look of surprise wash over her face.

Sera switched off the hairdryer. "What is it?"

"I've got so many calls from the Principe and Principessa."

"Shit. Check mine in my rucksack."

Bhal got it out and shook her head. "You too. The Principe's going to be so angry, and so worried about us. I was just caught up in you being unwell, and I forgot all about it."

"We both did," Sera said. "Give me the phone. She'll take it better from me."

Bhal paced nervously while the phone rang. Sera mouthed, *Calm down.*

"Sera? Where the hell have you been?"

"Doing mission stuff. I'm sorry, we both got caught up in"—Sera looked at Bhal for help, but she lifted her arms and shrugged—"pack stuff."

"Pack stuff? Great. Give me an update then, or hand me over to Bhal," Byron said.

"I'm perfectly capable of giving a mission update." Sera decided it was a good idea to steer the conversation herself. "We have the Ranwulf shield, and we are staying with the Wulvers. We arrived this morning, and we are going to meet the Alpha for dinner to talk about the sword, but there shouldn't be any problems. What about you?"

"We've found the coordinates for Lochlan. Once you have the Wulver weapon, we can meet you in Ireland."

"Okay. Oh, the Wolfgang Alpha, Dante, and her Second, Caden, have arrived with some of their elite wolves to help with our fight against Anka. Dante is cousins with Kenrick Wulver."

"Excellent. Things are looking up. Can I speak to Bhal?"

"She's not here with me at the moment." Bhal gave her a look, but Sera just waved her hand at her. "I'll get her to call you."

"Fine, let me know how your meeting with Kenrick goes," Byron said.

"I will. Love to Amelia."

When Sera hung up, Bhal said, "Why did you say I wasn't here? She's going to think I'm deliberately not bothering to take her calls."

"I don't know. I just panicked. I don't want her to get all big sisterly on me. If she knew we were sharing a place here..."

"You're going to have to tell her sometime. It's not easy for me either. I pledged my sword and my life to protect the Debreks, not to fall in love with one, but I will do it, as it's the only honourable thing to do."

Sera walked over and took her hand. "You make it sound as if this is wrong. It's not wrong. Our blood was compatible, and we fell in love. We were destined to be together."

"I know that." Bhal looked down as she held both her hands. "But you've seen where I came from. We didn't have anything. I'm just a warrior—you're too good for me."

"Don't be ludicrous. You are an immortal warrior who has saved countless lives, and I'm just a spoiled vampire," Sera said.

Bhal lifted both Sera's hands and kissed them in turn. "You are Serenity Debrek, of the most respected clan in the world. To the day we decide to leave this long, long life, I will forever try to deserve my Goddess."

Sera's heart melted. She placed her hands on Bhal's cheeks. "You are my dream come true, and you're making it so difficult to leave. Maybe just one kiss."

Their lips came together, but then Bhal pulled back. "No, don't tempt me. We are expected at dinner. Get ready, Goddess."

❖

A short time later Bhal and Sera sat together with Kenrick and Zaria while the barbecue food was being cooked.

The barbecue was in a community space set out for the purpose of eating together. In the middle of the large space was a bonfire, and wooden benches made out of tree trunks were placed around the perimeter. There were around five commercial-sized barbecue grills on one side of the clearing to feed a large number of wolves.

The space was filled with families, children racing around and adults chasing or yelling at them to be careful, and a few wolves playing guitars or traditional drums.

Bhal loved the family atmosphere. "This reminds me of my village," Bhal said, "gathering around the fire, enjoying stories, and singing songs together."

Sera grasped her hand and smiled adoringly at her. It was wonderful to be with Sera and not have to hide how she felt. If only they could have come to recognize their feelings quicker, then life would have been so much better.

"We love enjoying food together," Kenrick said. "Then when the cubs go to bed, we can enjoy some drinks under the stars."

"It is so peaceful compared to London," Sera said.

Rhuri, the pack Second, came over with bottles of beer for them all. "You'll like this. The Irish Filtiaran pack make it."

Rhuri sat down and Bhal lifted her bottle and took a sip. "I do love a good beer. This is good stuff."

"Later on, we can get the good whiskey out," Rhuri said. "The Alpha's got a nice aged malt for you to try."

Kenrick nodded. "Aye, I do. So tell me about the weapons. In fact, let me get my cousin. She needs to her this."

Kenrick came back in a few minutes with two tall good-looking wolves. One, clearly the more dominant, wore simple jeans and a shirt. The other had the look of an American cowboy, complete with boots and a Stetson.

"This is my cousin Dante, and her Second, Caden."

Bhal stood and thumped her chest. "Alpha, Second. Pleased to meet you."

"We've heard a lot about you, Bhal," Dante said.

Dante and Caden then leaned over and bowed their heads. "Ms. Debrek."

"Sera, please. Thank you for coming. It's so good to have you with us."

Kenrick sat back next to Zaria. "Sera and Bhal were just going to tell us what they knew so far."

Sera prodded Bhal. "You tell them."

"Okay. There was a tribe of people called the Tuatha De Danann, who my people called gods and goddesses. They had magical weapons with stones embedded in them, parts of a larger stone that Balor used to open the door of his reality to ours. We saw them as magical back then, but they could have just been technology."

"And this Balor," Zaria said, "was he a part of these Tuatha people?"

"We're not sure, but they knew him. They certainly thought he was breaking a rule by coming here."

Sera piped in, "The Celtic goddess Morrigan is his sister, as were the ancestors of our Principessa and her friend Daisy."

Bhal still felt uncomfortable hearing Morrigan's name. She continued, "When the Tuatha De Danann came to banish Balor to a prison realm, a void, they wanted the keys to the realm dispersed around the world. I don't know how your Great Mother got hold of them. Sounds to me that she was given the task of getting rid of the keys, then gave each of your packs a weapon. We know it's a big ask for the packs to give up their weapons," Bhal said, "but if Anka gets hold of them and lets Balor back into the world, she and he will devastate the land and your packs. He destroyed my village and killed my family."

Kenrick looked at Rhuri, then Dante, who nodded to her. "We have no choice. We will give you our sword tomorrow."

Rhuri added, "And we will fight side by side with you against this witch."

Zaria nodded in agreement.

Dante said, "If we didn't fight, they'd come attacking here next anyway. We must all stick together."

"Well said, Alpha," Kenrick said.

Bhal smiled at Sera. They were a good team.

Two wolves came over with plates of food for them. "First bite, Alpha?"

Bhal knew the ritual the wolves followed. In the wild, the Alpha got first bite and the best parts of the meat. The werewolf packs carried on this practice but made it more ritualized.

Kenrick took her plate but said, "Our guests get the honour tonight."

The wolves handed the burgers to Sera, Bhal, Dante, and Caden. "Venison burgers. Please take the first bite."

Bhal said, "Thank you," then tucked into the delicious food.

❖

How he had missed this, Gilbert thought as he led his team out into the Welsh countryside. He ducked down behind a dry stone wall and signalled his team to do the same. The Blaidds lived out in the middle of nowhere, to conceal their world from the human community in Wales, which suited Gilbert's plans.

Each werewolf family lived in a farmhouse near the place they worked the land. It was the evening now, and most families would be in their homes, give or take one or two.

Gilbert brought two vans full of vampires and shifters. She'd left the werewolves now in the Dred clan at home, since the Blaidds might be able to scent them quickly.

After spitting up into teams, Gilbert led his towards the Alpha's house. She spotted guards patrolling. She indicated for her team to split up and take care of the guards. Gilbert watched the vampires and shifter circle the house, then pull the guards into the undergrowth to kill them.

Gilbert thought of his other teams surrounding the pack Second's and the other elite wolves' houses and tearing them apart. It was time for him to do the same. This Alpha and Mater didn't have any cubs as yet, since they were newly married, so there wouldn't be many distractions.

She started to move towards the house with four vampires. There was a light in the kitchen, so someone was there, maybe both. Gilbert closed his eyes and heard a man's and a woman's voices.

Perfect. They were both there.

They moved to the kitchen door, and Gilbert counted down from five, using hand signals. Then two of her vampires burst through the door. He followed and helped rip out the throats of the two partially shifted wolves, until their bodies went limp.

Blood spattered across the kitchen and dripped down his face. Gilbert felt alive again.

"Spread out and look for any doors that might conceal a basement." With her vampire hearing, she could hear screams of pain and panic spread over the Blaidds' pack lands.

He licked the blood from his teeth and laughed.

"Principe, we've found something."

Gilbert followed them out into the hall of the farmhouse. The runner that covered the length of the hall was pulled back, revealing a heavy wooden trapdoor.

"Open it." He ordered his female vampire, Crane, down first.

"You can come down now, Principe."

Gilbert raced downstairs, and there in a display case on the wall was the Blaidds' spear. He punched his way through the glass and grasped the spear. He was bleeding from the cuts on his fist, but he would soon heal. Gilbert examined the tip of the spear and felt the heft of the wooden handle.

It was a good weapon, but Gilbert could only imagine the power in it when the Tuatha De Danann had used it. It must have looked remarkable. "One down, three to go."

Gilbert went back upstairs and outside into the garden. Bodies were strewn about, and the sound of screaming was still in the air.

"What a perfect evening."

❖

Torija climbed up Daisy's body, feeling wicked. Daisy was breathing heavily and holding tightly to the brass bedhead.

"You are just the best at that."

"I know," Torija said with an arrogant smile.

"You are far too cocky. Give me a hug."

Hugging was never a part of Torija's life until she met Daisy and, apart from the passion they shared, had become one of her favourite things.

The Debrek team had decided to have an early night and some alone time with their blood bonds.

"What were you thinking about downstairs, when we were having drinks?"

Torija didn't really want to talk about it now, but she had promised to be open and honest with Daisy. "It was when you went to get the wine. Amelia asked Byron not to smoke cigars around their baby."

"Yeah, and…?"

"It just made me think. We are Debreks now. I'm a Debrek born vampire, and I suppose we'll be able to, you know…"

Daisy feigned ignorance. "No, what?"

"You know." Torija pointed at her stomach. "We two could become three."

"I know, I know." Daisy laughed. "Don't worry, I asked Amelia. Yes, we could have kids, Amelia's life force gives us that, but we'd both have to want them, like, deep down."

"Is that something you'd ever want?" Torija said carefully.

"Wow, the atmosphere has really changed from a few minutes ago."

"I just think it needs to be talked about. Especially as it can happen so easily."

Daisy sat up, since this had now become a serious conversation. "You go first. You tell me what's in your heart."

"If you remember, I, like my father before me, was desperate for the Debrek secret of procreation, to sire an army of born vampires. Not children, but soldiers to be used to make the Dred clan more powerful."

"And now?"

"And now that I see the world differently, I feel guilty for the way I thought about children. Having kids makes me feel a sense of panic, to be honest. That might change, but not at the moment."

Torija was nervous of Daisy's reply. The last thing she wanted to do was upset her.

"I understand how you feel. I never really thought about it until Amelia became pregnant. I know I'm immortal now, but only just, and I'm young. I want to enjoy life with you after we stop Anka and Balor."

"You're sure?" Torija asked.

"Yeah, let's just leave the future to the future. I might never want any, so let's concentrate on us."

"Would you mind concentrating on my lips?" Torija said.

"That we can both agree on."

Torija was worryingly silent again. Then she said, "It won't be long until we meet Anka and her people in battle, until we meet my father again. I have to kill him, or find a way to kill him, or he will come after you. I know he will want to destroy anything I love."

"Remember, you are stronger than him. The next generation of born vampires is more powerful than the last." She pointed to her head. "Don't let him beat you in here."

"I won't—I'll try not to."

❖

Byron hung her suit up in the wardrobe and walked over to the bed. Amelia looked lost in her thoughts. She slipped into bed beside her. "What's wrong?"

"Sorry?" Amelia hadn't heard her.

"You seemed to be in a world of your own."

"Things are coming to a head. Bhal and Sera have two of the artifacts. Anka was ahead of us with finding Lochlan, and I'm sure she's going to come looking for a fight to get the weapons."

Byron said, "Probably, but we always knew it would come to this. We will overcome and protect the human population and our own. We have you and Daisy on our side. The descendants."

"That's what I'm worried about. What if Daisy and I are not good enough to stop them? We are only new to this, and it's up to us to save the world. It's frightening," Amelia said.

Byron pulled Amelia to her. "The last thing I want you to do is to be involved in a fight, especially now that you're pregnant. But I have to trust that Lucia, Magda, Sybil, and your mothers are all right, that you will prevail. And remember, I will be right by your side."

"I'm counting on it. So where did you say we'd meet up with Sera and Bhal?" Amelia said.

"If all goes well, in Ireland with the pack, then move to the Welsh pack lands. I said we'd call tomorrow and make definite plans. Sera sounded odd on the phone earlier," Byron said.

"What do you mean odd?"

"Stumbling over her words, cagey about what Bhal was doing. Bhal would never normally go this long without speaking to me."

Amelia joked, "Maybe she has killed Bhal at last and has hidden the body."

"There was something. I can feel it. I felt it the evening I went to speak to Sera in her room and Bhal was there. There was a tension in the room," Byron said.

"A sexual tension?"

"I prefer not to think of my sister being involved in sexual tension."

"Oh, come on," Amelia said, "you've both lived a long time. You must have seen Sera with people before?"

"Not really, she met people when she was out, she never brought them back home, and it was never someone who was part of the clan. We were both brought up to think that we shouldn't have anything other than friendship with our vampires, the warriors, or the human staff."

"Why?" Amelia asked.

"For one it would be uncomfortable for everyone if it went wrong, and most importantly, Sera, myself, and our parents and cousins, are in a position of power within the clan. The staff might feel pressured into things they don't want."

"That sounds healthy, but if two people fall in love—" Amelia said.

"You think they are in love?"

"I have no idea, but if there is something going on, I'll find out when we meet them next. I have a good eye for these things."

"Hmm," Byron said. "Sera said that Dante Wolfgang and her Second, Caden, were arriving in Scotland tonight. Ready to fight with us."

"It's really amazing the way the community has come together over this," Amelia said.

"And Daisy was right about Torija. Without her, there are a few groups who would never have promised to help us. Oh, and Brogan said she would come back with us when we leave."

Amelia gripped Byron tighter. "Like I said, things are rushing towards the end. It's scary."

Byron kissed her forehead. "Together good will prevail."

"Is this the first time Brogan has gone home to the Irish pack since she left?"

"Yes. It won't be easy for her," Byron said.

"What did they fall out about?"

"It's a bit delicate. Are you sure you want to know?"

"Yes, why wouldn't I?" Amelia asked.

Byron had a large exhale of breath. "You know the woman that she was in love with, and I had a—"

"Yes, I get the picture. Let's just call it a *dalliance*."

"You did ask. She didn't talk to me for years after, but I had no idea they were together. The woman, Gayle, certainly didn't give the impression that she was in a relationship. Well before that, Brogan had taken her home to her pack. They were like oil and water. Apparently her brother asked Gayle to leave after she said some nasty things to his Mater. Brogan didn't believe him. Gayle accused the wolf pack of not liking her because she was a human, and Brogan was so deeply in love with Gayle, she believed her."

"Poor Brogan, she lost her family, her whole pack?" Amelia said.

Byron nodded. "Then she was unceremoniously dumped after Gayle met this rich businesswoman. After that she was too embarrassed to go home."

"Did you explain to her about how she lied to you?" Amelia asked.

"Yes, then she felt even more of a fool."

"Maybe this is a chance to heal old wounds, then."

"Let's hope so," Byron said. "More than anyone else, wolves don't do well without their family."

❖

It was darker now, and the cubs had been taken off to bed, so the Wulver whiskey had come out. There was a case of it waiting to be drunk. Now that it was dark, the bonfire was all the more beautiful. The guitar playing, drumming, and singing had gotten louder, and Sera was having the best time ever.

She was sitting between Bhal's legs on a tree trunk seat, and Bhal was hugging her from behind. This sort of intimacy was new, and it was exhilarating.

Dante and Caden were talking with Rhuri and some of the elite wolves closer to the bonfire.

Kenrick came around with a top up of whiskey for them and a bottled fruit juice.

"Fantastic dram," Bhal said to Kenrick.

"There's plenty more where that came from, and this fruit juice is for you." He handed it to Zaria. "Did you tell them?"

"I hadn't found the right time. We are having a cub. Our first."

Sera squealed. "Congratulations, Zaria."

Bhal spoke her congratulations as well. "Wonderful news, Zaria."

"We're happy," Kenrick said, beaming with pride.

Sera said to Zaria, "Do you miss not having a drink?"

"No, I've never had a drink before. Only the Wulvers and the Irish pack have the adaptation or tolerance to drink alcohol."

"Really? Which pack do you come from?" Sera felt she'd said something wrong because Kenrick put her arms around Zaria protectively. "I'm sorry, did I say something out of line?"

"No, no, I'm fine to talk about it. I was from an Eastern European pack called the Lupas. The story goes that when Princess Scota left Egypt with her pack of werewolves, there was a rebellion, and a group of them were put on another ship and sailed east. The Lupas were not a good pack. The dominant wolves were aggressive and violent to submissive wolves. My sister and I ran away, and shortly after my sister died."

Sera knew better than to touch a pregnant wolf in the presence of its mate, but she wanted to show her comfort some way. "I'm so sorry to hear that."

"Aye, I'm sorry, Mater," Bhal said.

Kenrick rubbed Zaria's back. "But then Zaria came to my cousin Dante's pack lands, and I met the love of my life."

Zaria was smiling again. "Yes, and we both crossed paths with the witch Anka, didn't we?"

Kenrick nodded. "I didn't get the chance to tell you that, Bhal. Anka gave the Lupa Alpha a ring and asked her to attack the Wolfgangs—more particularly, Dante Wolfgang. When they fought, it was like the ring was draining Dante's strength."

Zaria then said, "We heard after that Anka had been collecting power and magic from powerful paranormals."

"Yes," Sera said, "she wanted to have a born vampire's strength too. She used it to open a portal to the other side."

"The whole picture is starting to fit together," Bhal said.

"If we all pull together, we can defeat her and this so-called God,

Balor," Kenrick said. She lifted her glass and proposed a toast. "To defeating evil in all its forms."

"Slainte," Bhal said.

❖

Gilbert walked into the throne room of the Dred castle with a feeling of being ten feet tall. The Vampires and other paranormals looked at him with awe. His face was covered with the blood of Welsh wolves, and he carried the spear he had stolen from them.

He could see Anka was on his throne, something that would be remedied when they carved up the world between them, but for now he was happy to come back the conquering hero.

Gilbert stopped at the steps that led up to the throne and banged the spear on the ground. "I have brought the Blaidds' spear, won in battle, won in our name and Balor's."

Anka stood up and raised her hand. "Bring it to me."

Gilbert walked up the steps slowly. When he gave it to Anka, it lit up like a thunderbolt. Those in the hall gasped.

"One down, Gilbert. Three to go."

❖

Bhal's hand grasped Sera's thigh and then squeezed her fleshy buttock. She wanted to make Sera feel everything that she was experiencing inside, like the thundering heavy beat in her core.

They returned to the tree house in the early hours of the morning, full of good whiskey and the joy of having fun with their new friends. Sera needed to feed, and it had driven their lovemaking to be even more passionate.

Bhal pulled away from the kiss and saw how turned on Sera was. "You are so beautiful."

"Don't stop. Touch me."

"You need to feed." Bhal would never have expected the drive to feed her blood bond would be so strong. It almost made her blood feel like it was burning hot, in a good way.

"No, make me wait for it," Sera pleaded.

Bhal grinned. "You like being made to wait, Goddess?"

"Not before, but with you? Yes, because I trust you."

Bhal wanted to kiss every part of her, and especially the part of Sera that used to drive her crazy in her tight jeans.

"Turn over."

"What?"

Bhal thwacked Sera's thigh, and she turned over. Bhal ran her hand down Sera's back and squeezed her buttock, and then every time she did it again, Bhal lingered near Sera's sex.

Sera pushed up her buttocks, as if trying to get closer to Bhal's fingers.

"Not yet, Goddess." Bhal stopped her teasing strokes and instead replaced them with her lips. She kissed down Sera's spine, and as she got closer to the base of her back, Sera squirmed. Bhal moved further down the bed so she could kiss the fleshy buttocks that she so loved. Bhal grasped two handfuls and squeezed. "Do you know how much I love these in your jeans?"

"Really?" Sera's hips were moving, and she hadn't even started with her yet.

"Yes." Bhal kissed and gave small bites.

Sera moaned and her hips were squirming a lot more.

"You're wet."

"Because I want you inside." Sera opened her hips.

Bhal teased Sera's clit, then suddenly pushed two fingers inside her. Sera groaned loudly. "Like that?"

"Yes."

Sera undulated her hips in time with Bhal's thrusts; all the while Bhal continued to kiss and tease with her tongue.

Sera's breathing became erratic as Bhal thrust faster. Bhal looked up and saw Sera grasp the pillows and covers with her clenched fists, and then she screamed loud and long as her whole body stiffened.

"Oh God, oh God—I need to feed, Bhal."

Bhal's body was so ready and hungry she had to come first. "Not yet."

She placed her sex on Sera's buttock, and thrust against her until a hot, painful pleasure rushed all over her. Bhal fell onto her hands and kissed Sera's back as she tried to get her breath.

"Turn over."

"Was that good?" Sera turned over and smiled.

"Can you not tell?" Bhal lowered her neck to Sera and said, "Feed, my Goddess. I love you."

"I love you," Sera replied, then sank her teeth into her neck.

Bhal got a second aftershock of an orgasm as Sera fed. It gave her such satisfaction to provide the lifeblood that her lover needed.

Bhal held Sera after and asked her, "Do you not feel any withdrawal symptoms now?"

"Not since yesterday when I've had your blood regularly. I don't know what would happen if we were apart for any time. If I would start to crave again."

"We won't be apart. Not any more."

Sera held Bhal's large and calloused hand above them and ran her fingertips over her fingers. "So after this is all over, and if we get back to normal life…"

"Not if. When we get back to normal life," Bhal said firmly.

"Okay, okay, when. Do you want to move your things into my room, or do you want your own space?"

"I want to be wherever you are. I don't know what Byron will say, though."

"Don't worry about Byron. I can handle my sister," Sera said.

They fell asleep in each other's arms, happy and contented, until Bhal's phone started to ring at six in the morning. Bhal awoke with a start and grabbed for her phone.

Sera rubbed her face. "Who is it at this time?"

"The Principe." She answered the call. "Principe?"

Sera heard every word of what Byron said. "The Blaidds have been massacred and their spear stolen by Gilbert."

"Fuck."

CHAPTER TWENTY-ONE

The distillery on the loch was a beautiful sight in the morning, but after hearing the terrible news about the Blaidds, Bhal and Sera couldn't enjoy it.

Kenrick led them through the whiskey pot still room. The wolves there nodded to them as they passed, but every wolf was feeling the pain of their brothers and sisters in Wales this morning.

They eventually came to a set of wooden stairs that took them down to a huge cellar filled with whiskey casks. "It's just down here." Kenrick led them to the back wall. There sitting on display was the Wulver sword.

"It's beautiful," Sera said.

"It is indeed," Bhal agreed.

Kenrick put her hand up to the security pad on the side and the glass slid open. "It wasn't too long ago that I was given the care of it in my Alpha ceremony, and I've got the stone of destiny in a trunk ready for you." She lifted it out and ran her hand along the flat of the blade. "It's been handed down Alpha to Alpha, from Princess Scota's own hand."

Bhal put her hand on Kenrick's shoulder. "I know how hard it is to hand over. I will do everything in my power to protect it."

"We all will," Sera added.

"I have no fears giving this over to you. What happened to the Blaidds makes it even more necessary to stop the Dreds and Anka."

"Thank you for your trust," Bhal said.

Kenrick took a case from the table beside them and set the sword in it. "Are you sure you want to go to Ireland alone?"

"Byron thinks after what happened to the Blaidds that you and the

Ranwulfs should stay on your pack lands," Sera said, "just till we work out what we do next."

Bhal nodded. "Protect your pack and your family first, especially with Zaria now pregnant. When the time is right, we will battle shoulder to shoulder."

"We will. It will be a glorious victory, Warrior," Kenrick said, "and we will avenge our wolf brothers and sisters."

Bhal lifted the sword case, and Kenrick picked up the trunk with the stone of destiny in it. They all made their way to Sera and Bhal's Jeep and packed the weapons with the Ranwulfs' shield. When Bhal and Sera got inside the Jeep, they waved goodbye to Kenrick, Zaria, Rhuri, and Hilda.

"They will be safe, won't they?" Sera said.

"They are werewolves and have the finest of warriors."

"That's what you would have said about the Blaidds."

Bhal started to drive away. "The Blaidds were hit at night in the most cowardly way possible. The Ranwulfs, Wulvers, and the Filtiaran have advance warning to be on their guard, and the Ranwulfs and Wulvers don't have their weapons any more. It wouldn't make sense for them to be attacked, other than vindictiveness."

"Anka and Gilbert are well capable of vindictiveness," Sera said.

"Have faith."

❖

Amelia sat with Erin Filtiaran on the porch of the Alpha and Mater's den, sharing a drink. The Irish pack lived on the coast of County Mayo. Their business and life was the Irish stout they made, and they lived in log cabins along the shore of the Atlantic Ocean. They were nicknamed the sea wolves, as they loved nothing more than to swim and hunt fish in the sea.

Amelia had taken to Erin immediately. She was in her forties and had the most beautiful auburn hair. And she had been extremely welcoming.

"I can't tell you how good it is to see Brogan back with us," Erin said as they watched her mate Colm play football with the cubs and Brogan, Bhal, and Torija.

Daisy was cheering on Torija, and Byron was standing on the sidelines, talking to Colm's father and Alexis.

"We missed her so much."

"I know she missed you too. Love can tangle feelings of hurt and anger, can't it?"

Erin nodded and laughed as she watched Brogan put one of her nephews on her shoulders.

"The cubs have missed out on so much with her, but let's hope after this business is done, we'll all have time to spend together as a pack."

"Let's pray for that," Amelia said.

Everyone stopped as they saw lights approach, and the dominant wolves circled the Mater.

"It's Sera and Bhal." Amelia got up and hurried over to meet them at the car.

Sera jumped out and threw her arms around Amelia, and Daisy followed soon after. Bhal took the weapons out of the boot and handed them to Alexis.

Amelia caught looks passing between Bhal and Sera. She was sure that there was something between them.

❖

A short time later Byron was pacing up and down the floor in her cabin, as Sera and Bhal explained what had happened.

"You tell me nothing? You get into drugs and don't come to me for help?" Byron shouted.

"Byron, stay calm," Amelia pleaded.

"And Bhal, you are my trusted warrior, and you didn't tell me?"

Sera was angry too. "Listen, we are giving you the courtesy of the truth because it's important for my recovery. I just wanted the space to get better with Bhal's help, not have your judgement."

Bhal stood and said, "I take full responsibility for both of our actions. I felt at the time that it would serve Sera better to have some space."

"That's understandable," Amelia said.

Then Bhal surprised everyone by dropping to one knee. "Principe, Sera and I have become blood bonds, and I ask for your blessing, to be your sister's protector, partner, and bond mate."

"I knew it." Amelia clapped her hands excitedly.

Byron looked up to the ceiling with a sigh.

"Don't ask for Byron's permission. Mine is the only one you need," Sera said.

"Bhal, get up," Byron said. "I understand now some of the choices you made. I made some reckless ones when I fell in love with Amelia." She held out her hand to Bhal. "There is no one finer to be my sister's blood bond."

Byron and Bhal hugged.

"Finally," Amelia said to Sera. "Do we get to hug now?"

❖

It was late, and Bhal, Byron, and the Alpha, Colm, were checking the security of the weapons.

"Our axe is under lock and key with the others," Colm said.

Bhal looked around the wooden building. It had a steel door, which was useful, and werewolf guards standing guard.

"Two guards front and back," Colm added.

Bhal would have liked more people on it, but she didn't want to step on the Alpha's toes.

"Good," Byron said. "We'll meet in the morning for the Zoom meeting with the other packs and see where we go from here. Thank you for your help, Colm."

"Pleasure. Goodnight then."

"Goodnight," both Bhal and Byron said.

Bhal walked Byron back to her cabin. There was an uneasy silence. So much had changed now.

"Principe, I'm sorry that things went the way they did, but I was just trying to do the best thing for Sera. She needed the time to work out her own problem this time, without running to her big sister for help."

Byron clapped her on the back. "I know that. I have just been getting her out of so many scrapes her whole life that I forgot she was a grown woman. Honestly, I'm so happy you are her blood bond because I know you will keep her safe."

They shook hands and Bhal said, "Thank you, Byron."

Bhal left Byron and walked to the cottage she was sharing with Sera. When she walked in, Sera was smiling.

"Did you do some warrior bonding?"

"Something like that. I take it you heard every word with that super vampire hearing?"

"Perhaps. Now I'm really hungry." Sera put her arms around Bhal's neck. "And you are the only one who can satisfy me."

❖

"Have they gone?" Gilbert said.

Anka walked into Gilbert's room and saw him sitting by the fire with a drink. She could tell how annoyed Gilbert was. He wanted to be the one gathering all the weapons and bringing them back like a hero.

"Several hours ago and don't pout like a schoolboy, emissary. This was not the job for you. This mission takes a very particular kind of person."

"Did you tell them to bring the extra prize that I want?"

Anka sat down in the armchair across from Gilbert. "I did, and they will deliver. Now just relax. We need you most of all for the final push."

"When we get to Norway?"

"When we get to Norway and enter the land of the Evergreen. There we'll bring back Balor," Anka said.

"And carve up the world between us?"

What a poor fool Gilbert was. When Balor returned, Gilbert would be lucky to be alive. Gilbert had his uses, and would in the future, if he played ball.

She raised her glass and said, "To the future."

"To the future," Gilbert echoed.

❖

Sera couldn't sleep. The truth was since she had become blood bonded to Bhal, she had such a surge in energy and good feeling that it was difficult to sleep. She turned over and stroked Bhal's cheek.

Bhal, on the other hand, did need her sleep. Sera decided to have a walk to calm her mind. She pulled on her clothes and shoes and exited the cabin. She could smell the salty sea air, and it started to calm her mind already.

Before she turned the corner, she heard hushed voices. She peeked around the corner and saw that the wolves around the weapons store had the metal door open and were moving cases out as quietly as possible.

Sera hurried over to them. "Is everything all right?"

They stopped dead and looked surprised at her appearance beside them. "What's your name?"

This wasn't right. She had met the wolves that were on guard earlier. They knew who she was, and she smelled blood coming from inside.

"Elor? Bring her in," a voice said.

One of the wolves held a gun at her chest, and although she could easily disarm and kill these apparent imposters, Sera wanted to find out what was going on first. She walked into the storage space and saw the duplicates of the wolves, the *real* wolves, dead on the floor.

Shifters. Of course.

One of the imposters looked exactly like Byron, and the other like the Alpha. The one posing as Byron transformed into a tall, thin silver-haired man. If anyone in the room looked sinister, then this shifter fit the bill.

"What's your name?"

"Who wants to know?"

The man grabbed her by her red leather jacket and yanked her forward. Again she let it happen to try to gauge what was happening here.

"She looks the right age for Daisy MacDougall," one of the others said.

Daisy? This was Anka and Gilbert's doing. She couldn't let them get hold of a descendant and couldn't let Gilbert get hold of Daisy, with his hatred for Torija.

"What is your name?" the man asked again.

Bhal was going to kill her for this, but she had to make this sacrifice. Daisy was too important to the plan.

"I am Daisy MacDougall."

❖

Bhal woke up slowly. She hadn't opened her eyes, but she knew where Sera would be and reached for her. But there was no one there. Bhal opened her eyes and saw that she wasn't in bed at all.

She pulled on some underwear and walked around the cabin. Bhal had a bad feeling. She couldn't feel Sera anywhere around. Then she heard raised voices outside. She ran to get dressed and ran equally as quickly outside.

Everyone was in panic. Colm was roaring at her guards, and werewolves were running around everywhere.

Bhal ran up to Byron. "What's going on?"

Byron brought her hands to her mouth. "Anka has the weapons."

"How could that happen? How could Gilbert get in here?"

"It wasn't Gilbert. Anka sent shifters. They posed as the Alpha and myself and took them away, easy as you like."

Then a thought hit Bhal. "Byron, Sera is gone. I can't feel her nearby."

"Fuck," Byron roared.

CHAPTER TWENTY-TWO

It took two days to gather up the Debreks' allies. Two days of Bhal in torture without Sera, two days of picturing all they could have done to her.

Alexis had gone ahead to organize a meeting place, and the town ten miles from the target at Lochlan was surprised at its sudden unusual visitors.

Alexis found a large industrial warehouse where they could meet.

Bhal watched from the side as Byron gave her speech to all that had gathered under their banner. Everyone who had promised to come, had done. The wolf packs, witches, fae, shifters including Slaine's family, and vampires who weren't affiliated with any clan but came to Torija's call for help, and Byron's cousin Angelo.

Brogan kept Bhal company. "Sera will be well, Bhal. Anka wants her alive for some reason. We will get her back."

Bhal nodded, but her stomach was a torment of worry.

"It is not too much to say that the fate of the world hangs in the balance today. Today we fight for freedom, for family, and for love," Byron said. "When we get to our target, and engage with the enemy, we must protect the descendants, Amelia and Daisy, at all costs. They are our only hope. We will take them to the coordinates and hopefully find Anka and Gilbert there. Good luck, everyone. Let's head out."

Bhal got into the car with Byron, Amelia, Torija, and Daisy. Amelia placed her hand on Bhal's.

"We will find her, Bhal. Believe in that."

"I just don't understand why they took Sera. They had the weapons. Why take her too?"

"I don't think they meant to," Torija said. "I think they mistook

Sera for Daisy. I think my father wants Daisy to torture me. It has Gilbert written all over it."

"We'll get her soon. I promise, Bhal," Byron said.

❖

The battle was fierce, as Byron said it would be. A large grassy open space lay above the lake below the town, and that's where the two forces collided. The fight was chaos, with blood and magic and wolves ripping each other apart.

Bhal and Byron's team was trying to find out Anka's location in the battle, but it was hard to see anything.

Angelo and Slaine came back from the fight and said to Byron, "They went down to the lake and we lost sight of them."

"Angelo, I'll leave you in command of our vampires. Alexis? Make sure that no one follows us."

"Yes, Principe."

Bhal led Byron, Torija, Amelia, Daisy, and Brogan down the right flank of the battle towards the lake. They made it down to the lake's edge. There was a wooden bridge that went out only a few metres into the lake. It was a dead end.

Out of the corner of Byron's eye she saw a vampire running towards Amelia. Byron intercepted it and threw it to the ground, and Bhal took its head off.

"Are you sure these are the coordinates?" Amelia asked.

Byron looked at the details again. "Yes, it says the land of the Evergreen is here."

Torija bent down and let water run through her fingers. "Under it? Over it? Where?"

"Let me try something." Daisy took a step on the wooden walkway and held the handrail.

Torija sped over to her. "Don't do that without telling me."

"Chill, Vamp. Just let me feel." Daisy closed her eyes. "Yep, my spidey sense says this thing is magic, or our paranormal friends have come this way."

"Principe, let me lead the way," Bhal said.

"Lead the way to what?" Brogan said. "There's nothing there."

"If Daisy can feel it, then there's something," Amelia said.

Byron moved behind Bhal. "Daisy, Amelia, you go behind me, and Torija, you bring up the rear with Brogan."

Bhal looked behind her and was sure she felt Sera, but of course she wasn't there. She heard Sera's voice in her head. *Be careful.*

Bhal walked to the edge of the walkway. Her heart thudded. What was she going to find through here? What *was* there. She took a breath and a step into what should have been the watery depths but instead was a green, sunny field. The battle outside was gone, and instead of chaos there was a calm ethereal atmosphere.

She was joined by the rest of the party, and Byron stepped up next to her. "What is this place?"

"The Evergreen," Bhal said. "A place with no age and no death."

Byron took a step forward. "They must be over the brow of the hill. Torija, I'll stay at one side of Daisy and Amelia and you at the other. Bhal, you and Brogan up front."

They walked up the hill, and Bhal saw Anka, Gilbert and some guards on a grassy area below, taking the weapons out of their cases.

The grassy area had an inner circle of raised plinths, and outside a large stone circle, similar to the ones that the ancient peoples of Europe built.

Over on the other side of grass she saw Sera on her knees, one vampire with a sword to her neck, and one with a dagger next to an urn billowing fire.

"Sera," Bhal shouted.

Anka and Gilbert looked up, and their vampires stood in front of them defensively. "Don't worry, they won't attack us," Anka said. "We have Sera Debrek. Come and join us," she called out, taunting Bhal.

Bhal ran down, and when she got close, the vampire holding a dagger put it at Sera's heart. Bhal stopped dead.

"I wouldn't come any closer," Anka said, "or my vampires will take her head and burn her heart in seconds."

That was the only way to kill a born vampire. Anka had thought this through.

Bhal. I love you. Just stay calm, Sera said with her mind.

I love you, Goddess.

Byron, Amelia, Daisy, and Torija stood beside her.

"I'm glad you could join us to watch the rebirth of our God, Balor. You can enjoy the show. But one wrong move and Serenity will lose her head and her heart."

Bhal had never felt so much fury in her long, long, existence. "If you hurt her, I will spend eternity torturing you."

Gilbert laughed and stepped forward. "Big words, eh, Madam

Anka? And my dear daughter has come to witness her father's finest work and brought her woman for me to kill. So good of you. I did want Daisy here with a sword at her throat, but we'll need to make do with a Debrek."

Torija ran and grabbed her father. "I'll tear you limb from limb."

Sera cried out as the knife sliced her skin.

"Torija, no," Brogan shouted.

Amelia held up her hands. "Let's just have everyone calm down."

Daisy stepped beside Torija and took her hand. "Don't worry about him, Tor. He's a pathetic excuse for a vampire."

"Am I? Because it looks like we are holding all the cards," Gilbert said.

"You think? Anka needs you right now, but what happens when Balor comes back to this world?"

"We will rule together and crush humans like you into the dust."

Daisy laughed. "You keep telling yourself that."

Gilbert snarled. "I'll kill you just like her first girlfriend."

"Gilbert," Anka shouted. "Enough. Let's get on with this."

As he walked away, Daisy called after him, "You know I'm right."

What are you doing? Torija spoke telepathically to Daisy.

Planting a seed.

Daisy walked over to Amelia, so they were ready to fight this.

Anka walked around, putting a weapon on each plinth. Each time she added one, the plinths would light up.

Gilbert lifted the final artifact. The stone of destiny.

Torija heard Gilbert say, "We will rule together when Balor comes through the portal, won't we?"

"Gilbert, we don't have time for this. Of course. Put the stone on."

He's questioning Anka, Torija said.

Daisy mouthed to Amelia, *Be ready.*

Gilbert placed the stone on, and between every pair of stones in the outer circle, a portal appeared. "We've done it."

"What is this place?" Byron asked Anka.

"The Evergreen is an airport, if you will, between universes, realms, whatever you want to call it."

Each portal had a different colour to it, but the most menacing one was the screaming void, filled with the sounds of despair and torment.

A rumble of thunder could be heard in the distance. It got louder and louder, closer and closer, until big fat drops of rain started to fall.

Bhal dropped to one knee and closed her eyes. This was a stronger version of what she'd felt when the Sluagh were close.

"Balor is coming, Principe."

Anka walked over and shouted, "Balor, come to your world."

What looked like ash spewed from the void. On the grass the ash formed into the shape of a large body, and the very earth beneath it was pulled from the ground to form what Bhal assumed was Balor made flesh.

Bhal had to act fast. She looked around at Byron, Brogan, and Amelia and Daisy. *Wait for it*, she mouthed.

The earth started to form the flesh of his hands and feet. They didn't have long.

Gilbert ran over to Anka. "Do you think this is the best idea? We could rule the world together, without Balor."

Anka didn't even turn to Gilbert. She just lifted her hand, and white light shot from her palm and encased Gilbert in a force field. "I don't have time for you."

This was the moment, Bhal knew. Anka was distracted. She nodded to her friends, pulled out her sword, and ran at the body of earth forming into Balor. She thrust her sword deep into where the chest was forming, hoping that her sword could do damage like it did with the Sluagh's dark spirits.

Meanwhile, Byron rushed over, dispatched the two vampires holding Sera, and helped her get up.

A crow swooped down from above and transformed into Morrigan. "The weapons will kill him. They open the portal but they are deadly to him."

"Brogan, Torija, grab a weapon," Sera shouted.

A high-pitched scream came from the body. And Anka turned her power on Bhal.

Bhal shouted in pain while trying to use all her strength to keep the sword in Balor's chest.

Amelia and Daisy stood nearby. Daisy turned to Amelia and said, "Are you ready?"

Amelia rubbed her baby bump and then took Daisy's hands. "We are."

Amelia and Daisy chanted the incantation they were taught. "We three come to send you to death, we three come to send you to death," they repeated and repeated.

Serenity took the shield, Brogan took the sword, and Byron lifted the spear and the axe. All three ran over and plunged the weapons into Balor's body.

The biggest howling noise came from Balor as his body broke up and started to return to ash.

Anka screamed and took a running jump onto Balor. Then she screamed again as her body started to turn to ash. It was as if she was burning from the inside out. A huge bang blew the allies from the disintegrating bodies. Byron, Sera, and Bhal were blown to the stones where the portals were, but the force of the blast sent Brogan flying through the blue-coloured portal.

"Brogan, no!" But she was gone.

Soon there was nothing left but a pile of smoking debris. Amelia and Daisy fell to their knees, and Byron and Torija ran to them.

"Are you okay?" Byron asked Amelia.

"I'm fine, I'm fine. I just need to catch my breath."

"The baby? Are they okay too?"

Amelia nodded. "Okay, I think."

Sera wrapped her arms around Bhal. "You did it."

Bhal kissed her and said, "We all did."

They stood up and Bhal said to Morrigan, "Thank you for helping us."

"I wasn't supposed to even give you a clue, but I'm fond of humans, no matter my reputation. I couldn't have my vicious brother let loose on you all."

Sera offered Morrigan her hand. "Thank you."

Bhal didn't think she'd see the day the love of her life was shaking hands with the Goddess Morrigan.

Byron and Amelia joined them and hugged each other.

Then Sera said to Morrigan, "Where is Brogan?"

"She could be anywhere. This place connects with many realms, many worlds."

Byron said, "We have to find her. She's one of us."

"You won't be able to find her, but if you wish, I could try to track her down," Morrigan said.

"Please, Morrigan," Amelia said.

"I'll try, but it's like looking for a needle in an infinite haystack."

"She's a brave wolf," Bhal said.

They heard Daisy shout, "Bhal? Byron?"

They turned around and saw Torija had taken Bhal's sword and had Gilbert on his knees.

"I don't know what to do," Daisy said. "I don't want Gilbert's death to bring out the old Victorija."

"Torija?" Byron said.

"He needs to die."

"You can't kill me. You don't have the guts to take my head and my heart," Gilbert taunted. "You're weak like your mother."

Torija drew the sword around his neck, slicing the skin. "I don't need to take your heart. You're in the body of Drasas, my weak turned vampire. All I need is"—she hesitated and then quickly sliced the sword through his neck—"your head."

"Torija, drop the sword now," Daisy pleaded.

Torija did as she was asked and turned to Daisy. "He had to die, but I won't change. You have changed me. Your love has."

"I can't believe it's over," Amelia said. "We did it." Amelia brought them into a group hug.

"Apart from Brogan. She lost her life to save the world," Byron said.

A whirl of wind blew the ash around them. The wind was coming from one of the portals and a tall blond man walked out of it.

"Morrigan," he said, "I see you just couldn't not interfere."

"They did it all themselves. I just pointed them in the right direction."

"Are you the Tuatha De Danann?" Sera asked.

He smiled. "I am Nuada, and these two brave women"—Nuada pointed at Amelia and Daisy—"are descendants of our people."

Daisy looked at Amelia, then said, "Hi, nice to meet you."

Nuada inclined his head. "My apologies that one of our kind has caused so much trouble."

Bhal tensed. She didn't like the word *trouble* being used as a description of what Balor had done. "He murdered my whole village, including my mother."

"Forgive me, Warrior. A poor choice of words. We should have taken more care to make sure Balor never got out again, but we thought dispersing the weapons would be enough."

"Will he be able to come back again?" Amelia asked.

He smiled and held out his hands. "Come here, daughters of Melusine."

Byron and Torija stepped in front of them, but Daisy pushed past. "We can trust him. I can feel it."

Amelia joined Daisy. He looked them both up and down. "Melusine would be so proud of you. You brought the whole paranormal world together to defeat the worst member of our people."

"What about our friend Brogan?" Sera said.

Nuada looked to Morrigan. She said, "She went through the west portal. I'll try to find her."

He nodded. "She may be lost, but she's not in the void. There are many different kinds of places through there, and Morrigan will try."

"What about the souls that Balor stole?" Bhal asked.

Nuada walked over to Bhal and raised his hand towards the void. It opened, and flashes of light shot from it and disappeared up into the sky above.

"They are free and will go to the other side."

He offered his hand to Bhal. "Warrior, you have stuck the task given to you by the Goddess Danu perfectly and saved so many souls from torment."

"I could have done more."

Sera elbowed Bhal. "No, she couldn't. She's given her long, long life to others."

Nuala chuckled. "You have your own protector now, Warrior. Well, I understand your priest offered you rest in death when the souls were freed. Is that what you want?"

Bhal grasped Sera's hand and looked into Sera's eyes. "No, I have more than enough to live for."

Byron put her arm around Amelia's middle and looked over to Daisy and Torija. "I think we all have everything to live for."

"I'm glad to hear it. Morrigan and I will take the artifacts so they can't be used again. Now go and try to live happy lives."

Morrigan came up to Bhal and Sera. She crossed her arms and with a half smile said, "So you are going to do the happy-every-after thing?"

"We are," Sera replied.

Morrigan brought her hand to her chest and said, "Have a happy life, Bhal. You deserve it."

"Thanks, Morrigan," Bhal said.

"Tell Brogan's brother, I'll find her if I can."

"If you do find her," Byron said, "tell her to come back to us. We'll never give up hope."

"I will."

Morrigan and Nuada walked to the furthest portal, but before going Nuada turned and said, "This place is called the Evergreen for a reason. Time works differently, slower in here. When you go out, things might be a bit different. Oh, and look after baby Debrek. She will be extraordinary."

Then they vanished into the light.

Amelia cried out in pain and fell to her knees.

"Amelia, what's wrong?"

"My waters have broken."

Sera and Daisy hurried to her side.

"You aren't due yet," Byron said with panic in her voice.

Sera shook her head. "Byron, vampire pregnancies can be one or two months shorter than a human's, and with witch blood thrown in, who knows."

"Bhal, Torija," Byron barked, "we need to get Amelia out of here."

"No," Amelia said, "it's coming too fast."

When Amelia cried out in pain, Byron looked to her sister. "Sera, what do we do? I don't know what to do."

Sera had never seen her sister look so helpless or confused. Sera had to step up to the plate. "Right. Everyone lay your jackets down over near the exit to the Evergreen. Daisy? Let's get Amelia over there. Amelia, we are going to get you through this, okay?"

They made a bed of jackets and helped Amelia lie down.

Amelia screamed, and Byron clutched her head in fright. "It's coming too fast."

Sera looked to Daisy. "We need to get her ready now."

Daisy turned to Torija and Bhal and said, "You two go and guard… somewhere over there. The Principessa needs some privacy."

Bhal and Torija scuttled away and seemed delighted to do so.

While Sera and Daisy undressed Amelia, Sera gave out more orders. "Byron, get down here and tell Amelia she's going to be fine."

Byron dropped to her knees and took Amelia's hand. "Everything will be okay. Take deep breaths like we practised."

Sera hoped the delivery would go well. Born vampire births usually did, but Amelia was part witch. Sera silently prayed to the Grand Duchess for a safe delivery. Lucia had also been a witch who gave birth to a born vampire. Hopefully she was watching over them.

Amelia let out an almighty scream.

❖

Amelia saw tears running down Byron's face. It was the most beautiful sight she had ever seen, watching her blood bond cradle their new baby in her arms. She was wrapped in Byron's jacket.

The birth had been extremely quick but went very smoothly. Daisy and Sera had helped her get dressed, and now it was important to get to safety.

"Are you happy?" Amelia said to Byron.

Byron looked at her and shook her head. "Can you not tell? Thank you, mia cara. You have given me a true gift. A beautiful baby girl."

"Thank our friends too. I couldn't have done it without them."

Byron walked over to Sera. "Thank you, friends, especially you, baby sister. You took charge and got us through it. I was lost."

"You're welcome."

Amelia watched Sera's face light up with pride. She really had found her place in the clan, and she couldn't have done it without Bhal.

Bhal helped Sera bring Amelia to her feet. She was shaky and tired beyond belief.

The baby cried and Bhal said, "We need to get Amelia and the baby out of here quickly. It's dangerous to stay in the Evergreen too long."

Byron nodded. "Amelia, we'll get you both to the nearest hotel and let you both rest."

"I need it. My legs feel like jelly."

"I'll hold the baby," Byron said. "Bhal, you lead us out. There is a battle outside here, remember? Torija, you take the rear."

"Oui. Be careful, everyone," Torija said.

Sera and Daisy helped Amelia walk. She couldn't wait to get to a soft bed and hold her baby in her arms.

"Let's go home," Byron said to everyone.

"Yes," Torija said, "we saved the world. We deserve it."

Daisy laughed.

Bhal led them through the barrier back to the lake bridge.

❖

Amelia took a step through, and the pain and weakness she had felt was gone.

Byron fell to one knee after she stepped through. "Amelia!"

Amelia looked at their baby girl in Byron's arms, and the child wasn't a newborn any more.

"Byron? What's happening? The baby can't be—" The baby held its hands up to Amelia, and she scooped it into her arms. "What's happened to our little girl, Byron?"

Sera and Daisy got down on their hands and knees.

"She looks as if she's aged to a toddler," Sera said.

Byron leaned over and kissed her baby daughter's head. "Nuada said that time works differently in there. Look, everyone's gone, there's no battle."

"How much time has passed?"

Almost immediately everyone's phone started buzzing with missed messages and phone calls.

"What's the date?" Amelia asked. "Please? How much time has passed?"

Torija looked over at Bhal with worry etched on her features.

Bhal said, "Two years, Principe."

Amelia felt like all the air had been stolen from her lungs.

CHAPTER TWENTY-THREE

D aisy pushed Torija from her. Even though Torija could overpower her, she fell back on the bed as if a truck had hit her.

"I can never have enough of you, cherie, and I have two years of feeding and touching you to make up for."

"I think we've managed to catch up. We have a birth ceremony present to go and buy."

Torija threw her arm over her face theatrically. "You want me to leave our bed to go shopping?"

"Yes." Daisy slipped on her nightdress and walked to the kitchen to make coffee.

"All right, cherie. As long as I'm with you and I can take you for an exquisite lunch."

Daisy added sugar to her coffee and lifted her cup. "I might allow that." She took her coffee over to the balcony, her favourite morning spot. "It's so strange that we've missed two whole years," Daisy said.

"At least the humans didn't find out about our world."

"Yeah, that little false-flag terrorist incident in Norway seemed to fool the world's media. It's scary how easily they can do that."

Torija shrugged. "It's in the humans' interest to keep our world secret. Governments don't like panic."

Daisy felt Torija hug her from behind. "We've got a happy future to look forward to now."

"I can't wait, Vamp."

❖

Byron popped her head around the nursery door and saw Amelia there as she expected. She sat at the side of the cot while baby Lucia

Debrek slept. Amelia had hardly left their little girl's side since they got home, and Byron didn't blame her. She had missed the whole bonding period because of the effects of the Evergreen.

Amelia turned her head and smiled. "Hi."

Byron walked in and pulled up a chair beside Amelia. "How is little Luc?"

"Just perfect. She's so well behaved." Amelia sighed.

"What is it?" Byron asked.

"I've missed out on so much."

Byron took her hand. "I know, but she's safe and she's happy. And because of what you and Daisy did, she will have a safe future."

"I know, I do. It was worth the sacrifice, but it's still sad." Amelia put her head on Byron's shoulder.

At that moment Katie and Alexis whispered, "Is she asleep?"

"Yes," Amelia whispered back. "Come in."

"She's beautiful," Katie said.

Alexis smiled. "Sometimes I think she looks like Byron and some days like you, Amelia."

"A perfect mix of both," Byron said.

"Have you heard from Sera and Bhal?" Katie asked.

"Oh yes," Amelia said. "They are living it up in Monaco. I don't think Bhal has ever experienced a holiday like that."

❖

Sera lay on the deck of the Debrek superyacht. It was bobbing about on the bay in front of the family's Monaco home.

She heard a splash and lifted her sun hat. Sera was glad she had. Bhal was climbing back into the boat after swimming, and she loved to see Bhal with water dripping down her body. It was so sexy.

"How can you lie there all day, doing nothing?" Bhal said as she dried herself on a towel.

"I haven't been doing *nothing*. In fact if you think about it, I've been very active most of every day. I need to recover somehow."

Bhal sat down beside her.

"Is this the first time you've worn shorts?" Sera said with a smile.

"Yes, and just for you."

"They are very sexy."

Bhal had been horrified at the selection of shorts that Sera had bought her. Today's offering had a light blue background with large pineapples on them.

"They are not. Just don't tell my warriors. I'll never live it down," Bhal said.

Sera sighed. "This has just been bliss, hasn't it? No clan, no bad guy coming to destroy the world. Just you and me, and the sun."

Bhal took off Sera's hat and flung it to the side, then rolled on top of her.

"Ah, you're still wet."

Bhal trailed her fingers down Sera's skimpy bikini top. "Yes, it has been perfect, and seeing you in this makes up for the pineapples."

Sera kissed her and bit her lip.

"I love you, Goddess. I always have," Bhal said.

"I love you, Warrior, but I want to get you out of those pineapples. Let's go to our room."

Bhal let herself be dragged off with Sera. Bhal might have waited forever to find the one her heart yearned for, but it was well worth the wait.

Forever was going to be fun.

About the Author

Jenny Frame is from the small town of Motherwell in Scotland, where she lives with her partner, Lou, and their well-loved and very spoiled dog.

She has a diverse range of qualifications, including a BA in public management and a diploma in acting and performance. Nowadays, she likes to put her creative energies into writing rather than treading the boards.

When not writing or reading, Jenny loves cheering on her local football team, cooking, and spending time with her family.

Jenny can be contacted at www.jennyframe.com.

Books Available From Bold Strokes Books

A Talent Ignited by Suzanne Lenoir. When Evelyne is abducted and Annika believes she has been abandoned, they must risk everything to find each other again. (978-1-63679-483-9)

All Things Beautiful by Alaina Erdell. Casey Norford only planned to learn to paint like her mentor, Leighton Vaughn, not sleep with her. (978-1-63679-479-2)

An Atlas to Forever by Krystina Rivers. Can Atlas, a difficult dog Ellie inherits after the death of her best friend, help the busy hopeless romantic find forever love with commitment-phobic animal behaviorist Hayden Brandt? (978-1-63679-451-8)

Bait and Witch by Clifford Mae Henderson. When Zeddi gets an unexpected inheritance from her client Mags, she discovers that Mags served as high priestess to a dwindling coven of old witches—who are positive that Mags was murdered. Zeddi owes it to her to uncover the truth. (978-1-63679-535-5)

Buried Secrets by Sheri Lewis Wohl. Tuesday and Addie, along with Tuesday's dog, Tripper, struggle to solve a twenty-five-year-old mystery while searching for love and redemption along the way. (978-1-63679-396-2)

Come Find Me in the Midnight Sun by Bailey Bridgewater. In Alaska, disappearing is the easy part. When two men go missing, state trooper Louisa Linebach must solve the case, and when she thinks she's coming close, she's wrong. (978-1-63679-566-9)

Death on the Water by CJ Birch. The Ocean Summit's authorities have ruled a death on board its inaugural cruise as a suicide, but Claire suspects murder, and with the help of Assistant Cruise Director Moira, Claire conducts her own investigation. (978-1-63679-497-6)

Living For You by Jenny Frame. Can Sera Debrek face real and personal demons to help save the world from darkness and open her heart to love? (978-1-63679-491-4)

Ride with Me by Jenna Jarvis. When Lucy's vacation to find herself becomes Emma's chance to remember herself, they realize that everything they're looking for might already be sitting right next to them—if they're willing to reach for it. (978-1-63679-499-0)

Rivals for Love by Ali Vali. Brooks Boseman's brother Curtis is getting married, and Brooks needs to be at the engagement party. Only she can't possibly go, not with Curtis set to marry the secret love of her youth, Fallon Goodwin. (978-1-63679-384-9)

Whiskey and Wine by Kelly and Tana Fireside. Winemaker Tessa Williams and sex toy shop owner Lace Reynolds are both used to taking risks, but will they be willing to put their friendship on the line if it gives them a shot at finding forever love? (978-1-63679-531-7)

Hands of the Morri by Heather K O'Malley. Discovering she is a Lost Sister and growing acquainted with her new body, Asche learns how to be a warrior and commune with the Goddess the Hands serve, the Morri. (978-1-63679-465-5)

I Know About You by Erin Kaste. With her stalker inching closer to the truth, Cary Smith is forced to face the past she's tried desperately to forget. (978-1-63679-513-3)

Mate of Her Own by Elena Abbott. When Heather McKenna finally confronts the family who cursed her, her werewolf is shocked to discover her one true mate, and that's only the beginning. (978-1-63679-481-5)

Pumpkin Spice by Tagan Shepard. For Nicki, new love is making this pumpkin spice season sweeter than expected. (978-1-63679-388-7)

Sweat Equity by Aurora Rey. When cheesemaker Sy Travino takes a job in rural Vermont and hires contractor Maddie Barrow to rehab a house she buys sight unseen, they both wind up with a lot more than they bargained for. (978-1-63679-487-7)

Taking the Plunge by Amanda Radley. When Regina Avery meets model Grace Holland—the most beautiful woman she's ever seen—she doesn't have a clue how to flirt, date, or hold on to a relationship. But Regina must take the plunge with Grace and hope she manages to swim. (978-1-63679-400-6)

We Met in a Bar by Claire Forsythe. Wealthy nightclub owner Erica turns undercover bartender on a mission to catch a thief where she meets no-strings, no-commitments Charlie, who couldn't be further from Erica's type. Right? (978-1-63679-521-8)

Western Blue by Suzie Clarke. Step back in time to this historic western filled with heroism, loyalty, friendship, and love. The odds are against this unlikely group—but never underestimate women who have nothing to lose. (978-1-63679-095-4)

Windswept by Patricia Evans. The windswept shores of the Scottish Highlands weave magic for two people convinced they'd never fall in love again. (978-1-63679-382-5)

A Calculated Risk by Cari Hunter. Detective Jo Shaw doesn't need complications, but the stabbing of a young woman brings plenty of those, and Jo will have to risk everything if she's going to make it through the case alive. (978-1-63679-477-8)

An Independent Woman by Kit Meredith. Alex and Rebecca's attraction won't stop smoldering, despite their reluctance to act on it and incompatible poly relationship styles. (978-1-63679-553-9)

Cherish by Kris Bryant. Josie and Olivia cherish the time spent together, but when the summer ends and their temporary romance melts into the real deal, reality gets complicated. (978-1-63679-567-6)

Cold Case Heat by Mary P. Burns. Sydney Hansen receives a threat in a very cold murder case that sends her to the police for help, where she finds more than justice with Detective Gale Sterling. (978-1-63679-374-0)

Proximity by Jordan Meadows. Joan really likes Ellie, but being alone with her could turn deadly unless she can keep her dangerous powers under control. (978-1-63679-476-1)

Sweet Spot by Kimberly Cooper Griffin. Pro surfer Shia Turning will have to take a chance if she wants to find the sweet spot. (978-1-63679-418-1)

The Haunting of Oak Springs by Crin Claxton. Ghosts and the past haunt the supernatural detective in a race to save the lesbians of Oak Springs farm. (978-1-63679-432-7)

Transitory by J.M. Redmann. The cops blow it off as a customer surprised by what was under the dress, but PI Micky Knight knows they're wrong—she either makes it her case or lets a murderer go free to kill again. (978-1-63679-251-4)

Unexpectedly Yours by Toni Logan. A private resort on a tropical island, a feisty old chief, and a kleptomaniac pet pig bring Suzanne and Allie together for unexpected love. (978-1-63679-160-9)

Crush by Ana Hartnett Reichardt. Josie Sanchez worked for years for the opportunity to create her own wine label, and nothing will stand in her way. Not even Mac, the owner's annoyingly beautiful niece Josie's forced to hire as her harvest intern. (978-1-63679-330-6)

Decadence by Ronica Black, Renee Roman & Piper Jordan. You are cordially invited to Decadence, Las Vegas's most talked about invitation-only Masquerade Ball. Come for the entertainment and stay for the erotic indulgence. We guarantee it'll be a party that lives up to its name. (978-1-63679-361-0)

Gimmicks and Glamour by Lauren Melissa Ellzey. Ashly has learned to hide her Sight, but as she speeds toward high school graduation she must protect the classmates she claims to hate from an evil that no one else sees. (978-1-63679-401-3)

Heart of Stone by Sam Ledel. Princess Keeva Glantor meets Maeve, a gorgon forced to live alone thanks to a decades-old lie, and together the two women battle forces they formerly thought to be good in the hopes of leading lives they can finally call their own. (978-1-63679-407-5)

Peaches and Cream by Georgia Beers. Adley Purcell is living her dreams owning Get the Scoop ice cream shop until national dessert chain Sweet Heaven opens less than two blocks away and Adley has to compete with the far too heavenly Sabrina James. (978-1-63679-412-9)

The Only Fish in the Sea by Angie Williams. Will love overcome years of bitter rivalry for the daughters of two crab fishing families in this queer modern-day spin on Romeo and Juliet? (978-1-63679-444-0)